HARRY POTTER

and the Philosopher's Stone

DRAGO DORMIENS NUNQUAM TITILLANDUS

HARRY POTTER

and the Philosopher's Stone

J. K. ROWLING

RAINCOAST BOOKS

Vancouver

BLOOMSBURY

First published in hardcover in Great Britain in 1997 by Bloomsbury Publishing Plc

This paperback edition first published in Canada in 2004 by

Raincoast Books
9050 Shaughnessy Street
Vancouver, B.C.
V6P 6E5
www.raincoast.com

Bloomsbury Publishing Plc
38 Soho Square
London
W1D 3HB
www.bloomsbury.com

Copyright © J.K. Rowling 1997

Typeset by Dorchester Typesetting

Harry Potter, names, characters and related indicia are copyright and trademark Warner Bros., 2000™

The moral right of the author has been asserted

National Library of Canada Cataloguing in Publication Data

Rowling, J. K.
Harry Potter and the philosopher's stone
ISBN 1-55192-700-4
I. Title.

PZ7.R79835Harp 2000   J823'.914   C00-910940-4

04 05 06 07 08 09 • 10 9 8 7 6 5 4 3 2 1

At Raincoast Books we are committed to protecting the environment and to the responsible use of natural resources. We are acting on this commitment by working with suppliers and printers to phase out our use of paper produced from ancient forests – this book is one step towards that goal. It is printed on 100% ancient-forest-free paper (100% recycled, 40% post-consumer), processed chlorine-free, and supplied by New Leaf Paper. For further information, visit our website at www.raincoast.com. We are working with Markets Initiative (www.oldgrowthfree.com) on this project.

Printed and bound in the United States by Quebecor World.

for Jessica, who loves stories,
for Anne, who loved them too,
and for Di, who heard this one first.

— CHAPTER ONE —

The Boy Who Lived

Mr and Mrs Dursley, of number four, Privet Drive, were proud to say that they were perfectly normal, thank you very much. They were the last people you'd expect to be involved in anything strange or mysterious, because they just didn't hold with such nonsense.

Mr Dursley was the director of a firm called Grunnings, which made drills. He was a big, beefy man with hardly any neck, although he did have a very large moustache. Mrs Dursley was thin and blonde and had nearly twice the usual amount of neck, which came in very useful as she spent so much of her time craning over garden fences, spying on the neighbours. The Dursleys had a small son called Dudley and in their opinion there was no finer boy anywhere.

The Dursleys had everything they wanted, but they also had a secret, and their greatest fear was that somebody would discover it. They didn't think they could bear it if anyone found out about the Potters. Mrs Potter was Mrs Dursley's sister, but they hadn't met for several years; in fact, Mrs Dursley pretended she didn't have a sister, because her sister and her good-for-nothing husband were as unDursleyish as it was possible to be. The Dursleys shuddered to think what the neighbours would say if the Potters arrived in the street. The Dursleys knew that the Potters had a small son, too, but they had never even seen him. This boy was another good reason for keeping the Potters away; they didn't want Dudley mixing with a child like that.

When Mr and Mrs Dursley woke up on the dull, grey Tuesday our story starts, there was nothing about the cloudy sky outside to suggest that strange and mysterious things would soon be happening all over the country. Mr Dursley hummed as he picked out his most boring tie for work and Mrs Dursley gossiped away happily as she wrestled a screaming Dudley into his high chair.

None of them noticed a large tawny owl flutter past the window.

At half past eight, Mr Dursley picked up his briefcase, pecked Mrs Dursley on the cheek and tried to kiss Dudley goodbye but missed, because Dudley was now having a tantrum and throwing his cereal at the walls. 'Little tyke,' chortled Mr Dursley as he left the house. He got into his car and backed out of number four's drive.

It was on the corner of the street that he noticed the first sign of something peculiar – a cat reading a map. For a second, Mr Dursley didn't realise what he had seen – then he jerked his head around to look again. There was a tabby cat standing on the corner of Privet Drive, but there wasn't a map in sight. What could he have been thinking of? It must have been a trick of the light. Mr Dursley blinked and stared at the cat. It stared back. As Mr Dursley drove around the corner and up the road, he watched the cat in his mirror. It was now reading the sign that said *Privet Drive* – no, *looking* at the sign; cats couldn't read maps *or* signs. Mr Dursley gave himself a little shake and put the cat out of his mind. As he drove towards town he thought of nothing except a large order of drills he was hoping to get that day.

But on the edge of town, drills were driven out of his mind by something else. As he sat in the usual morning traffic jam, he couldn't help noticing that there seemed to be a lot of strangely dressed people about. People in cloaks. Mr Dursley couldn't bear people who dressed in funny clothes – the get-ups you saw on young people! He supposed this was some stupid new fashion. He drummed his fingers on the steering wheel and his eyes fell on a huddle of these weirdos standing quite close by. They were whispering excitedly together. Mr Dursley was enraged to see that a couple of them weren't young at all; why, that man had to be older than he was, and wearing an emerald-green cloak! The nerve of him! But then it struck Mr Dursley that this was probably some silly stunt – these people were obviously collecting for something ... yes, that would be it. The traffic moved on, and a few minutes later, Mr Dursley arrived in the Grunnings car park, his mind back on drills.

Mr Dursley always sat with his back to the window in his office on the ninth floor. If he hadn't, he might have found it harder to concentrate on drills that morning. *He* didn't see the owls swooping past in broad daylight, though people down in the street did; they pointed and gazed open-mouthed as owl after owl sped overhead. Most of them had never seen an owl even at night-time. Mr Dursley, however, had a perfectly normal, owl-free morning. He yelled at five different people. He made several important telephone calls and shouted a bit more. He was in a very good mood until lunch-time, when he thought he'd stretch his legs and walk across the road to buy himself a bun from the baker's opposite.

He'd forgotten all about the people in cloaks until he passed a group of them next to the baker's. He eyed them angrily as he passed. He didn't know why, but they made him uneasy. This lot were whispering excitedly, too, and he couldn't see a single collecting tin. It was on his way back past them, clutching a large doughnut in a bag, that he caught a few words of what they were saying.

'The Potters, that's right, that's what I heard –'

'– yes, their son, Harry –'

Mr Dursley stopped dead. Fear flooded him. He looked back at the whisperers as if he wanted to say something to them, but thought better of it.

He dashed back across the road, hurried up to his office, snapped at his secretary not to disturb him, seized his telephone and had almost finished dialling his home number when he changed his mind. He put the receiver back down and stroked his moustache, thinking ... no, he was being stupid. Potter wasn't such an unusual name. He was sure there were lots of people called Potter who had a son called Harry. Come to think of it, he wasn't even sure his nephew *was* called Harry. He'd never even seen the boy. It might have been Harvey. Or Harold. There was no point in worrying Mrs Dursley, she always got so upset at any mention of her sister. He didn't blame her – if *he'd* had a sister like that ... but all the same, those people in cloaks ...

He found it a lot harder to concentrate on drills that afternoon, and when he left the building at five o'clock, he was still so worried that he walked straight into someone just outside the door.

'Sorry,' he grunted, as the tiny old man stumbled and almost fell. It was a few seconds before Mr Dursley realised that the man was wearing a violet cloak. He didn't seem at all upset at being almost knocked to the ground. On the contrary, his face split into a wide smile and he said in a squeaky voice that made passers-by stare: 'Don't be sorry, my dear sir, for nothing could upset me today! Rejoice, for You-Know-Who has gone at last! Even Muggles like yourself should be celebrating, this happy, happy day!'

And the old man hugged Mr Dursley around the middle and walked off.

Mr Dursley stood rooted to the spot. He had been hugged by a complete stranger. He also thought he had been called a Muggle, whatever that was. He was rattled. He hurried to his car and set off home, hoping he was imagining things, which he had never hoped before, because he didn't approve of imagination.

As he pulled into the driveway of number four, the first thing he saw – and it didn't improve his mood – was the tabby cat he'd spotted that morning. It was now sitting on his garden wall. He was sure it was the same one; it had the same markings around its eyes.

'Shoo!' said Mr Dursley loudly.

The cat didn't move. It just gave him a stern look. Was this normal cat behaviour, Mr Dursley wondered. Trying to pull himself together, he let himself into the house. He was still determined not to mention anything to his wife.

Mrs Dursley had had a nice, normal day. She told him over dinner all about Mrs Next Door's problems with her daughter and how Dudley had learnt a new word ('Shan't!'). Mr Dursley tried to act normally. When Dudley had been put to bed, he went into the living-room in time to catch the last report on the evening news:

'And finally, bird-watchers everywhere have reported that the nation's owls have been behaving very unusually today. Although owls normally hunt at night and are hardly ever seen in daylight, there have been hundreds of sightings of these birds flying in every direction since sunrise. Experts are unable to explain why the owls have suddenly changed their sleeping pattern.' The news reader allowed himself a grin. 'Most mysterious. And now, over to Jim McGuffin with the weather. Going to be any more showers of owls tonight, Jim?'

'Well, Ted,' said the weatherman, 'I don't know about that, but it's not only the owls that have been acting oddly today. Viewers as far apart as Kent, Yorkshire and Dundee have been phoning in to tell me that instead of the rain I promised yesterday, they've had a downpour of shooting stars! Perhaps people have been celebrating Bonfire Night early – it's not until next week, folks! But I can promise a wet night tonight.'

Mr Dursley sat frozen in his armchair. Shooting stars all over Britain? Owls flying by daylight? Mysterious people in cloaks all over the place? And a whisper, a whisper about the Potters ...

Mrs Dursley came into the living-room carrying two cups of tea. It was no good. He'd have to say something to her. He cleared his throat nervously. 'Er – Petunia, dear – you haven't heard from your sister lately, have you?'

As he had expected, Mrs Dursley looked shocked and angry. After all, they normally pretended she didn't have a sister.

'No,' she said sharply. 'Why?'

'Funny stuff on the news,' Mr Dursley mumbled. 'Owls ... shooting stars ... and there were a lot of funny-looking people in town today ...'

'So?' snapped Mrs Dursley.

'Well, I just thought ... maybe ... it was something to do with ... you know ... *her lot.*'

Mrs Dursley sipped her tea through pursed lips. Mr Dursley wondered whether he dared tell her he'd heard the name 'Potter'. He decided he didn't dare. Instead he said, as casually as he could, 'Their son – he'd be about Dudley's age now, wouldn't he?'

'I suppose so,' said Mrs Dursley stiffly.

'What's his name again? Howard, isn't it?'

'Harry. Nasty, common name, if you ask me.'

'Oh, yes,' said Mr Dursley, his heart sinking horribly. 'Yes, I quite agree.'

He didn't say another word on the subject as they went upstairs to bed. While Mrs Dursley was in the bathroom, Mr Dursley crept to the bedroom window and peered down into the front garden. The cat was still there. It was staring down Privet Drive as though it was waiting for something.

Was he imagining things? Could all this have anything to do with the Potters? If it did ... if it got out that they were related to a pair of – well, he didn't think he could bear it.

The Dursleys got into bed. Mrs Dursley fell asleep quickly but Mr Dursley lay awake, turning it all over in his mind. His last, comforting thought before he fell asleep was that even if the Potters *were* involved, there was no reason for them to come near him and Mrs Dursley. The Potters knew very well what he and Petunia thought about them and their kind ... He couldn't see how he and Petunia could get mixed up in anything that might be going on. He yawned and turned over. It couldn't affect *them* ...

How very wrong he was.

Mr Dursley might have been drifting into an uneasy sleep, but the cat on the wall outside was showing no sign of sleepiness. It was sitting as still as a statue, its eyes fixed unblinkingly on the far corner of Privet Drive. It didn't so much as quiver when a car door slammed in the next street, nor when two owls swooped overhead. In fact, it was nearly midnight before the cat moved at all.

A man appeared on the corner the cat had been watching, appeared so suddenly and silently you'd have thought he'd just popped out of the ground.

The cat's tail twitched and its eyes narrowed.

Nothing like this man had ever been seen in Privet Drive. He was tall, thin and very old, judging by the silver of his hair and beard, which were both long enough to tuck into his belt. He was wearing long robes, a purple cloak which swept the ground and high-heeled, buckled boots. His blue eyes were light, bright and sparkling behind half-moon spectacles and his nose was very long and crooked, as though it had been broken at least twice. This man's name was Albus Dumbledore.

Albus Dumbledore didn't seem to realise that he had just arrived in a street where everything from his name to his boots was unwelcome. He was busy rummaging in his cloak, looking for something. But he did seem to realise he was being watched, because he looked up suddenly at the cat, which was still staring at him from the other end of the street. For some reason, the sight of the cat seemed to amuse him. He chuckled and muttered, 'I should have known.'

He had found what he was looking for in his inside pocket. It seemed to be a silver cigarette lighter. He flicked it open, held it up in the air and clicked it. The nearest street lamp went out with a little pop. He clicked it again – the next lamp flickered into darkness. Twelve times he clicked the Put-Outer, until the only lights left in the whole street were two tiny pinpricks in the distance, which were the eyes of the cat watching him. If anyone looked out of their window now, even beady-eyed Mrs Dursley, they wouldn't be able to see anything that was happening down on the pavement. Dumbledore slipped the Put-Outer back inside his cloak and set off down the street towards number four, where he sat down on the wall next to the cat. He didn't look at it, but after a moment he spoke to it.

'Fancy seeing you here, Professor McGonagall.'

He turned to smile at the tabby, but it had gone. Instead he was smiling at a rather severe-looking woman who was wearing square glasses exactly the shape of the markings the cat had had around its eyes. She, too, was wearing a cloak, an emerald one. Her black hair was drawn into a tight bun. She looked distinctly ruffled.

'How did you know it was me?' she asked.

'My dear Professor, I've never seen a cat sit so stiffly.'

'You'd be stiff if you'd been sitting on a brick wall all day,' said Professor McGonagall.

'All day? When you could have been celebrating? I must have passed a dozen feasts and parties on my way here.'

Professor McGonagall sniffed angrily.

'Oh yes, everyone's celebrating, all right,' she said impatiently. 'You'd think they'd be a bit more careful, but no – even the Muggles have noticed something's going on. It was on their news.' She jerked her head back at the Dursleys' dark living-room window. 'I heard it. Flocks of owls ... shooting stars ... Well, they're not completely stupid. They were bound to notice something. Shooting stars down in Kent – I'll bet that was Dedalus Diggle. He never had much sense.'

'You can't blame them,' said Dumbledore gently.

'We've had precious little to celebrate for eleven years.'

'I know that,' said Professor McGonagall irritably. 'But that's no reason to lose our heads. People are being downright careless, out on the streets in broad daylight, not even dressed in Muggle clothes, swapping rumours.'

She threw a sharp, sideways glance at Dumbledore here, as though hoping he was going to tell her something, but he didn't, so she went on: 'A fine thing it would be if, on the very day You-Know-Who seems to have disappeared at last, the Muggles found out about us all. I suppose he really *has* gone, Dumbledore?'

'It certainly seems so,' said Dumbledore. 'We have much to be thankful for. Would you care for a sherbet lemon?'

'A *what*?'

'A sherbet lemon. They're a kind of Muggle sweet I'm rather fond of.'

'No, thank you,' said Professor McGonagall coldly, as though she didn't think this was the moment for sherbet lemons. 'As I say, even if You-Know-Who *has* gone –'

'My dear Professor, surely a sensible person like yourself can call him by his name? All this "You-Know-Who" nonsense – for eleven years I have been trying to persuade people to call him by his proper name: *Voldemort*.' Professor McGonagall flinched, but Dumbledore, who was unsticking two sherbet lemons, seemed not to notice. 'It all gets so confusing if we keep saying "You-Know-Who".' I have never seen any reason to be frightened of saying Voldemort's name.'

'I know you haven't,' said Professor McGonagall, sounding half-exasperated, half-admiring. 'But you're different. Everyone knows you're the only one You-Know – oh, all right, *Voldemort* – was frightened of.'

'You flatter me,' said Dumbledore calmly. 'Voldemort had powers I will never have.'

'Only because you're too – well – *noble* to use them.'

'It's lucky it's dark. I haven't blushed so much since Madam Pomfrey told me she liked my new earmuffs.'

Professor McGonagall shot a sharp look at Dumbledore and said, 'The owls are nothing to the *rumours* that are flying around. You know what everyone's saying? About why he's disappeared? About what finally stopped him?'

It seemed that Professor McGonagall had reached the point she was most anxious to discuss, the real reason she had been waiting on a cold hard wall all day, for neither as a cat nor as a woman had she fixed Dumbledore with such a piercing stare as she did now. It was plain that whatever 'everyone' was saying, she was not going to believe it until Dumbledore told her it was true. Dumbledore, however, was choosing another sherbet lemon and did not answer.

'What they're *saying*,' she pressed on, 'is that last night Voldemort turned up in Godric's Hollow. He went to find the Potters. The rumour is that Lily and James Potter are – are – that they're – *dead*.'

Dumbledore bowed his head. Professor McGonagall gasped.

'Lily and James ... I can't believe it ... I didn't want to believe it ... Oh, Albus ...'

Dumbledore reached out and patted her on the shoulder. 'I know ... I know ...' he said heavily.

Professor McGonagall's voice trembled as she went on. 'That's not all. They're saying he tried to kill the Potters' son, Harry. But – he couldn't. He couldn't kill that little boy. No one knows why, or how, but they're saying that when he couldn't kill Harry Potter, Voldemort's power somehow broke – and that's why he's gone.'

Dumbledore nodded glumly.

'It's – it's *true*?' faltered Professor McGonagall. 'After all he's done ... all the people he's killed ... he couldn't kill a little boy? It's just astounding ... of all the things to stop him ... but how in the name of heaven did Harry survive?'

'We can only guess,' said Dumbledore. 'We may never know.'

Professor McGonagall pulled out a lace handkerchief and dabbed at her eyes beneath her spectacles. Dumbledore gave a great sniff as he took a golden watch from his pocket and examined it. It was a very odd watch. It had twelve hands but no numbers; instead, little planets were moving around the edge. It must have made sense to Dumbledore, though, because he put it back in his pocket and said, 'Hagrid's late. I suppose it was he who told you I'd be here, by the way?'

'Yes,' said Professor McGonagall. 'And I don't

suppose you're going to tell me *why* you're here, of all places?'

'I've come to bring Harry to his aunt and uncle. They're the only family he has left now.'

'You don't mean – you *can't* mean the people who live *here*?' cried Professor McGonagall, jumping to her feet and pointing at number four. 'Dumbledore – you can't. I've been watching them all day. You couldn't find two people who are less like us. And they've got this son – I saw him kicking his mother all the way up the street, screaming for sweets. Harry Potter come and live here!'

'It's the best place for him,' said Dumbledore firmly. 'His aunt and uncle will be able to explain everything to him when he's older. I've written them a letter.'

'A letter?' repeated Professor McGonagall faintly, sitting back down on the wall. 'Really, Dumbledore, you think you can explain all this in a letter? These people will never understand him! He'll be famous – a legend – I wouldn't be surprised if today was known as Harry Potter Day in future – there will be books written about Harry – every child in our world will know his name!'

'Exactly,' said Dumbledore, looking very serious-ly over the top of his half-moon glasses. 'It would be enough to turn any boy's head. Famous before he can walk and talk! Famous for something he won't even remember! Can't you see how much better off he'll be, growing up away from all that until he's ready to take it?'

Professor McGonagall opened her mouth,

changed her mind, swallowed and then said, 'Yes –
yes, you're right, of course. But how is the boy
getting here, Dumbledore?' She eyed his cloak
suddenly as though she thought he might be hiding
Harry underneath it.

'Hagrid's bringing him.'

'You think it – *wise* – to trust Hagrid with something as important as this?'

'I would trust Hagrid with my life,' said
Dumbledore.

'I'm not saying his heart isn't in the right place,'
said Professor McGonagall grudgingly, 'but you
can't pretend he's not careless. He does tend to –
what was that?'

A low rumbling sound had broken the silence
around them. It grew steadily louder as they looked
up and down the street for some sign of a head-
light; it swelled to a roar as they both looked up at
the sky – and a huge motorbike fell out of the air
and landed on the road in front of them.

If the motorbike was huge, it was nothing to the
man sitting astride it. He was almost twice as tall as
a normal man and at least five times as wide. He
looked simply too big to be allowed, and so *wild* –
long tangles of bushy black hair and beard hid
most of his face, he had hands the size of dustbin
lids and his feet in their leather boots were like
baby dolphins. In his vast, muscular arms he was
holding a bundle of blankets.

'Hagrid,' said Dumbledore, sounding relieved. 'At
last. And where did you get that motorbike?'

'Borrowed it, Professor Dumbledore, sir,' said the
giant, climbing carefully off the motorbike as he

spoke. 'Young Sirius Black lent it me. I've got him, sir.'

'No problems, were there?'

'No, sir – house was almost destroyed but I got him out all right before the Muggles started swarmin' around. He fell asleep as we was flyin' over Bristol.'

Dumbledore and Professor McGonagall bent forward over the bundle of blankets. Inside, just visible, was a baby boy, fast asleep. Under a tuft of jet-black hair over his forehead they could see a curiously shaped cut, like a bolt of lightning.

'Is that where – ?' whispered Professor McGonagall.

'Yes,' said Dumbledore. 'He'll have that scar for ever.'

'Couldn't you do something about it, Dumbledore?'

'Even if I could, I wouldn't. Scars can come in useful. I have one myself above my left knee which is a perfect map of the London Underground. Well – give him here, Hagrid – we'd better get this over with.'

Dumbledore took Harry in his arms and turned towards the Dursleys' house.

'Could I – could I say goodbye to him, sir?' asked Hagrid.

He bent his great, shaggy head over Harry and gave him what must have been a very scratchy, whiskery kiss. Then, suddenly, Hagrid let out a howl like a wounded dog.

'Shhh!' hissed Professor McGonagall. 'You'll wake the Muggles!'

'S-s-sorry,' sobbed Hagrid, taking out a large spotted handkerchief and burying his face in it. 'But I c-c-can't stand it – Lily an' James dead – an' poor little Harry off ter live with Muggles –'

'Yes, yes, it's all very sad, but get a grip on yourself, Hagrid, or we'll be found,' Professor McGonagall whispered, patting Hagrid gingerly on the arm as Dumbledore stepped over the low garden wall and walked to the front door. He laid Harry gently on the doorstep, took a letter out of his cloak, tucked it inside Harry's blankets and then came back to the other two. For a full minute the three of them stood and looked at the little bundle; Hagrid's shoulders shook, Professor McGonagall blinked furiously and the twinkling light that usually shone from Dumbledore's eyes seemed to have gone out.

'Well,' said Dumbledore finally, 'that's that. We've no business staying here. We may as well go and join the celebrations.'

'Yeah,' said Hagrid in a very muffled voice. 'I'd best get this bike away. G'night, Professor McGonagall – Professor Dumbledore, sir.'

Wiping his streaming eyes on his jacket sleeve, Hagrid swung himself on to the motorbike and kicked the engine into life; with a roar it rose into the air and off into the night.

'I shall see you soon, I expect, Professor McGonagall,' said Dumbledore, nodding to her. Professor McGonagall blew her nose in reply.

Dumbledore turned and walked back down the street. On the corner he stopped and took out the silver Put-Outer. He clicked it once and twelve balls of light sped back to their street lamps so that Privet Drive glowed suddenly orange and he could make out a tabby cat slinking around the corner at the other end of the street. He could just see the bundle of blankets on the step of number four.

'Good luck, Harry,' he murmured. He turned on his heel and with a swish of his cloak he was gone.

A breeze ruffled the neat hedges of Privet Drive, which lay silent and tidy under the inky sky, the very last place you would expect astonishing things to happen. Harry Potter rolled over inside his blankets without waking up. One small hand closed on the letter beside him and he slept on, not knowing he was special, not knowing he was famous, not knowing he would be woken in a few hours' time by Mrs Dursley's scream as she opened the front door to put out the milk bottles, nor that he would spend the next few weeks being prodded and pinched by his cousin Dudley ... He couldn't know that at this very moment, people meeting in secret all over the country were holding up their glasses and saying in hushed voices: 'To Harry Potter – the boy who lived!'

— CHAPTER TWO —

The Vanishing Glass

Nearly ten years had passed since the Dursleys had woken up to find their nephew on the front step, but Privet Drive had hardly changed at all. The sun rose on the same tidy front gardens and lit up the brass number four on the Dursleys' front door; it crept into their living-room, which was almost exactly the same as it had been on the night when Mr Dursley had seen that fateful news report about the owls. Only the photographs on the mantelpiece really showed how much time had passed. Ten years ago, there had been lots of pictures of what looked like a large pink beach ball wearing different-coloured bobble hats – but Dudley Dursley was no longer a baby, and now the photographs showed a large, blond boy riding his first bicycle, on a roundabout at the fair, playing a computer game with his father, being hugged and kissed by his mother. The room held no sign at all that another boy lived in the house, too.

Yet Harry Potter was still there, asleep at the moment, but not for long. His Aunt Petunia was awake and it was her shrill voice which made the first noise of the day.

'Up! Get up! Now!'

Harry woke with a start. His aunt rapped on the door again.

'Up!' she screeched. Harry heard her walking towards the kitchen and then the sound of the frying pan being put on the cooker. He rolled on to his back and tried to remember the dream he had been having. It had been a good one. There had been a flying motorbike in it. He had a funny feeling he'd had the same dream before.

His aunt was back outside the door.

'Are you up yet?' she demanded.

'Nearly,' said Harry.

'Well, get a move on, I want you to look after the bacon. And don't you dare let it burn, I want everything perfect on Duddy's birthday.'

Harry groaned.

'What did you say?' his aunt snapped through the door.

'Nothing, nothing ...'

Dudley's birthday – how could he have forgotten? Harry got slowly out of bed and started looking for socks. He found a pair under his bed and, after pulling a spider off one of them, put them on. Harry was used to spiders, because the cupboard under the stairs was full of them, and that was where he slept.

When he was dressed he went down the hall into the kitchen. The table was almost hidden beneath all Dudley's birthday presents. It looked as though Dudley had got the new computer he wanted, not to mention the second television and the racing bike. Exactly why Dudley wanted a racing bike was a mystery to Harry, as Dudley was very fat and hated exercise – unless of course it involved punching somebody. Dudley's favourite punch-bag was Harry, but he couldn't often catch him. Harry didn't look it, but he was very fast.

Perhaps it had something to do with living in a dark cupboard, but Harry had always been small and skinny for his age. He looked even smaller and skinnier than he really was because all he had to wear were old clothes of Dudley's and Dudley was about four times bigger than he was. Harry had a thin face, knobbly knees, black hair and bright-green eyes. He wore round glasses held together with a lot of Sellotape because of all the times Dudley had punched him on the nose. The only thing Harry liked about his own appearance was a very thin scar on his forehead which was shaped like a bolt of lightning. He had had it as long as he could remember and the first question he could ever remember asking his Aunt Petunia was how he had got it.

'In the car crash when your parents died,' she had said. 'And don't ask questions.'

Don't ask questions – that was the first rule for a quiet life with the Dursleys.

Uncle Vernon entered the kitchen as Harry was turning over the bacon.

'Comb your hair!' he barked, by way of a morning greeting.

About once a week, Uncle Vernon looked over the top of his newspaper and shouted that Harry needed a haircut. Harry must have had more haircuts than the rest of the boys in his class put together, but it made no difference, his hair simply grew that way – all over the place.

Harry was frying eggs by the time Dudley arrived in the kitchen with his mother. Dudley looked a lot like Uncle Vernon. He had a large, pink face, not much neck, small, watery blue eyes and thick, blond hair that lay smoothly on his thick, fat head. Aunt Petunia often said that Dudley looked like a baby angel – Harry often said that Dudley looked like a pig in a wig.

Harry put the plates of egg and bacon on the table, which was difficult as there wasn't much room. Dudley, meanwhile, was counting his presents. His face fell.

'Thirty-six,' he said, looking up at his mother and father. 'That's two less than last year.'

'Darling, you haven't counted Auntie Marge's present, see, it's here under this big one from Mummy and Daddy.'

'All right, thirty-seven then,' said Dudley, going red in the face. Harry, who could see a huge Dudley tantrum coming on, began wolfing down his bacon as fast as possible in case Dudley turned the table over.

Aunt Petunia obviously scented danger too, because she said quickly, 'And we'll buy you another *two* presents while we're out today. How's that, popkin? *Two* more presents. Is that all right?'

Dudley thought for a moment. It looked like hard work. Finally he said slowly, 'So I'll have thirty ... thirty ...'

'Thirty-nine, sweetums,' said Aunt Petunia.

'Oh.' Dudley sat down heavily and grabbed the

nearest parcel. 'All right then.'

Uncle Vernon chuckled.

'Little tyke wants his money's worth, just like his father. Atta boy, Dudley!' He ruffled Dudley's hair.

At that moment the telephone rang and Aunt Petunia went to answer it while Harry and Uncle Vernon watched Dudley unwrap the racing bike, a cine-camera, a remote-control aeroplane, sixteen new computer games and a video recorder. He was ripping the paper off a gold wristwatch when Aunt Petunia came back from the telephone, looking both angry and worried.

'Bad news, Vernon,' she said. 'Mrs Figg's broken her leg. She can't take him.' She jerked her head in Harry's direction.

Dudley's mouth fell open in horror but Harry's heart gave a leap. Every year on Dudley's birthday his parents took him and a friend out for the day, to adventure parks, hamburger bars or the cinema. Every year, Harry was left behind with Mrs Figg, a mad old lady who lived two streets away. Harry hated it there. The whole house smelled of cabbage and Mrs Figg made him look at photographs of all the cats she'd ever owned.

'Now what?' said Aunt Petunia, looking furiously at Harry as though he'd planned this. Harry knew he ought to feel sorry that Mrs Figg had broken her leg, but it wasn't easy when he reminded himself it would be a whole year before he had to look at Tibbles, Snowy, Mr Paws and Tufty again.

'We could phone Marge,' Uncle Vernon suggested.

'Don't be silly, Vernon, she hates the boy.'

The Dursleys often spoke about Harry like this, as though he wasn't there – or rather, as though he was something very nasty that couldn't understand them, like a slug.

'What about what's-her-name, your friend – Yvonne?'

'On holiday in Majorca,' snapped Aunt Petunia.

'You could just leave me here,' Harry put in hopefully (he'd be able to watch what he wanted on television for a change and maybe even have a go on Dudley's computer).

Aunt Petunia looked as though she'd just swallowed a lemon.

'And come back and find the house in ruins?' she snarled.

'I won't blow up the house,' said Harry, but they weren't listening.

'I suppose we could take him to the zoo,' said Aunt Petunia slowly, '… and leave him in the car …'

'That car's new, he's not sitting in it alone …'

Dudley began to cry loudly. In fact, he wasn't really crying, it had been years since he'd really cried, but he knew that if he screwed up his face and wailed, his mother would give him anything he wanted.

'Dinky Duddydums, don't cry, Mummy won't let him spoil your special day!' she cried, flinging her arms around him.

'I … don't … want … him … t-t-to come!' Dudley yelled between huge pretend sobs. 'He always sp-spoils everything!' He shot Harry a nasty grin through the gap in his mother's arms.

Just then, the doorbell rang – 'Oh, Good Lord,

they're here!' said Aunt Petunia frantically – and a
moment later, Dudley's best friend, Piers Polkiss,
walked in with his mother. Piers was a scrawny boy
with a face like a rat. He was usually the one who
held people's arms behind their backs while Dudley
hit them. Dudley stopped pretending to cry at
once.

Half an hour later, Harry, who couldn't believe
his luck, was sitting in the back of the Dursleys' car
with Piers and Dudley, on the way to the zoo for
the first time in his life. His aunt and uncle hadn't
been able to think of anything else to do with him,
but before they'd left, Uncle Vernon had taken
Harry aside.

'I'm warning you,' he had said, putting his large
purple face right up close to Harry's, 'I'm warning
you now, boy – any funny business, anything at all
– and you'll be in that cupboard from now until
Christmas.'

'I'm not going to do anything,' said Harry, 'honestly ...'

But Uncle Vernon didn't believe him. No one
ever did.

The problem was, strange things often happened
around Harry and it was just no good telling the
Dursleys he didn't make them happen.

Once, Aunt Petunia, tired of Harry coming back
from the barber's looking as though he hadn't been
at all, had taken a pair of kitchen scissors and cut
his hair so short he was almost bald except for his
fringe, which she left 'to hide that horrible scar'.
Dudley had laughed himself silly at Harry, who
spent a sleepless night imagining school the next

day, where he was already laughed at for his baggy clothes and Sellotaped glasses. Next morning, however, he had got up to find his hair exactly as it had been before Aunt Petunia had sheared it off. He had been given a week in his cupboard for this, even though he had tried to explain that he *couldn't* explain how it had grown back so quickly.

Another time, Aunt Petunia had been trying to force him into a revolting old jumper of Dudley's (brown with orange bobbles). The harder she tried to pull it over his head, the smaller it seemed to become, until finally it might have fitted a glove puppet, but certainly wouldn't fit Harry. Aunt Petunia had decided it must have shrunk in the wash and, to his great relief, Harry wasn't punished.

On the other hand, he'd got into terrible trouble for being found on the roof of the school kitchens. Dudley's gang had been chasing him as usual when, as much to Harry's surprise as anyone else's, there he was sitting on the chimney. The Dursleys had received a very angry letter from Harry's headmistress telling them Harry had been climbing school buildings. But all he'd tried to do (as he shouted at Uncle Vernon through the locked door of his cupboard) was jump behind the big bins outside the kitchen doors. Harry supposed that the wind must have caught him in mid-jump.

But today, nothing was going to go wrong. It was even worth being with Dudley and Piers to be spending the day somewhere that wasn't school, his cupboard or Mrs Figg's cabbage-smelling living-room.

While he drove, Uncle Vernon complained to

Aunt Petunia. He liked to complain about things: people at work, Harry, the council, Harry, the bank and Harry were just a few of his favourite subjects. This morning, it was motorbikes.

' ... roaring along like maniacs, the young hoodlums,' he said, as a motorbike overtook them.

'I had a dream about a motorbike,' said Harry, remembering suddenly. 'It was flying.'

Uncle Vernon nearly crashed into the car in front. He turned right around in his seat and yelled at Harry, his face like a gigantic beetroot with a moustache, 'MOTORBIKES DON'T FLY!'

Dudley and Piers sniggered.

'I know they don't,' said Harry. 'It was only a dream.'

But he wished he hadn't said anything. If there was one thing the Dursleys hated even more than his asking questions, it was his talking about anything acting in a way it shouldn't, no matter if it was in a dream or even a cartoon – they seemed to think he might get dangerous ideas.

It was a very sunny Saturday and the zoo was crowded with families. The Dursleys bought Dudley and Piers large chocolate ice-creams at the entrance and then, because the smiling lady in the van had asked Harry what he wanted before they could hurry him away, they bought him a cheap lemon ice lolly. It wasn't bad either, Harry thought, licking it as they watched a gorilla scratching its head and looking remarkably like Dudley, except that it wasn't blond.

Harry had the best morning he'd had in a long time. He was careful to walk a little way apart from the Dursleys so that Dudley and Piers, who were starting to get bored with the animals by lunch-time, wouldn't fall back on their favourite hobby of hitting him. They ate in the zoo restaurant and when Dudley had a tantrum because his knicker-bocker glory wasn't big enough, Uncle Vernon bought him another one and Harry was allowed to finish the first.

Harry felt, afterwards, that he should have known it was all too good to last.

After lunch they went to the reptile house. It was cool and dark in here, with lit windows all along the walls. Behind the glass, all sorts of lizards and snakes were crawling and slithering over bits of wood and stone. Dudley and Piers wanted to see huge, poisonous cobras and thick, man-crushing pythons. Dudley quickly found the largest snake in the place. It could have wrapped its body twice around Uncle Vernon's car and crushed it into a dustbin – but at the moment it didn't look in the mood. In fact, it was fast asleep.

Dudley stood with his nose pressed against the glass, staring at the glistening brown coils.

'Make it move,' he whined at his father. Uncle Vernon tapped on the glass, but the snake didn't budge.

'Do it again,' Dudley ordered. Uncle Vernon rapped the glass smartly with his knuckles, but the snake just snoozed on.

'This is boring,' Dudley moaned. He shuffled away.

Harry moved in front of the tank and looked intently at the snake. He wouldn't have been surprised if it had died of boredom itself – no company except stupid people drumming their fingers on the glass trying to disturb it all day long. It was worse than having a cupboard as a bedroom, where the only visitor was Aunt Petunia hammering on the door to wake you up – at least he got to visit the rest of the house.

The snake suddenly opened its beady eyes. Slowly, very slowly, it raised its head until its eyes were on a level with Harry's.

It winked.

Harry stared. Then he looked quickly around to see if anyone was watching. They weren't. He looked back at the snake and winked, too.

The snake jerked its head towards Uncle Vernon and Dudley, then raised its eyes to the ceiling. It gave Harry a look that said quite plainly: *'I get that all the time.'*

'I know,' Harry murmured through the glass, though he wasn't sure the snake could hear him. 'It must be really annoying.'

The snake nodded vigorously.

'Where do you come from, anyway?' Harry asked.

The snake jabbed its tail at a little sign next to the glass. Harry peered at it.

Boa Constrictor, Brazil.

'Was it nice there?'

The boa constrictor jabbed its tail at the sign again and Harry read on: *This specimen was bred in the zoo.* 'Oh, I see – so you've never been to Brazil?'

As the snake shook its head, a deafening shout behind Harry made both of them jump. 'DUDLEY!

MR DURSLEY! COME AND LOOK AT THIS
SNAKE! YOU WON'T *BELIEVE* WHAT IT'S
DOING!'

Dudley came waddling towards them as fast as
he could.

'Out of the way, you,' he said, punching Harry in
the ribs. Caught by surprise, Harry fell hard on the
concrete floor. What came next happened so fast
no one saw how it happened – one second, Piers
and Dudley were leaning right up close to the glass,
the next, they had leapt back with howls of horror.

Harry sat up and gasped; the glass front of the
boa constrictor's tank had vanished. The great
snake was uncoiling itself rapidly, slithering out on
to the floor – people throughout the reptile house
screamed and started running for the exits.

As the snake slid swiftly past him, Harry could
have sworn a low, hissing voice said, 'Brazil, here I
come ... Thanksss, amigo.'

The keeper of the reptile house was in shock.

'But the glass,' he kept saying, 'where did the
glass go?'

The zoo director himself made Aunt Petunia a
cup of strong sweet tea while he apologised over
and over again. Piers and Dudley could only gibber.
As far as Harry had seen, the snake hadn't done
anything except snap playfully at their heels as it
passed, but by the time they were all back in Uncle
Vernon's car, Dudley was telling them how it had
nearly bitten off his leg, while Piers was swearing it
had tried to squeeze him to death. But worst of all,
for Harry at least, was Piers calming down enough
to say, 'Harry was talking to it, weren't you, Harry?'

Uncle Vernon waited until Piers was safely out of the house before starting on Harry. He was so angry he could hardly speak. He managed to say, 'Go – cupboard – stay – no meals,' before he collapsed into a chair and Aunt Petunia had to run and get him a large brandy.

*

Harry lay in his dark cupboard much later, wishing he had a watch. He didn't know what time it was and he couldn't be sure the Dursleys were asleep yet. Until they were, he couldn't risk sneaking to the kitchen for some food.

He'd lived with the Dursleys almost ten years, ten miserable years, as long as he could remember, ever since he'd been a baby and his parents had died in that car crash. He couldn't remember being in the car when his parents had died. Sometimes, when he strained his memory during long hours in his cupboard, he came up with a strange vision: a blinding flash of green light and a burning pain on his forehead. This, he supposed, was the crash, though he couldn't imagine where all the green light came from. He couldn't remember his parents at all. His aunt and uncle never spoke about them, and of course he was forbidden to ask questions. There were no photographs of them in the house.

When he had been younger, Harry had dreamed and dreamed of some unknown relation coming to take him away, but it had never happened; the Dursleys were his only family. Yet sometimes he thought (or maybe hoped) that strangers in the street seemed to know him. Very strange strangers they were, too. A tiny man in a violet top hat had bowed to him once while out shopping with Aunt Petunia and Dudley. After asking Harry furiously if he knew the man, Aunt Petunia had rushed them out of the shop without buying anything. A wild-looking old woman dressed all in green had waved merrily at him once on a bus. A bald man in a very long purple coat had actually shaken his hand in the street the other day and then walked away without a word. The weirdest thing about all these people was the way they seemed to vanish the second Harry tried to get a closer look.

At school, Harry had no one. Everybody knew that Dudley's gang hated that odd Harry Potter in his baggy old clothes and broken glasses, and nobody liked to disagree with Dudley's gang.

CHAPTER THREE

The Letters from No One

The escape of the Brazilian boa constrictor earned Harry his longest-ever punishment. By the time he was allowed out of his cupboard again, the summer holidays had started and Dudley had already broken his new cine-camera, crashed his remote-control aeroplane and, first time on his racing bike, knocked down old Mrs Figg as she crossed Privet Drive on her crutches.

Harry was glad school was over, but there was no escaping Dudley's gang, who visited the house every single day. Piers, Dennis, Malcolm and Gordon were all big and stupid, but as Dudley was the biggest and stupidest of the lot, he was the leader. The rest of them were all quite happy to join in Dudley's favourite sport: Harry-hunting.

This was why Harry spent as much time as possible out of the house, wandering around and thinking about the end of the holidays, where he could see a tiny ray of hope. When September came he would be going off to secondary school and, for the first time in his life, he wouldn't be with Dudley.

Dudley had a place at Uncle Vernon's old school, Smeltings. Piers Polkiss was going there, too. Harry, on the other hand, was going to Stonewall High, the local comprehensive. Dudley thought this was very funny.

'They stuff people's heads down the toilet first day at Stonewall,' he told Harry. 'Want to come upstairs and practise?'

'No thanks,' said Harry. 'The poor toilet's never had anything as horrible as your head down it – it might be sick.' Then he ran, before Dudley could work out what he'd said.

One day in July, Aunt Petunia took Dudley to London to buy his Smeltings uniform, leaving Harry at Mrs Figg's. Mrs Figg wasn't as bad as usual. It turned out she'd broken her leg tripping over one of her cats and she didn't seem quite as fond of them as before. She let Harry watch television and gave him a bit of chocolate cake that tasted as though she'd had it for several years.

That evening, Dudley paraded around the living-room for the family in his brand-new uniform. Smeltings boys wore maroon tailcoats, orange knickerbockers and flat straw hats called boaters. They also carried knobbly sticks, used for hitting each other while the teachers weren't looking. This was supposed to be good training for later life.

As he looked at Dudley in his new knickerbockers, Uncle Vernon said gruffly that it was the proudest moment of his life. Aunt Petunia burst into tears and said she couldn't believe it was her Ickle Dudleykins, he looked so handsome and grown-up. Harry didn't trust himself to speak. He thought two of his ribs might already have cracked from trying not to laugh.

There was a horrible smell in the kitchen next morning when Harry went in for breakfast. It seemed to be coming from a large metal tub in the sink. He went to have a look. The tub was full of what looked like dirty rags swimming in grey water.

'What's this?' he asked Aunt Petunia. Her lips tightened as they always did if he dared to ask a question.

'Your new school uniform,' she said.

Harry looked in the bowl again.

'Oh,' he said. 'I didn't realise it had to be so wet.'

'Don't be stupid,' snapped Aunt Petunia. 'I'm dyeing some of Dudley's old things grey for you. It'll look just like everyone else's when I've finished.'

Harry seriously doubted this, but thought it best not to argue. He sat down at the table and tried not to think about how he was going to look on his first day at Stonewall High – like he was wearing bits of old elephant skin, probably.

Dudley and Uncle Vernon came in, both with wrinkled noses because of the smell from Harry's new uniform. Uncle Vernon opened his newspaper as usual and Dudley banged his Smeltings stick, which he carried everywhere, on the table.

They heard the click of the letter-box and flop of letters on the doormat.

'Get the post, Dudley,' said Uncle Vernon from behind his paper.

'Make Harry get it.'

'Get the post, Harry.'

'Make Dudley get it.'

'Poke him with your Smeltings stick, Dudley.'

Harry dodged the Smeltings stick and went to get the post. Three things lay on the doormat: a postcard from Uncle Vernon's sister Marge, who was holidaying on the Isle of Wight, a brown envelope that looked like a bill and – *a letter for Harry*.

Harry picked it up and stared at it, his heart twanging like a giant elastic band. No one, ever, in his whole life, had written to him. Who would? He had no friends, no other relatives – he didn't belong to the library so he'd never even got rude notes asking for books back. Yet here it was, a letter, addressed so plainly there could be no mistake:

> *Mr H. Potter*
> *The Cupboard under the Stairs*
> *4 Privet Drive*
> *Little Whinging*
> *Surrey*

The envelope was thick and heavy, made of yellowish parchment, and the address was written in emerald-green ink. There was no stamp.

Turning the envelope over, his hand trembling, Harry saw a purple wax seal bearing a coat of arms; a lion, an eagle, a badger and a snake surrounding a large letter 'H'.

'Hurry up, boy!' shouted Uncle Vernon from the kitchen. 'What are you doing, checking for letter-bombs?' He chuckled at his own joke.

Harry went back to the kitchen, still staring at

his letter. He handed Uncle Vernon the bill and the postcard, sat down and slowly began to open the yellow envelope.

Uncle Vernon ripped open the bill, snorted in disgust and flipped over the postcard.

'Marge's ill,' he informed Aunt Petunia. 'Ate a funny whelk ...'

'Dad!' said Dudley suddenly. 'Dad, Harry's got something!'

Harry was on the point of unfolding his letter, which was written on the same heavy parchment as the envelope, when it was jerked sharply out of his hand by Uncle Vernon.

'That's *mine*!' said Harry, trying to snatch it back.

'Who'd be writing to you?' sneered Uncle Vernon, shaking the letter open with one hand and glancing at it. His face went from red to green faster than a set of traffic lights. And it didn't stop there. Within seconds it was the greyish white of old porridge.

'P-P-Petunia!' he gasped.

Dudley tried to grab the letter to read it, but Uncle Vernon held it high out of his reach. Aunt Petunia took it curiously and read the first line. For a moment it looked as though she might faint. She clutched her throat and made a choking noise.

'Vernon! Oh my goodness – Vernon!'

They stared at each other, seeming to have forgotten that Harry and Dudley were still in the room. Dudley wasn't used to being ignored. He gave his father a sharp tap on the head with his Smeltings stick.

'I want to read that letter,' he said loudly.

'*I* want to read it,' said Harry furiously, 'as it's *mine*.'

'Get out, both of you,' croaked Uncle Vernon, stuffing the letter back inside its envelope.

Harry didn't move.

'I WANT MY LETTER!' he shouted.

'Let *me* see it!' demanded Dudley.

'OUT!' roared Uncle Vernon, and he took both Harry and Dudley by the scruffs of their necks and threw them into the hall, slamming the kitchen door behind them. Harry and Dudley promptly had a furious but silent fight over who would listen at the keyhole; Dudley won, so Harry, his glasses dangling from one ear, lay flat on his stomach to listen at the crack between door and floor.

'Vernon,' Aunt Petunia was saying in a quivering voice, 'look at the address – how could they possibly know where he sleeps? You don't think they're watching the house?'

'Watching – spying – might be following us,' muttered Uncle Vernon wildly.

'But what should we do, Vernon? Should we write back? Tell them we don't want –'

Harry could see Uncle Vernon's shiny black shoes pacing up and down the kitchen.

'No,' he said finally. 'No, we'll ignore it. If they don't get an answer ... yes, that's best ... we won't do anything ...'

'But –'

'I'm not having one in the house, Petunia! Didn't we swear when we took him in we'd stamp out that dangerous nonsense?'

*

That evening when he got back from work, Uncle Vernon did something he'd never done before; he visited Harry in his cupboard.

'Where's my letter?' said Harry, the moment Uncle Vernon had squeezed through the door. 'Who's writing to me?'

'No one. It was addressed to you by mistake,' said Uncle Vernon shortly. 'I have burned it.'

'It was *not* a mistake,' said Harry angrily. 'It had my cupboard on it.'

'SILENCE!' yelled Uncle Vernon, and a couple of spiders fell from the ceiling. He took a few deep breaths and then forced his face into a smile, which looked quite painful.

'Er – yes, Harry – about this cupboard. Your aunt and I have been thinking ... you're really getting a bit big for it ... we think it might be nice if you moved into Dudley's second bedroom.'

'Why?' said Harry.

'Don't ask questions!' snapped his uncle. 'Take this stuff upstairs, now.'

The Dursleys' house had four bedrooms: one for Uncle Vernon and Aunt Petunia, one for visitors (usually Uncle Vernon's sister, Marge), one where Dudley slept and one where Dudley kept all the toys and things that wouldn't fit into his first bedroom. It only took Harry one trip upstairs to move everything he owned from the cupboard to this room. He sat down on the bed and stared around him. Nearly everything in here was broken. The month-old cine-camera was lying on top of a small, working tank Dudley had once driven over next door's dog; in the corner was Dudley's first-ever television set, which he'd put his foot through when his favourite programme had been cancelled; there was a large bird-cage which had once held a parrot that Dudley had swapped at school for a real air-rifle, which was up on a shelf with the end all bent because Dudley had sat on it. Other shelves were full of books. They were the only things in the room that looked as though they'd never been touched.

From downstairs came the sound of Dudley bawling at his mother: 'I don't *want* him in there ... I *need* that room ... make him get out ...'

Harry sighed and stretched out on the bed. Yesterday he'd have given anything to be up here. Today he'd rather be back in his cupboard with that letter than up here without it.

Next morning at breakfast, everyone was rather quiet. Dudley was in shock. He'd screamed, whacked his father with his Smeltings stick, been sick on purpose, kicked his mother and thrown his tortoise through the greenhouse roof and he still didn't have his room back. Harry was thinking about this time yesterday and bitterly wishing he'd opened the letter in the hall. Uncle Vernon and Aunt Petunia kept looking at each other darkly.

When the post arrived, Uncle Vernon, who seemed to be trying to be nice to Harry, made Dudley go and get it. They heard him banging things with his Smeltings stick all the way down the hall. Then he shouted, 'There's another one! *Mr H. Potter, The Smallest Bedroom, 4 Privet Drive –*'

With a strangled cry, Uncle Vernon leapt from his seat and ran down the hall, Harry right behind him. Uncle Vernon had to wrestle Dudley to the ground to get the letter from him, which was made difficult by the fact that Harry had grabbed Uncle Vernon around the neck from behind. After a minute of confused fighting, in which everyone got hit a lot by the Smeltings stick, Uncle Vernon straightened up, gasping for breath, with Harry's letter clutched in his hand.

'Go to your cupboard – I mean, your bedroom,' he wheezed at Harry. 'Dudley – go – just go.'

Harry walked round and round his new room. Someone knew he had moved out of his cupboard and they seemed to know he hadn't received his first letter. Surely that meant they'd try again? And this time he'd make sure they didn't fail. He had a plan.

*

The repaired alarm clock rang at six o'clock the next morning. Harry turned it off quickly and dressed silently. He mustn't wake the Dursleys. He stole downstairs without turning on any of the lights.

He was going to wait for the postman on the corner of Privet Drive and get the letters for number four first. His heart hammered as he crept across the dark hall towards the front door –

'AAAAARRRGH!'

Harry leapt into the air – he'd trodden on something big and squashy on the doormat – something *alive*!

Lights clicked on upstairs and to his horror Harry realised that the big squashy something had been his uncle's face. Uncle Vernon had been lying

at the foot of the front door in a sleeping bag, clearly making sure that Harry didn't do exactly what
he'd been trying to do. He shouted at Harry for
about half an hour and then told him to go and
make a cup of tea. Harry shuffled miserably off into
the kitchen, and by the time he got back, the post
had arrived, right into Uncle Vernon's lap. Harry
could see three letters addressed in green ink.

'I want –' he began, but Uncle Vernon was tearing the letters into pieces before his eyes.

Uncle Vernon didn't go to work that day. He
stayed at home and nailed up the letter-box.

'See,' he explained to Aunt Petunia through a
mouthful of nails, 'if they can't *deliver* them they'll
just give up.'

'I'm not sure that'll work, Vernon.'

'Oh, these people's minds work in strange ways,
Petunia, they're not like you and me,' said Uncle
Vernon, trying to knock in a nail with the piece of
fruit cake Aunt Petunia had just brought him.

*

On Friday, no fewer than twelve letters arrived for
Harry. As they couldn't go through the letter-box
they had been pushed under the door, slotted
through the sides and a few even forced through
the small window in the downstairs toilet.

Uncle Vernon stayed at home again. After burning all the letters, he got out a hammer and nails
and boarded up the cracks around the front and
back doors so no one could go out. He hummed
'Tiptoe through the Tulips' as he worked, and
jumped at small noises.

*

On Saturday, things began to get out of hand. Twenty-four letters to Harry found their way into the house, rolled up and hidden inside each of the two dozen eggs that their very confused milkman had handed Aunt Petunia through the living-room window. While Uncle Vernon made furious telephone calls to the post office and the dairy trying to find someone to complain to, Aunt Petunia shredded the letters in her food mixer.

'Who on earth wants to talk to *you* this badly?' Dudley asked Harry in amazement.

*

On Sunday morning, Uncle Vernon sat down at the breakfast table looking tired and rather ill, but happy.

'No post on Sundays,' he reminded them happily as he spread marmalade on his newspapers, 'no damn letters today –'

Something came whizzing down the kitchen chimney as he spoke and caught him sharply on the back of the head. Next moment, thirty or forty letters came pelting out of the fireplace like bullets. The Dursleys ducked, but Harry leapt into the air trying to catch one –

'Out! OUT!'

Uncle Vernon seized Harry around the waist and threw him into the hall. When Aunt Petunia and Dudley had run out with their arms over their faces, Uncle Vernon slammed the door shut. They could hear the letters still streaming into the room, bouncing off the walls and floor.

'That does it,' said Uncle Vernon, trying to speak calmly but pulling great tufts out of his moustache at the same time. 'I want you all back here in five minutes, ready to leave. We're going away. Just pack some clothes. No arguments!'

He looked so dangerous with half his moustache missing that no one dared argue. Ten minutes later they had wrenched their way through the boarded-up doors and were in the car, speeding towards the motorway. Dudley was sniffling in the back seat; his father had hit him round the head for holding them up while he tried to pack his television, video and computer in his sports bag.

They drove. And they drove. Even Aunt Petunia didn't dare ask where they were going. Every now and then Uncle Vernon would take a sharp turning and drive in the opposite direction for a while.

'Shake 'em off ... shake 'em off,' he would mutter whenever he did this.

They didn't stop to eat or drink all day. By nightfall Dudley was howling. He'd never had such a bad day in his life. He was hungry, he'd missed five television programmes he'd wanted to see and he'd never gone so long without blowing up an alien on his computer.

Uncle Vernon stopped at last outside a gloomy-looking hotel on the outskirts of a big city. Dudley and Harry shared a room with twin beds and damp, musty sheets. Dudley snored but Harry stayed awake, sitting on the window-sill, staring down at the lights of passing cars and wondering ...

*

They ate stale cornflakes and cold tinned tomatoes on toast for breakfast next day. They had just finished when the owner of the hotel came over to their table.

' 'Scuse me, but is one of you Mr H. Potter? Only I got about an 'undred of these at the front desk.'

She held up a letter so they could read the green ink address:

Mr H. Potter
Room 17
Railview Hotel
Cokeworth

Harry made a grab for the letter but Uncle Vernon knocked his hand out of the way. The woman stared.

'I'll take them,' said Uncle Vernon, standing up quickly and following her from the dining-room.

*

'Wouldn't it be better just to go home, dear?' Aunt Petunia suggested timidly, hours later, but Uncle Vernon didn't seem to hear her. Exactly what he was looking for, none of them knew. He drove them into the middle of a forest, got out, looked around, shook his head, got back in the car and off they went again. The same thing happened in the middle of a ploughed field, halfway across a sus-pension bridge and at the top of a multi-storey car park.

'Daddy's gone mad, hasn't he?' Dudley asked Aunt Petunia dully late that afternoon. Uncle Vernon had parked at the coast, locked them all inside the car and disappeared.

It started to rain. Great drops beat on the roof of the car. Dudley snivelled.

'It's Monday,' he told his mother. 'The Great

Humberto's on tonight. I want to stay somewhere with a *television*.'

Monday. This reminded Harry of something. If it *was* Monday – and you could usually count on Dudley to know the days of the week, because of television – then tomorrow, Tuesday, was Harry's eleventh birthday. Of course, his birthdays were never exactly fun – last year, the Dursleys had given him a coat-hanger and a pair of Uncle Vernon's old socks. Still, you weren't eleven every day.

Uncle Vernon was back and he was smiling. He was also carrying a long, thin package and didn't answer Aunt Petunia when she asked what he'd bought.

'Found the perfect place!' he said. 'Come on! Everyone out!'

It was very cold outside the car. Uncle Vernon was pointing at what looked like a large rock way out to sea. Perched on top of the rock was the most miserable little shack you could imagine. One thing was certain, there was no television in there.

'Storm forecast for tonight!' said Uncle Vernon gleefully, clapping his hands together. 'And this gentleman's kindly agreed to lend us his boat!'

A toothless old man came ambling up to them, pointing, with a rather wicked grin, at an old rowing boat bobbing in the iron-grey water below them.

'I've already got us some rations,' said Uncle Vernon, 'so all aboard!'

It was freezing in the boat. Icy sea spray and rain crept down their necks and a chilly wind whipped their faces. After what seemed like hours they reached the rock, where Uncle Vernon, slipping and sliding, led the way to the broken-down house.

The inside was horrible; it smelled strongly of seaweed, the wind whistled through the gaps in the wooden walls and the fireplace was damp and empty. There were only two rooms.

Uncle Vernon's rations turned out to be a packet of crisps each and four bananas. He tried to start a fire but the empty crisp packets just smoked and shrivelled up.

'Could do with some of those letters now, eh?' he said cheerfully.

He was in a very good mood. Obviously he thought nobody stood a chance of reaching them here in a storm to deliver post. Harry privately agreed, though the thought didn't cheer him up at all.

As night fell, the promised storm blew up around them. Spray from the high waves splattered the walls of the hut and a fierce wind rattled the filthy windows. Aunt Petunia found a few mouldy blankets in the second room and made up a bed for Dudley on the moth-eaten sofa. She and Uncle Vernon went off to the lumpy bed next door and Harry was left to find the softest bit of floor he could and to curl up under the thinnest, most ragged blanket.

The storm raged more and more ferociously as the night went on. Harry couldn't sleep. He shivered and turned over, trying to get comfortable, his stomach rumbling with hunger. Dudley's snores were drowned by the low rolls of thunder that started near midnight. The lighted dial of Dudley's watch, which was dangling over the edge of the sofa on his fat wrist, told Harry he'd be eleven in ten minutes' time. He lay and watched his birthday tick nearer, wondering if the Dursleys would remember at all, wondering where the letter-writer was now.

Five minutes to go. Harry heard something creak outside. He hoped the roof wasn't going to fall in, although he might be warmer if it did. Four minutes to go. Maybe the house in Privet Drive would be so full of letters when they got back that he'd be able to steal one somehow.

Three minutes to go. Was that the sea, slapping hard on the rock like that? And (two minutes to go) what was that funny crunching noise? Was the rock crumbling into the sea?

One minute to go and he'd be eleven. Thirty seconds ... twenty ... ten – nine – maybe he'd wake Dudley up, just to annoy him – three – two – one –

BOOM.

The whole shack shivered and Harry sat bolt upright, staring at the door. Someone was outside, knocking to come in.

— CHAPTER FOUR —

The Keeper of the Keys

BOOM. They knocked again. Dudley jerked awake.

'Where's the cannon?' he said stupidly.

There was a crash behind them and Uncle Vernon came skidding into the room. He was holding a rifle in his hands – now they knew what had been in the long, thin package he had brought with them.

'Who's there?' he shouted. 'I warn you – I'm armed!'

There was a pause. Then –

SMASH!

The door was hit with such force that it swung clean off its hinges and with a deafening crash landed flat on the floor.

A giant of a man was standing in the doorway. His face was almost completely hidden by a long, shaggy mane of hair and a wild, tangled beard, but you could make out his eyes, glinting like black beetles under all the hair.

The giant squeezed his way into the hut, stooping so that his head just brushed the ceiling. He bent down, picked up the door and fitted it easily back into its frame. The noise of the storm outside dropped a little. He turned to look at them all.

'Couldn't make us a cup o' tea, could yeh? It's not been an easy journey ...'

He strode over to the sofa where Dudley sat frozen with fear.

'Budge up, yeh great lump,' said the stranger.

Dudley squeaked and ran to hide behind his mother, who was crouching, terrified, behind Uncle Vernon.

'An' here's Harry!' said the giant.

Harry looked up into the fierce, wild, shadowy face and saw that the beetle eyes were crinkled in a smile.

'Las' time I saw you, you was only a baby,' said the giant. 'Yeh look a lot like yer dad, but yeh've got yer mum's eyes.'

Uncle Vernon made a funny rasping noise.

'I demand that you leave at once, sir!' he said. 'You are breaking and entering!'

'Ah, shut up, Dursley, yeh great prune,' said the giant. He reached over the back of the sofa, jerked the gun out of Uncle Vernon's hands, bent it into a knot as easily as if it had been made of rubber, and threw it into a corner of the room.

Uncle Vernon made another funny noise, like a mouse being trodden on.

'Anyway – Harry,' said the giant, turning his back on the Dursleys, 'a very happy birthday to yeh. Got summat fer yeh here – I mighta sat on it at some point, but it'll taste all right.'

From an inside pocket of his black overcoat he pulled a slightly squashed box. Harry opened it with trembling fingers. Inside was a large, sticky chocolate cake with *Happy Birthday Harry* written on it in green icing.

Harry looked up at the giant. He meant to say thank you, but the words got lost on the way to his mouth, and what he said instead was, 'Who are you?'

The giant chuckled.

'True, I haven't introduced meself. Rubeus Hagrid, Keeper of Keys and Grounds at Hogwarts.'

He held out an enormous hand and shook Harry's whole arm.

'What about that tea then, eh?' he said, rubbing his hands together. 'I'd not say no ter summat stronger if yeh've got it, mind.'

His eyes fell on the empty grate with the shrivelled crisp packets in it and he snorted. He bent down over the fireplace; they couldn't see what he was doing but when he drew back a second later, there was a roaring fire there. It filled the whole damp hut with flickering light and Harry felt the warmth wash over him as though he'd sunk into a hot bath.

The giant sat back down on the sofa, which sagged under his weight, and began taking all sorts of things out of the pockets of his coat: a copper kettle, a squashy package of sausages, a poker, a teapot, several chipped mugs and a bottle of some amber liquid which he took a swig from before starting to make tea. Soon the hut was full of the sound and smell of sizzling sausage. Nobody said a thing while the giant was working, but as he slid the first six fat, juicy, slightly burnt sausages from the poker, Dudley fidgeted a little. Uncle Vernon said sharply, 'Don't touch anything he gives you, Dudley.'

The giant chuckled darkly.

'Yer great puddin' of a son don' need fattenin' any more, Dursley, don' worry.'

He passed the sausages to Harry, who was so hungry he had never tasted anything so wonderful, but he still couldn't take his eyes off the giant. Finally, as nobody seemed about to explain anything, he said, 'I'm sorry, but I still don't really know who you are.'

The giant took a gulp of tea and wiped his mouth with the back of his hand.

'Call me Hagrid,' he said, 'everyone does. An' like I told yeh, I'm Keeper of Keys at Hogwarts – yeh'll know all about Hogwarts, o' course.'

'Er – no,' said Harry.

Hagrid looked shocked.

'Sorry,' Harry said quickly.

'*Sorry?*' barked Hagrid, turning to stare at the Dursleys, who shrank back into the shadows. 'It's them as should be sorry! I knew yeh weren't gettin' yer letters but I never thought yeh wouldn't even know abou' Hogwarts, fer cryin' out loud! Did yeh never wonder where yer parents learnt it all?'

'All what?' asked Harry.

'ALL WHAT?' Hagrid thundered. 'Now wait jus' one second!'

He had leapt to his feet. In his anger he seemed to fill the whole hut. The Dursleys were cowering against the wall.

'Do you mean ter tell me,' he growled at the

Dursleys, 'that this boy – this boy! – knows nothin' abou' – about ANYTHING?'

Harry thought this was going a bit far. He had been to school, after all, and his marks weren't bad.

'I know *some* things,' he said. 'I can, you know, do maths and stuff.'

But Hagrid simply waved his hand and said, 'About *our* world, I mean. *Your* world. *My* world. *Yer parents' world.*'

'What world?'

Hagrid looked as if he was about to explode.

'DURSLEY!' he boomed.

Uncle Vernon, who had gone very pale, whispered something that sounded like 'Mimblewimble'. Hagrid stared wildly at Harry.

'But yeh must know about yer mum and dad,' he said. 'I mean, they're *famous. You're* famous.'

'What? My – my mum and dad weren't famous, were they?'

'Yeh don' know ... yeh don' know ...' Hagrid ran his fingers through his hair, fixing Harry with a bewildered stare.

'Yeh don' know what yeh *are?*' he said finally.

Uncle Vernon suddenly found his voice.

'Stop!' he commanded. 'Stop right there, sir! I forbid you to tell the boy anything!'

A braver man than Vernon Dursley would have quailed under the furious look Hagrid now gave him; when Hagrid spoke, his every syllable trembled with rage.

'You never told him? Never told him what was in the letter Dumbledore left fer him? I was there! I saw Dumbledore leave it, Dursley! An' you've kept it from him all these years?'

'Kept *what* from me?' said Harry eagerly.

'STOP! I FORBID YOU!' yelled Uncle Vernon in panic.

Aunt Petunia gave a gasp of horror.

'Ah, go boil yer heads, both of yeh,' said Hagrid. 'Harry – yer a wizard.'

There was silence inside the hut. Only the sea and the whistling wind could be heard.

'I'm a *what*?' gasped Harry.

'A wizard, o' course,' said Hagrid, sitting back down on the sofa, which groaned and sank even lower, 'an' a thumpin' good'un, I'd say, once yeh've been trained up a bit. With a mum an' dad like yours, what else would yeh be? An' I reckon it's abou' time yeh read yer letter.'

Harry stretched out his hand at last to take the yellowish envelope, addressed in emerald green to *Mr H. Potter, The Floor, Hut-on-the-Rock, The Sea.* He pulled out the letter and read:

HOGWARTS SCHOOL OF WITCHCRAFT AND WIZARDRY

Headmaster: Albus Dumbledore
(Order of Merlin, First Class, Grand Sorc.,
Chf. Warlock, Supreme Mugwump, International
Confed. of Wizards)

Dear Mr Potter,
  We are pleased to inform you that you have a place at Hogwarts School of Witchcraft and

Wizardry. Please find enclosed a list of all neces-
sary books and equipment.

   Term begins on 1 September. We await your
owl by no later than 31 July.

Yours sincerely,

Minerva McGonagall
Deputy Headmistress

Questions exploded inside Harry's head like fire-
works and he couldn't decide which to ask first.
After a few minutes he stammered, 'What does it
mean, they await my owl?'

'Gallopin' Gorgons, that reminds me,' said
Hagrid, clapping a hand to his forehead with
enough force to knock over a cart horse, and from
yet another pocket inside his overcoat he pulled an
owl – a real, live, rather ruffled-looking owl – a
long quill and a roll of parchment. With his tongue
between his teeth he scribbled a note which Harry
could read upside-down:

Dear Mr Dumbledore,
   Given Harry his letter. Taking him to buy his
things tomorrow.
   Weather's horrible. Hope you're well.
   Hagrid

Hagrid rolled up the note, gave it to the owl, which
clamped it in its beak, went to the door and threw
the owl out into the storm. Then he came back and

sat down as though this was as normal as talking on the telephone.

Harry realised his mouth was open and closed it quickly.

'Where was I?' said Hagrid, but at that moment, Uncle Vernon, still ashen-faced but looking very angry, moved into the firelight.

'He's not going,' he said.

Hagrid grunted.

'I'd like ter see a great Muggle like you stop him,' he said.

'A what?' said Harry, interested.

'A Muggle,' said Hagrid. 'It's what we call non-magic folk like them. An' it's your bad luck you grew up in a family o' the biggest Muggles I ever laid eyes on.'

'We swore when we took him in we'd put a stop to that rubbish,' said Uncle Vernon, 'swore we'd stamp it out of him! Wizard, indeed!'

'You *knew*?' said Harry. 'You *knew* I'm a – a wizard?'

'Knew!' shrieked Aunt Petunia suddenly. '*Knew!* Of course we knew! How could you not be, my dratted sister being what she was? Oh, she got a letter just like that and disappeared off to that – that *school* – and came home every holiday with her pockets full of frog-spawn, turning teacups into rats. I was the only one who saw her for what she was – a freak! But for my mother and father, oh no, it was Lily this and Lily that, they were proud of having a witch in the family!'

She stopped to draw a deep breath and then went ranting on. It seemed she had been wanting to say all this for years.

'Then she met that Potter at school and they left and got married and had you, and of course I knew you'd be just the same, just as strange, just as – as – *abnormal* – and then, if you please, she went and got herself blown up and we got landed with you!'

Harry had gone very white. As soon as he found his voice he said, 'Blown up? You told me they died in a car crash!'

'CAR CRASH!' roared Hagrid, jumping up so angrily that the Dursleys scuttled back to their corner. 'How could a car crash kill Lily an' James Potter? It's an outrage! A scandal! Harry Potter not knowin' his own story when every kid in our world knows his name!'

'But why? What happened?' Harry asked urgently.

The anger faded from Hagrid's face. He looked suddenly anxious.

'I never expected this,' he said, in a low, worried voice. 'I had no idea, when Dumbledore told me there might be trouble gettin' hold of yeh, how much yeh didn't know. Ah, Harry, I don' know if I'm the right person ter tell yeh – but someone's gotta – yeh can't go off ter Hogwarts not knowin'.'

He threw a dirty look at the Dursleys.

'Well, it's best yeh know as much as I can tell yeh – mind, I can't tell yeh everythin', it's a great myst'ry, parts of it ...'

He sat down, stared into the fire for a few seconds and then said, 'It begins, I suppose, with – with a person called – but it's incredible yeh don't know his name, everyone in our world knows –'

'Who?'

'Well – I don' like sayin' the name if I can help it. No one does.'

'Why not?'

'Gulpin' gargoyles, Harry, people are still scared. Blimey, this is difficult. See, there was this wizard who went ... bad. As bad as you could go. Worse. Worse than worse. His name was ...'

Hagrid gulped, but no words came out.

'Could you write it down?' Harry suggested.

'Nah – can't spell it. All right – *Voldemort*.' Hagrid shuddered. 'Don' make me say it again. Anyway, this – this wizard, about twenty years ago now, started lookin' fer followers. Got 'em, too – some were afraid, some just wanted a bit o' his power, 'cause he was gettin' himself power, all right. Dark days, Harry. Didn't know who ter trust, didn't dare get friendly with strange wizards or witches ... Terrible things happened. He was takin' over. 'Course, some stood up to him – an' he killed 'em. Horribly. One o' the only safe places left was Hogwarts. Reckon Dumbledore's the only one You-Know-Who was afraid of. Didn't dare try takin' the school, not jus' then, anyway.

'Now, yer mum an' dad were as good a witch an' wizard as I ever knew. Head Boy an' Girl at Hog-warts in their day! Suppose the myst'ry is why You-Know-Who never tried to get 'em on his side before ... probably knew they were too close ter Dumbledore ter want anythin' ter do with the Dark Side.

'Maybe he thought he could persuade 'em ... maybe he just wanted 'em outta the way. All any-one knows is, he turned up in the village where you was all living, on Hallowe'en ten years ago. You was just a year old. He came ter yer house an' – an' –'

Hagrid suddenly pulled out a very dirty, spotted handkerchief and blew his nose with a sound like a foghorn.

'Sorry,' he said. 'But it's that sad – knew yer mum an' dad, an' nicer people yeh couldn't find – anyway –

'You-Know-Who killed 'em. An' then – an' this is the real myst'ry of the thing – he tried to kill you, too. Wanted ter make a clean job of it, I suppose, or maybe he just liked killin' by then. But he couldn't do it. Never wondered how you got that mark on yer forehead? That was no ordinary cut. That's what yeh get when a powerful, evil curse touches yeh – took care of yer mum an' dad an' yer house, even – but it didn't work on you, an' that's why yer famous, Harry. No one ever lived after he decided ter kill 'em, no one except you, an' he'd killed some o' the best witches an' wizards of the age – the McKinnons, the Bones, the Prewetts – an' you was only a baby, an' you lived.'

Something very painful was going on in Harry's mind. As Hagrid's story came to a close, he saw again the blinding flash of green light, more clearly than he had ever remembered it before – and he remembered something else, for the first time in his life – a high, cold, cruel laugh.

Hagrid was watching him sadly.

'Took yeh from the ruined house myself, on Dumbledore's orders. Brought yeh ter this lot ...'

'Load of old tosh,' said Uncle Vernon. Harry jumped, he had almost forgotten that the Dursleys were there. Uncle Vernon certainly seemed to have got back his courage. He was glaring at Hagrid and his fists were clenched.

'Now, you listen here, boy,' he snarled. 'I accept there's something strange about you, probably nothing a good beating wouldn't have cured – and as for all this about your parents, well, they were weirdos, no denying it, and the world's better off without them in my opinion – asked for all they got, getting mixed up with these wizarding types – just what I expected, always knew they'd come to a sticky end –'

But at that moment, Hagrid leapt from the sofa and drew a battered pink umbrella from inside his coat. Pointing this at Uncle Vernon like a sword, he said, 'I'm warning you, Dursley – I'm warning you – one more word ...'

In danger of being speared on the end of an umbrella by a bearded giant, Uncle Vernon's courage failed again; he flattened himself against the wall and fell silent.

'That's better,' said Hagrid, breathing heavily and sitting back down on the sofa, which this time sagged right down to the floor.

Harry, meanwhile, still had questions to ask, hundreds of them.

'But what happened to Vol – sorry – I mean, You-Know-Who?'

'Good question, Harry. Disappeared. Vanished. Same night he tried ter kill you. Makes yeh even more famous. That's the biggest myst'ry, see ... he was gettin' more an' more powerful – why'd he go?

'Some say he died. Codswallop, in my opinion.

Dunno if he had enough human left in him to die. Some say he's still out there, bidin' his time, like, but I don' believe it. People who was on his side came back ter ours. Some of 'em came outta kinda trances. Don' reckon they could've done if he was comin' back.

'Most of us reckon he's still out there somewhere but lost his powers. Too weak to carry on. 'Cause somethin' about you finished him, Harry. There was somethin' goin' on that night he hadn't counted on — I dunno what it was, no one does — but somethin' about you stumped him, all right.'

Hagrid looked at Harry with warmth and respect blazing in his eyes, but Harry, instead of feeling pleased and proud, felt quite sure there had been a horrible mistake. A wizard? Him? How could he possibly be? He'd spent his life being clouted by Dudley and bullied by Aunt Petunia and Uncle Vernon; if he was really a wizard, why hadn't they been turned into warty toads every time they'd tried to lock him in his cupboard? If he'd once defeated the greatest sorcerer in the world, how come Dudley had always been able to kick him around like a football?

'Hagrid,' he said quietly, 'I think you must have made a mistake. I don't think I can be a wizard.'

To his surprise, Hagrid chuckled.

'Not a wizard, eh? Never made things happen when you was scared, or angry?'

Harry looked into the fire. Now he came to think about it ... every odd thing that had ever made his aunt and uncle furious with him had happened when he, Harry, had been upset or angry ... chased by Dudley's gang, he had somehow found himself out of their reach ... dreading going to school with that ridiculous haircut, he'd managed to make it grow back ... and the very last time Dudley had hit him, hadn't he got his revenge, without even realising he was doing it? Hadn't he set a boa constrictor on him?

Harry looked back at Hagrid, smiling, and saw that Hagrid was positively beaming at him.

'See?' said Hagrid. 'Harry Potter, not a wizard – you wait, you'll be right famous at Hogwarts.'

But Uncle Vernon wasn't going to give in without a fight.

'Haven't I told you he's not going?' he hissed. 'He's going to Stonewall High and he'll be grateful for it. I've read those letters and he needs all sorts of rubbish – spell books and wands and –'

'If he wants ter go, a great Muggle like you won't stop him,' growled Hagrid. 'Stop Lily an' James Potter's son goin' ter Hogwarts! Yer mad. His name's been down ever since he was born. He's off ter the finest school of witchcraft and wizardry in the world. Seven years there and he won't know himself. He'll be with youngsters of his own sort, fer a change, an' he'll be under the greatest Headmaster Hogwarts ever had, Albus Dumbled–'

'I AM NOT PAYING FOR SOME CRACKPOT OLD FOOL TO TEACH HIM MAGIC TRICKS!' yelled Uncle Vernon.

But he had finally gone too far. Hagrid seized his umbrella and whirled it over his head. 'NEVER –' he thundered, '– INSULT – ALBUS – DUMBLE-DORE – IN – FRONT – OF – ME!'

He brought the umbrella swishing down through the air to point at Dudley – there was a flash of violet light, a sound like a firecracker, a sharp squeal and next second, Dudley was dancing on the spot with his hands clasped over his fat bottom, howling in pain. When he turned his back on them, Harry saw a curly pig's tail poking through a hole in his trousers.

Uncle Vernon roared. Pulling Aunt Petunia and Dudley into the other room, he cast one last terrified look at Hagrid and slammed the door behind them.

Hagrid looked down at his umbrella and stroked his beard.

'Shouldn'ta lost me temper,' he said ruefully, 'but it didn't work anyway. Meant ter turn him into a pig, but I suppose he was so much like a pig anyway there wasn't much left ter do.'

He cast a sideways look at Harry under his bushy eyebrows.

'Be grateful if yeh didn't mention that ter anyone at Hogwarts,' he said. 'I'm – er – not supposed ter do magic, strictly speakin'. I was allowed ter do a bit ter follow yeh an' get yer letters to yeh an' stuff – one o' the reasons I was so keen ter take on the job –'

'Why aren't you supposed to do magic?' asked Harry.

'Oh, well – I was at Hogwarts meself but I – er – got expelled, ter tell yeh the truth. In me third year. They snapped me wand in half an' everything. But Dumbledore let me stay on as gamekeeper. Great man, Dumbledore.'

'Why were you expelled?'

'It's gettin' late and we've got lots ter do tomorrow,' said Hagrid loudly. 'Gotta get up ter town, get all yer books an' that.'

He took off his thick black coat and threw it to Harry.

'You can kip under that,' he said. 'Don' mind if it wriggles a bit, I think I still got a couple o' dormice in one o' the pockets.'

CHAPTER FIVE

Diagon Alley

Harry woke early the next morning. Although he could tell it was daylight, he kept his eyes shut tight.

'It was a dream,' he told himself firmly. 'I dreamed a giant called Hagrid came to tell me I was going to a school for wizards. When I open my eyes I'll be at home in my cupboard.'

There was suddenly a loud tapping noise.

'And there's Aunt Petunia knocking on the door,' Harry thought, his heart sinking. But he still didn't open his eyes. It had been such a good dream.

Tap. Tap. Tap.

'All right,' Harry mumbled, 'I'm getting up.'

He sat up and Hagrid's heavy coat fell off him. The hut was full of sunlight, the storm was over, Hagrid himself was asleep on the collapsed sofa and there was an owl rapping its claw on the window, a newspaper held in its beak.

Harry scrambled to his feet, so happy he felt as though a large balloon was swelling inside him. He went straight to the window and jerked it open. The owl swooped in and dropped the newspaper on top of Hagrid, who didn't wake up. The owl then fluttered on to the floor and began to attack Hagrid's coat.

'Don't do that.'

Harry tried to wave the owl out of the way, but it snapped its beak fiercely at him and carried on savaging the coat.

'Hagrid!' said Harry loudly. 'There's an owl –'

'Pay him,' Hagrid grunted into the sofa.

'What?'

'He wants payin' fer deliverin' the paper. Look in the pockets.'

Hagrid's coat seemed to be made of nothing *but* pockets – bunches of keys, slug pellets, balls of string, mint humbugs, tea-bags ... finally, Harry pulled out a handful of strange-looking coins.

'Give him five Knuts,' said Hagrid sleepily.

'Knuts?'

'The little bronze ones.'

Harry counted out five little bronze coins and the owl held out its leg so he could put the money into a small leather pouch tied to it. Then it flew off through the open window.

Hagrid yawned loudly, sat up and stretched.

'Best be off, Harry, lots ter do today, gotta get up ter London an' buy all yer stuff fer school.'

Harry was turning over the wizard coins and looking at them. He had just thought of something which made him feel as though the happy balloon inside him had got a puncture.

'Um – Hagrid?'

'Mm?' said Hagrid, who was pulling on his huge boots.

'I haven't got any money – and you heard Uncle

Vernon last night – he won't pay for me to go and learn magic. '

'Don't worry about that,' said Hagrid, standing up and scratching his head. 'D'yeh think yer parents didn't leave yeh anything?'

'But if their house was destroyed –'

'They didn' keep their gold in the house, boy! Nah, first stop fer us is Gringotts. Wizards' bank. Have a sausage, they're not bad cold – an' I wouldn' say no teh a bit o' yer birthday cake, neither.'

'Wizards have *banks*?'

'Just the one. Gringotts. Run by goblins.'

Harry dropped the bit of sausage he was holding. '*Goblins?*'

'Yeah – so yeh'd be mad ter try an' rob it, I'll tell yeh that. Never mess with goblins, Harry. Gringotts is the safest place in the world fer anything yeh want ter keep safe – 'cept maybe Hogwarts. As a matter o' fact, I gotta visit Gringotts anyway. Fer Dumbledore. Hogwarts business.' Hagrid drew himself up proudly. 'He usually gets me ter do important stuff fer him. Fetchin' you – gettin' things from Gringotts – knows he can trust me, see.

'Got everythin'? Come on, then.'

Harry followed Hagrid out on to the rock. The sky was quite clear now and the sea gleamed in the sunlight. The boat Uncle Vernon had hired was still there, with a lot of water in the bottom after the storm.

'How did you get here?' Harry asked, looking around for another boat.

'Flew,' said Hagrid.

'*Flew?*'

'Yeah – but we'll go back in this. Not s'pposed ter use magic now I've got yeh.'

They settled down in the boat, Harry still staring at Hagrid, trying to imagine him flying.

'Seems a shame ter row, though,' said Hagrid, giving Harry another of his sideways looks. 'If I was ter – er – speed things up a bit, would yeh mind not mentionin' it at Hogwarts?'

'Of course not,' said Harry, eager to see more magic. Hagrid pulled out the pink umbrella again, tapped it twice on the side of the boat and they sped off towards land.

'Why would you be mad to try and rob Gringotts?' Harry asked.

'Spells – enchantments,' said Hagrid, unfolding his newspaper as he spoke. 'They say there's dragons guardin' the high-security vaults. And then yeh gotta find yer way – Gringotts is hundreds of miles under London, see. Deep under the Underground. Yeh'd die of hunger tryin' ter get out, even if yeh did manage ter get yer hands on summat.'

Harry sat and thought about this while Hagrid read his newspaper, the *Daily Prophet*. Harry had learnt from Uncle Vernon that people liked to be left alone while they did this, but it was very difficult, he'd never had so many questions in his life.

'Ministry o' Magic messin' things up as usual,' Hagrid muttered, turning the page.

'There's a Ministry of Magic?' Harry asked, before he could stop himself.

''Course,' said Hagrid. 'They wanted Dumbledore fer Minister, o' course, but he'd never leave

Hogwarts, so old Cornelius Fudge got the job. Bungler if ever there was one. So he pelts Dumbledore with owls every morning, askin' fer advice.'

'But what does a Ministry of Magic *do*?'

'Well, their main job is to keep it from the Muggles that there's still witches an' wizards up an' down the country.'

'Why?'

'*Why?* Blimey, Harry, everyone'd be wantin' magic solutions to their problems. Nah, we're best left alone.'

At this moment the boat bumped gently into the harbour wall. Hagrid folded up his newspaper and they clambered up the stone steps on to the street.

Passers-by stared a lot at Hagrid as they walked through the little town to the station. Harry couldn't blame them. Not only was Hagrid twice as tall as anyone else, he kept pointing at perfectly ordinary things like parking meters and saying loudly, 'See that, Harry? Things these Muggles dream up, eh?'

'Hagrid,' said Harry, panting a bit as he ran to keep up, 'did you say there are *dragons* at Gringotts?'

'Well, so they say,' said Hagrid. 'Crikey, I'd like a dragon.'

'You'd *like* one?'

'Wanted one ever since I was a kid – here we go.'

They had reached the station. There was a train to London in five minutes' time. Hagrid, who didn't understand 'Muggle money', as he called it, gave the notes to Harry so he could buy their tickets.

People stared more than ever on the train. Hagrid took up two seats and sat knitting what looked like a canary-yellow circus tent.

'Still got yer letter, Harry?' he asked as he counted stitches.

Harry took the parchment envelope out of his pocket.

'Good,' said Hagrid. 'There's a list there of everything yeh need.'

Harry unfolded a second piece of paper he hadn't noticed the night before and read:

HOGWARTS SCHOOL OF WITCHCRAFT AND WIZARDRY

Uniform
First-year students will require:
1. *Three sets of plain work robes (black)*
2. *One plain pointed hat (black) for day wear*
3. *One pair of protective gloves (dragon hide or similar)*
4. *One winter cloak (black, silver fastenings)*
Please note that all pupils' clothes should carry name tags

Set Books
All students should have a copy of each of the following:
The Standard Book of Spells (Grade 1) *by Miranda Goshawk*
A History of Magic *by Bathilda Bagshot*
Magical Theory *by Adalbert Waffling*
A Beginners' Guide to Transfiguration *by*

Emeric Switch
One Thousand Magical Herbs and Fungi *by Phyllida Spore*
Magical Drafts and Potions *by Arsenius Jigger*
Fantastic Beasts and Where to Find Them *by Newt Scamander*
The Dark Forces: A Guide to Self-Protection *by Quentin Trimble*

Other Equipment
1 wand
1 cauldron (pewter, standard size 2)
1 set glass or crystal phials
1 telescope
1 set brass scales

Students may also bring an owl OR a cat OR a toad

PARENTS ARE REMINDED THAT FIRST-YEARS ARE NOT ALLOWED THEIR OWN BROOMSTICKS

'Can we buy all this in London?' Harry wondered aloud.

'If yeh know where to go,' said Hagrid.

*

Harry had never been to London before. Although Hagrid seemed to know where he was going, he was obviously not used to getting there in an ordinary way. He got stuck in the ticket barrier on the Underground and complained loudly that the seats were too small and the trains too slow.

'I don't know how the Muggles manage without

magic,' he said, as they climbed a broken-down escalator which led up to a bustling road lined with shops.

Hagrid was so huge that he parted the crowd easily; all Harry had to do was keep close behind him. They passed book shops and music stores, hamburger bars and cinemas, but nowhere that looked as if it could sell you a magic wand. This was just an ordinary street full of ordinary people. Could there really be piles of wizard gold buried miles beneath them? Were there really shops that sold spell books and broomsticks? Might this not all be some huge joke that the Dursleys had cooked up? If Harry hadn't known that the Dursleys had no sense of humour, he might have thought so; yet somehow, even though everything Hagrid had told him so far was unbelievable, Harry couldn't help trusting him.

'This is it,' said Hagrid, coming to a halt, 'the Leaky Cauldron. It's a famous place.'

It was a tiny, grubby-looking pub. If Hagrid hadn't pointed it out, Harry wouldn't have noticed it was there. The people hurrying by didn't glance at it. Their eyes slid from the big book shop on one side to the record shop on the other as if they couldn't see the Leaky Cauldron at all. In fact, Harry had the most peculiar feeling that only he and Hagrid could see it. Before he could mention this, Hagrid had steered him inside.

For a famous place, it was very dark and shabby. A few old women were sitting in a corner, drinking tiny glasses of sherry. One of them was smoking a long pipe. A little man in a top hat was talking to the old barman, who was quite bald and looked like a gummy walnut. The low buzz of chatter stopped when they walked in. Everyone seemed to know Hagrid; they waved and smiled at him, and the barman reached for a glass, saying, 'The usual, Hagrid?'

'Can't, Tom, I'm on Hogwarts business,' said Hagrid, clapping his great hand on Harry's shoulder and making Harry's knees buckle.

'Good Lord,' said the barman, peering at Harry, 'is this – can this be –?'

The Leaky Cauldron had suddenly gone completely still and silent.

'Bless my soul,' whispered the old barman. 'Harry Potter ... what an honour.'

He hurried out from behind the bar, rushed towards Harry and seized his hand, tears in his eyes.

'Welcome back, Mr Potter, welcome back.'

Harry didn't know what to say. Everyone was looking at him. The old woman with the pipe was puffing on it without realising it had gone out. Hagrid was beaming.

Then there was a great scraping of chairs and, next moment, Harry found himself shaking hands with everyone in the Leaky Cauldron.

'Doris Crockford, Mr Potter, can't believe I'm meeting you at last.'

'So proud, Mr Potter, I'm just so proud.'

'Always wanted to shake your hand – I'm all of a flutter.'

'Delighted, Mr Potter, just can't tell you. Diggle's the name, Dedalus Diggle.'

'I've seen you before!' said Harry, as Dedalus Diggle's top hat fell off in his excitement. 'You bowed to me once in a shop.'

'He remembers!' cried Dedalus Diggle, looking around at everyone. 'Did you hear that? He remembers me!'

Harry shook hands again and again – Doris Crockford kept coming back for more.

A pale young man made his way forward, very nervously. One of his eyes was twitching.

'Professor Quirrell!' said Hagrid. 'Harry, Professor Quirrell will be one of your teachers at Hogwarts.'

'P-P-Potter,' stammered Professor Quirrell, grasping Harry's hand, 'c-can't t-tell you how p-pleased I am to meet you.'

'What sort of magic do you teach, Professor Quirrell?'

'D-Defence Against the D-D-Dark Arts,' muttered Professor Quirrell, as though he'd rather not think about it. 'N-not that you n-need it, eh, P-P-Potter?' He laughed nervously. 'You'll be g-getting all your equipment, I suppose? I've g-got to p-pick up a new b-book on vampires, m-myself.' He looked terrified at the very thought.

But the others wouldn't let Professor Quirrell keep Harry to himself. It took almost ten minutes to get away from them all. At last, Hagrid managed to make himself heard over the babble.

'Must get on – lots ter buy. Come on, Harry.'

Doris Crockford shook Harry's hand one last time and Hagrid led them through the bar and out into a small, walled courtyard, where there was nothing but a dustbin and a few weeds.

Hagrid grinned at Harry.

'Told yeh, didn't I? Told yeh you was famous. Even Professor Quirrell was tremblin' ter meet yeh – mind you, he's usually tremblin'.'

'Is he always that nervous?'

'Oh, yeah. Poor bloke. Brilliant mind. He was fine while he was studyin' outta books but then he took a year off ter get some first-hand experience ... They say he met vampires in the Black Forest and there was a nasty bit o' trouble with a hag – never been the same since. Scared of the students, scared of his own subject – now, where's me umbrella?'

Vampires? Hags? Harry's head was swimming. Hagrid, meanwhile, was counting bricks in the wall above the dustbin.

'Three up ... two across ...' he muttered. 'Right, stand back, Harry.'

He tapped the wall three times with the point of his umbrella.

The brick he had touched quivered – it wriggled – in the middle, a small hole appeared – it grew wider and wider – a second later they were facing an archway large enough even for Hagrid, an archway on to a cobbled street which twisted and turned out of sight.

'Welcome,' said Hagrid, 'to Diagon Alley.'

He grinned at Harry's amazement. They stepped through the archway. Harry looked quickly over his shoulder and saw the archway shrink instantly back into solid wall.

The sun shone brightly on a stack of cauldrons outside the nearest shop. *Cauldrons – All Sizes – Copper, Brass, Pewter, Silver – Self-Stirring –*

Collapsible said a sign hanging over them.

'Yeah, you'll be needin' one,' said Hagrid, 'but we gotta get yer money first.'

Harry wished he had about eight more eyes. He turned his head in every direction as they walked up the street, trying to look at everything at once: the shops, the things outside them, the people doing their shopping. A plump woman outside an apothecary's was shaking her head as they passed, saying, 'Dragon liver, seventeen Sickles an ounce, they're mad ...'

A low, soft hooting came from a dark shop with a sign saying *Eeylops Owl Emporium – Tawny, Screech, Barn, Brown and Snowy*. Several boys of about Harry's age had their noses pressed against a window with broomsticks in it. 'Look,' Harry heard one of them say, 'the new Nimbus Two Thousand – fastest ever –' There were shops selling robes, shops selling telescopes and strange silver instruments Harry had never seen before, windows stacked with barrels of bat spleens and eels' eyes, tottering piles of spell books, quills and rolls of parchment, potion bottles, globes of the moon ...

'Gringotts,' said Hagrid.

They had reached a snowy-white building which towered over the other little shops. Standing beside its burnished bronze doors, wearing a uniform of scarlet and gold, was –

'Yeah, that's a goblin,' said Hagrid quietly as they walked up the white stone steps towards him. The goblin was about a head shorter than Harry. He had a swarthy, clever face, a pointed beard and, Harry noticed, very long fingers and feet. He bowed as they walked inside. Now they were facing a second pair of doors, silver this time, with words engraved upon them:

> *Enter, stranger, but take heed*
> *Of what awaits the sin of greed,*
> *For those who take, but do not earn,*
> *Must pay most dearly in their turn,*
> *So if you seek beneath our floors*
> *A treasure that was never yours,*
> *Thief, you have been warned, beware*
> *Of finding more than treasure there.*

'Like I said, yeh'd be mad ter try an' rob it,' said Hagrid.

A pair of goblins bowed them through the silver doors and they were in a vast marble hall. About a hundred more goblins were sitting on high stools behind a long counter, scribbling in large ledgers, weighing coins on brass scales, examining precious stones through eyeglasses. There were too many doors to count leading off the hall, and yet more goblins were showing people in and out of these. Hagrid and Harry made for the counter.

'Morning,' said Hagrid to a free goblin. 'We've come ter take some money outta Mr Harry Potter's safe.'

'You have his key, sir?'

'Got it here somewhere,' said Hagrid and he started emptying his pockets on to the counter, scattering a handful of mouldy dog-biscuits over the goblin's book of numbers. The goblin wrinkled his nose. Harry watched the goblin on their right weighing a pile of rubies as big as glowing coals.

'Got it,' said Hagrid at last, holding up a tiny golden key.

The goblin looked at it closely.

'That seems to be in order.'

'An' I've also got a letter here from Professor Dumbledore,' said Hagrid importantly, throwing out his chest. 'It's about the You-Know-What in vault seven hundred and thirteen.'

The goblin read the letter carefully.

'Very well,' he said, handing it back to Hagrid, 'I will have someone take you down to both vaults. Griphook!'

Griphook was yet another goblin. Once Hagrid had crammed all the dog-biscuits back inside his pockets, he and Harry followed Griphook towards one of the doors leading off the hall.

'What's the You-Know-What in vault seven hundred and thirteen?' Harry asked.

'Can't tell yeh that,' said Hagrid mysteriously. 'Very secret. Hogwarts business. Dumbledore's trusted me. More'n my job's worth ter tell yeh that.'

Griphook held the door open for them. Harry, who had expected more marble, was surprised. They were in a narrow stone passageway lit with flaming torches. It sloped steeply downwards and there were little railway tracks on the floor. Griphook whistled and a small cart came hurtling up the tracks towards them. They climbed in – Hagrid with some difficulty – and were off.

At first they just hurtled through a maze of twisting passages. Harry tried to remember, left, right, right, left, middle fork, right, left, but it was impossible. The rattling cart seemed to know its own way, because Griphook wasn't steering.

Harry's eyes stung as the cold air rushed past them, but he kept them wide open. Once, he thought he saw a burst of fire at the end of a passage and twisted around to see if it was a dragon, but too late – they plunged even deeper, passing an underground lake where huge stalactites and stalagmites grew from the ceiling and floor.

'I never know,' Harry called to Hagrid over the noise of the cart, 'what's the difference between a stalagmite and a stalactite?'

'Stalagmite's got an "m" in it,' said Hagrid. 'An' don' ask me questions just now, I think I'm gonna be sick.'

He did look very green and when the cart stopped at last beside a small door in the passage wall, Hagrid got out and had to lean against the wall to stop his knees trembling.

Griphook unlocked the door. A lot of green smoke came billowing out, and as it cleared, Harry gasped. Inside were mounds of gold coins. Columns of silver. Heaps of little bronze Knuts.

'All yours,' smiled Hagrid.

All Harry's – it was incredible. The Dursleys couldn't have known about this or they'd have had it from him faster than blinking. How often had they complained how much Harry cost them to keep? And all the time there had been a small fortune belonging to him, buried deep under London.

Hagrid helped Harry pile some of it into a bag.

'The gold ones are Galleons,' he explained. 'Seventeen silver Sickles to a Galleon and twenty-nine Knuts to a Sickle, it's easy enough. Right, that should be enough fer a couple o' terms, we'll keep the rest safe for yeh.' He turned to Griphook. 'Vault seven hundred and thirteen now, please, and can we go more slowly?'

'One speed only,' said Griphook.

They were going even deeper now and gathering speed. The air became colder and colder as they hurtled round tight corners. They went rattling over an underground ravine and Harry leant over the side to try and see what was down at the dark bottom but Hagrid groaned and pulled him back by the scruff of his neck.

Vault seven hundred and thirteen had no key-hole.

'Stand back,' said Griphook importantly. He stroked the door gently with one of his long fingers and it simply melted away.

'If anyone but a Gringotts goblin tried that, they'd be sucked through the door and trapped in there,' said Griphook.

'How often do you check to see if anyone's inside?' Harry asked.

'About once every ten years,' said Griphook, with a rather nasty grin.

Something really extraordinary had to be inside this top-security vault, Harry was sure, and he leant forward eagerly, expecting to see fabulous jewels at the very least – but at first he thought it was empty. Then he noticed a grubby little package wrapped up in brown paper lying on the floor. Hagrid picked it up and tucked it deep inside his coat. Harry longed to know what it was, but knew better than to ask.

'Come on, back in this infernal cart, and don't talk to me on the way back, it's best if I keep me mouth shut,' said Hagrid.

*

One wild cart-ride later they stood blinking in the sunlight outside Gringotts. Harry didn't know where to run first now that he had a bag full of money. He didn't have to know how many Galleons there were to a pound to know that he was holding more money than he'd had in his whole life – more money than even Dudley had ever had.

'Might as well get yer uniform,' said Hagrid, nodding towards Madam Malkin's Robes for All Occasions. 'Listen, Harry, would yeh mind if I slipped off fer a pick-me-up in the Leaky Cauldron? I hate them Gringotts carts.' He did still look a bit sick, so Harry entered Madam Malkin's shop alone, feeling nervous.

Madam Malkin was a squat, smiling witch dressed all in mauve.

'Hogwarts, dear?' she said, when Harry started to speak. 'Got the lot here – another young man being fitted up just now, in fact.'

In the back of the shop, a boy with a pale, pointed face was standing on a footstool while a second witch pinned up his long black robes. Madam Malkin stood Harry on a stool next to him, slipped a long robe over his head and began to pin it to the right length.

'Hullo,' said the boy, 'Hogwarts too?'

'Yes,' said Harry.

'My father's next door buying my books and mother's up the street looking at wands,' said the boy. He had a bored, drawling voice. 'Then I'm going to drag them off to look at racing brooms. I don't see why first-years can't have their own. I think I'll bully father into getting me one and I'll smuggle it in somehow.'

Harry was strongly reminded of Dudley.

'Have *you* got your own broom?' the boy went on.

'No,' said Harry.

'Play Quidditch at all?'

'No,' Harry said again, wondering what on earth Quidditch could be.

'I do – Father says it's a crime if I'm not picked to play for my house, and I must say, I agree. Know what house you'll be in yet?'

'No,' said Harry, feeling more stupid by the minute.

'Well, no one really knows until they get there, do they, but I know I'll be in Slytherin, all our family have been – imagine being in Hufflepuff, I think I'd leave, wouldn't you?'

'Mmm,' said Harry, wishing he could say something a bit more interesting.

'I say, look at that man!' said the boy suddenly, nodding towards the front window. Hagrid was standing there, grinning at Harry and pointing at two large ice-creams to show he couldn't come in.

'That's Hagrid,' said Harry, pleased to know something the boy didn't. 'He works at Hogwarts.'

'Oh,' said the boy, 'I've heard of him. He's a sort of servant, isn't he?'

'He's the gamekeeper,' said Harry. He was liking the boy less and less every second.

'Yes, exactly. I heard he's a sort of *savage* – lives in a hut in the school grounds and every now and then he gets drunk, tries to do magic and ends up setting fire to his bed.'

'I think he's brilliant,' said Harry coldly.

'*Do* you?' said the boy, with a slight sneer. 'Why is he with you? Where are your parents?'

'They're dead,' said Harry shortly. He didn't feel much like going into the matter with this boy.

'Oh, sorry,' said the other, not sounding sorry at all. 'But they were *our* kind, weren't they?'

'They were a witch and wizard, if that's what you mean.'

'I really don't think they should let the other sort in, do you? They're just not the same, they've never been brought up to know our ways. Some of them have never even heard of Hogwarts until they get the letter, imagine. I think they should keep it in the old wizarding families. What's your surname, anyway?'

But before Harry could answer, Madam Malkin said, 'That's you done, my dear,' and Harry, not sorry for an excuse to stop talking to the boy, hopped down from the footstool.

'Well, I'll see you at Hogwarts, I suppose,' said the drawling boy.

Harry was rather quiet as he ate the ice-cream Hagrid had bought him (chocolate and raspberry with chopped nuts).

'What's up?' said Hagrid.

'Nothing,' Harry lied. They stopped to buy parchment and quills. Harry cheered up a bit when he found a bottle of ink that changed colour as you

wrote. When they had left the shop, he said,
'Hagrid, what's Quidditch?'

'Blimey, Harry, I keep forgettin' how little yeh
know – not knowin' about Quidditch!'

'Don't make me feel worse,' said Harry. He told
Hagrid about the pale boy in Madam Malkin's.

'– and he said people from Muggle families
shouldn't even be allowed in –'

'Yer not *from* a Muggle family. If he'd known who
yeh *were* – he's grown up knowin' yer name if his
parents are wizardin' folk – you saw 'em in the
Leaky Cauldron. Anyway, what does he know
about it, some o' the best I ever saw were the only
ones with magic in 'em in a long line o' Muggles –
look at yer mum! Look what she had fer a sister!'

'So what *is* Quidditch?'

'It's our sport. Wizard sport. It's like – like football in the Muggle world – everyone follows
Quidditch – played up in the air on broomsticks
and there's four balls – sorta hard ter explain the
rules.'

'And what are Slytherin and Hufflepuff?'

'School houses. There's four. Everyone says
Hufflepuff are a lot o' duffers, but –'

'I bet I'm in Hufflepuff,' said Harry gloomily.

'Better Hufflepuff than Slytherin,' said Hagrid
darkly. 'There's not a single witch or wizard who
went bad who wasn't in Slytherin. You-Know-Who
was one.'

'Vol– sorry – You-Know-Who was at Hogwarts?'

'Years an' years ago,' said Hagrid.

They bought Harry's school books in a shop
called Flourish and Blotts where the shelves were

stacked to the ceiling with books as large as paving stones bound in leather; books the size of postage stamps in covers of silk; books full of peculiar symbols and a few books with nothing in them at all. Even Dudley, who never read anything, would have been wild to get his hands on some of these. Hagrid almost had to drag Harry away from *Curses and Counter-Curses* (*Bewitch your Friends and Befuddle your Enemies with the Latest Revenges: Hair Loss, Jelly-Legs, Tongue-Tying and much, much more*) by Professor Vindictus Viridian.

'I was trying to find out how to curse Dudley.'

'I'm not sayin' that's not a good idea, but yer not ter use magic in the Muggle world except in very special circumstances,' said Hagrid. 'An' anyway, yeh couldn' work any of them curses yet, yeh'll need a lot more study before yeh get ter that level.'

Hagrid wouldn't let Harry buy a solid gold cauldron, either ('It says pewter on yer list'), but they got a nice set of scales for weighing potion ingredients and a collapsible brass telescope. Then they visited the apothecary's, which was fascinating enough to make up for its horrible smell, a mixture of bad eggs and rotted cabbages. Barrels of slimy stuff stood on the floor, jars of herbs, dried roots and bright powders lined the walls, bundles of feathers, strings of fangs and snarled claws hung from the ceiling. While Hagrid asked the man behind the counter for a supply of some basic potion ingredients for Harry, Harry himself examined silver unicorn horns at twenty-one Galleons each and minuscule, glittery black beetle eyes (five Knuts a scoop).

Outside the apothecary's, Hagrid checked Harry's list again.

'Just yer wand left – oh yeah, an' I still haven't got yeh a birthday present.'

Harry felt himself go red.

'You don't have to –'

'I know I don't have to. Tell yeh what, I'll get yer animal. Not a toad, toads went outta fashion years ago, yeh'd be laughed at – an' I don' like cats, they make me sneeze. I'll get yer an owl. All the kids want owls, they're dead useful, carry yer post an' everythin'.'

Twenty minutes later, they left Eeylops Owl Emporium, which had been dark and full of rustling and flickering, jewel-bright eyes. Harry now carried a large cage which held a beautiful snowy owl, fast asleep with her head under her wing. He couldn't stop stammering his thanks, sounding just like Professor Quirrell.

'Don' mention it,' said Hagrid gruffly. 'Don' expect you've had a lotta presents from them Dursleys. Just Ollivanders left now – only place fer wands, Ollivanders, and yeh gotta have the best wand.'

A magic wand ... this was what Harry had been really looking forward to.

The last shop was narrow and shabby. Peeling gold letters over the door read *Ollivanders: Makers of Fine Wands since 382 BC*. A single wand lay on a faded purple cushion in the dusty window.

A tinkling bell rang somewhere in the depths of the shop as they stepped inside. It was a tiny place, empty except for a single spindly chair which

Hagrid sat on to wait. Harry felt strangely as though he had entered a very strict library; he swallowed a lot of new questions which had just occurred to him and looked instead at the thousands of narrow boxes piled neatly right up to the ceiling. For some reason, the back of his neck prickled. The very dust and silence in here seemed to tingle with some secret magic.

'Good afternoon,' said a soft voice. Harry jumped. Hagrid must have jumped, too, because there was a loud crunching noise and he got quickly off the spindly chair.

An old man was standing before them, his wide, pale eyes shining like moons through the gloom of the shop.

'Hello,' said Harry awkwardly.

'Ah yes,' said the man. 'Yes, yes. I thought I'd be seeing you soon. Harry Potter.' It wasn't a question. 'You have your mother's eyes. It seems only yesterday she was in here herself, buying her first wand. Ten and a quarter inches long, swishy, made of willow. Nice wand for charm work.'

Mr Ollivander moved closer to Harry. Harry wished he would blink. Those silvery eyes were a bit creepy.

'Your father, on the other hand, favoured a mahogany wand. Eleven inches. Pliable. A little more power and excellent for transfiguration. Well, I say your father favoured it – it's really the wand that chooses the wizard, of course.'

Mr Ollivander had come so close that he and Harry were almost nose to nose. Harry could see himself reflected in those misty eyes.

'And that's where ...'

Mr Ollivander touched the lightning scar on Harry's forehead with a long, white finger.

'I'm sorry to say I sold the wand that did it,' he said softly. 'Thirteen and a half inches. Yew. Powerful wand, very powerful, and in the wrong hands ... Well, if I'd known what that wand was going out into the world to do ...'

He shook his head and then, to Harry's relief, spotted Hagrid.

'Rubeus! Rubeus Hagrid! How nice to see you again ... Oak, sixteen inches, rather bendy, wasn't it?'

'It was, sir, yes,' said Hagrid.

'Good wand, that one. But I suppose they snapped it in half when you got expelled?' said Mr Ollivander, suddenly stern.

'Er – yes, they did, yes,' said Hagrid, shuffling his feet. 'I've still got the pieces, though,' he added brightly.

'But you don't *use* them?' said Mr Ollivander sharply.

'Oh, no, sir,' said Hagrid quickly. Harry noticed he gripped his pink umbrella very tightly as he spoke.

'Hmmm,' said Mr Ollivander, giving Hagrid a piercing look. 'Well, now – Mr Potter. Let me see.' He pulled a long tape measure with silver markings out of his pocket. 'Which is your wand arm?'

'Er – well, I'm right-handed,' said Harry.

'Hold out your arm. That's it.' He measured Harry from shoulder to finger, then wrist to elbow, shoulder to floor, knee to armpit and round his head. As he measured, he said, 'Every Ollivander wand has a core of a powerful magical substance, Mr Potter. We use unicorn hairs, phoenix tail feathers and the heartstrings of dragons. No two Ollivander wands are the same, just as no two unicorns, dragons or phoenixes are quite the same. And of course, you will never get such good results with another wizard's wand.'

Harry suddenly realised that the tape measure, which was measuring between his nostrils, was doing this on its own. Mr Ollivander was flitting around the shelves, taking down boxes.

'That will do,' he said, and the tape measure crumpled into a heap on the floor. 'Right then, Mr Potter. Try this one. Beechwood and dragon heartstring. Nine inches. Nice and flexible. Just take it and give it a wave.'

Harry took the wand and (feeling foolish) waved it around a bit, but Mr Ollivander snatched it out of his hand almost at once.

'Maple and phoenix feather. Seven inches. Quite whippy. Try –'

Harry tried – but he had hardly raised the wand when it, too, was snatched back by Mr Ollivander.

'No, no – here, ebony and unicorn hair, eight and a half inches, springy. Go on, go on, try it out.'

Harry tried. And tried. He had no idea what Mr Ollivander was waiting for. The pile of tried wands was mounting higher and higher on the spindly chair, but the more wands Mr Ollivander pulled from the shelves, the happier he seemed to become.

'Tricky customer, eh? Not to worry, we'll find the perfect match here somewhere – I wonder, now –

yes, why not – unusual combination – holly and phoenix feather, eleven inches, nice and supple.'

Harry took the wand. He felt a sudden warmth in his fingers. He raised the wand above his head, brought it swishing down through the dusty air and a stream of red and gold sparks shot from the end like a firework, throwing dancing spots of light on to the walls. Hagrid whooped and clapped and Mr Ollivander cried, 'Oh, bravo! Yes, indeed, oh, very good. Well, well, well ... how curious ... how very curious ...'

He put Harry's wand back into its box and wrapped it in brown paper, still muttering, 'Curious ... curious ...'

'Sorry,' said Harry, 'but *what's* curious?'

Mr Ollivander fixed Harry with his pale stare.

'I remember every wand I've ever sold, Mr Potter. Every single wand. It so happens that the phoenix whose tail feather is in your wand, gave another feather – just one other. It is very curious indeed that you should be destined for this wand when its brother – why, its brother gave you that scar.'

Harry swallowed.

'Yes, thirteen and a half inches. Yew. Curious indeed how these things happen. The wand chooses the wizard, remember ... I think we must expect great things from you, Mr Potter ... After all, He Who Must Not Be Named did great things – terrible, yes, but great.'

Harry shivered. He wasn't sure he liked Mr Ollivander too much. He paid seven gold Galleons for his wand and Mr Ollivander bowed them from his shop.

*

The late-afternoon sun hung low in the sky as Harry and Hagrid made their way back down Diagon Alley, back through the wall, back through the Leaky Cauldron, now empty. Harry didn't speak at all as they walked down the road; he didn't even notice how much people were gawping at them on the Underground, laden as they were with all their funny-shaped packages, with the sleeping snowy owl on Harry's lap. Up another escalator, out into Paddington station; Harry only realised where they were when Hagrid tapped him on the shoulder.

'Got time fer a bite to eat before yer train leaves,' he said.

He bought Harry a hamburger and they sat down on plastic seats to eat them. Harry kept looking around. Everything looked so strange, somehow.

'You all right, Harry? Yer very quiet,' said Hagrid.

Harry wasn't sure he could explain. He'd just had the best birthday of his life – and yet – he chewed his hamburger, trying to find the words.

'Everyone thinks I'm special,' he said at last. 'All those people in the Leaky Cauldron, Professor Quirrell, Mr Ollivander ... but I don't know anything about magic at all. How can they expect great things? I'm famous and I can't even remember what I'm famous for. I don't know what happened when Vol– sorry – I mean, the night my parents died.'

Hagrid leant across the table. Behind the wild beard and eyebrows he wore a very kind smile.

'Don' you worry, Harry. You'll learn fast enough. Everyone starts at the beginning at Hogwarts, you'll be just fine. Just be yerself. I know it's hard. Yeh've been singled out, an' that's always hard. But yeh'll have a great time at Hogwarts – I did – still do, 'smatter of fact.'

Hagrid helped Harry on to the train that would take him back to the Dursleys, then handed him an envelope.

'Yer ticket fer Hogwarts,' he said. 'First o' September – King's Cross – it's all on yer ticket. Any problems with the Dursleys, send me a letter with yer owl, she'll know where to find me ... See yeh soon, Harry.'

The train pulled out of the station. Harry wanted to watch Hagrid until he was out of sight; he rose in his seat and pressed his nose against the window, but he blinked and Hagrid had gone.

— CHAPTER SIX —

The Journey from Platform Nine and Three-Quarters

Harry's last month with the Dursleys wasn't fun. True, Dudley was now so scared of Harry he wouldn't stay in the same room, while Aunt Petunia and Uncle Vernon didn't shut Harry in his cupboard, force him to do anything or shout at him – in fact, they didn't speak to him at all. Half-terrified, half-furious, they acted as though any chair with Harry in it was empty. Although this was an improvement in many ways, it did become a bit depressing after a while.

Harry kept to his room, with his new owl for company. He had decided to call her Hedwig, a name he had found in *A History of Magic*. His school books were very interesting. He lay on his bed reading late into the night, Hedwig swooping in and out of the open window as she pleased. It was lucky that Aunt Petunia didn't come in to hoover any more, because Hedwig kept bringing back dead mice. Every night before he went to sleep, Harry ticked off another day on the piece of paper he had pinned to the wall, counting down to September the first.

On the last day of August he thought he'd better speak to his aunt and uncle about getting to King's Cross station next day, so he went down to the living-room, where they were watching a quiz show on television. He cleared his throat to let them know he was there, and Dudley screamed and ran from the room.

'Er – Uncle Vernon?'

Uncle Vernon grunted to show he was listening.

'Er – I need to be at King's Cross tomorrow to – to go to Hogwarts.'

Uncle Vernon grunted again.

'Would it be all right if you gave me a lift?'

Grunt. Harry supposed that meant yes.

'Thank you.'

He was about to go back upstairs when Uncle Vernon actually spoke.

'Funny way to get to a wizards' school, the train. Magic carpets all got punctures, have they?'

Harry didn't say anything.

'Where is this school, anyway?'

'I don't know,' said Harry, realising this for the first time. He pulled the ticket Hagrid had given him out of his pocket.

'I just take the train from platform nine and three-quarters at eleven o'clock,' he read.

His aunt and uncle stared.

'Platform what?'

'Nine and three-quarters.'

'Don't talk rubbish,' said Uncle Vernon, 'there is

no platform nine and three-quarters.'

'It's on my ticket.'

'Barking,' said Uncle Vernon, 'howling mad, the lot of them. You'll see. You just wait. All right, we'll take you to King's Cross. We're going up to London tomorrow anyway, or I wouldn't bother.'

'Why are you going to London?' Harry asked, trying to keep things friendly.

'Taking Dudley to hospital,' growled Uncle Vernon. 'Got to have that ruddy tail removed before he goes to Smeltings.'

*

Harry woke at five o'clock the next morning and was too excited and nervous to go back to sleep. He got up and pulled on his jeans because he didn't want to walk into the station in his wizard's robes – he'd change on the train. He checked his Hogwarts list yet again to make sure he had everything he needed, saw that Hedwig was shut safely in her cage and then paced the room, waiting for the Dursleys to get up. Two hours later, Harry's huge, heavy trunk had been loaded into the Dursleys' car, Aunt Petunia had talked Dudley into sitting next to Harry and they had set off.

They reached King's Cross at half past ten. Uncle Vernon dumped Harry's trunk on to a trolley and wheeled it into the station for him. Harry thought this was strangely kind until Uncle Vernon stopped dead, facing the platforms with a nasty grin on his face.

'Well, there you are, boy. Platform nine – platform ten. Your platform should be somewhere in the middle, but they don't seem to have built it yet, do they?'

He was quite right, of course. There was a big plastic number nine over one platform and a big plastic number ten over the one next to it, and in the middle, nothing at all.

'Have a good term,' said Uncle Vernon with an even nastier smile. He left without another word. Harry turned and saw the Dursleys drive away. All three of them were laughing. Harry's mouth went rather dry. What on earth was he going to do? He was starting to attract a lot of funny looks, because of Hedwig. He'd have to ask someone.

He stopped a passing guard, but didn't dare mention platform nine and three-quarters. The guard had never heard of Hogwarts and when Harry couldn't even tell him what part of the country it was in, he started to get annoyed, as though Harry was being stupid on purpose. Getting desperate, Harry asked for the train that left at eleven o'clock, but the guard said there wasn't one. In the end the guard strode away, muttering about time-wasters. Harry was now trying hard not to panic. According to the large clock over the arrivals board, he had ten minutes left to get on the train to Hogwarts and he had no idea how to do it; he was stranded in the middle of a station with a trunk he could hardly lift, a pocket full of wizard money and a large owl.

Hagrid must have forgotten to tell him something you had to do, like tapping the third brick on the left to get into Diagon Alley. He wondered if he should get out his wand and start tapping the ticket box between platforms nine and ten.

At that moment a group of people passed just behind him and he caught a few words of what they were saying.

'– packed with Muggles, of course –'

Harry swung round. The speaker was a plump woman who was talking to four boys, all with flaming red hair. Each of them was pushing a trunk like Harry's in front of him – and they had an *owl*.

Heart hammering, Harry pushed his trolley after them. They stopped and so did he, just near enough to hear what they were saying.

'Now, what's the platform number?' said the boys' mother.

'Nine and three-quarters!' piped a small girl, also red-headed, who was holding her hand. 'Mum, can't I go ...'

'You're not old enough, Ginny, now be quiet. All right, Percy, you go first.'

What looked like the oldest boy marched towards platforms nine and ten. Harry watched, careful not to blink in case he missed it – but just as the boy reached the divide between the two platforms, a large crowd of tourists came swarming in front of him, and by the time the last rucksack had cleared away, the boy had vanished.

'Fred, you next,' the plump woman said.

'I'm not Fred, I'm George,' said the boy. 'Honestly, woman, call yourself our mother? Can't you *tell* I'm George?'

'Sorry, George, dear.'

'Only joking, I am Fred,' said the boy, and off he went. His twin called after him to hurry up, and he must have done, because a second later, he had gone – but how had he done it?

Now the third brother was walking briskly

towards the ticket barrier – he was almost there – and then, quite suddenly, he wasn't anywhere.

There was nothing else for it.

'Excuse me,' Harry said to the plump woman.

'Hullo, dear,' she said. 'First time at Hogwarts? Ron's new, too.'

She pointed at the last and youngest of her sons. He was tall, thin and gangling, with freckles, big hands and feet and a long nose.

'Yes,' said Harry. 'The thing is – the thing is, I don't know how to –'

'How to get on to the platform?' she said kindly, and Harry nodded.

'Not to worry,' she said. 'All you have to do is walk straight at the barrier between platforms nine and ten. Don't stop and don't be scared you'll crash into it, that's very important. Best do it at a bit of a run if you're nervous. Go on, go now before Ron.'

'Er – OK,' said Harry.

He pushed his trolley round and stared at the barrier. It looked very solid.

He started to walk towards it. People jostled him on their way to platforms nine and ten. Harry walked more quickly. He was going to smash right into that ticket box and then he'd be in trouble – leaning forward on his trolley he broke into a heavy run – the barrier was coming nearer and nearer – he wouldn't be able to stop – the trolley was out of control – he was a foot away – he closed his eyes ready for the crash –

It didn't come ... he kept on running ... he opened his eyes.

A scarlet steam engine was waiting next to a

platform packed with people. A sign overhead said *Hogwarts Express, 11 o'clock*. Harry looked behind him and saw a wrought-iron archway where the ticket box had been, with the words *Platform Nine and Three-Quarters* on it. He had done it.

Smoke from the engine drifted over the heads of the chattering crowd, while cats of every colour wound here and there between their legs. Owls hooted to each other in a disgruntled sort of way over the babble and the scraping of heavy trunks.

The first few carriages were already packed with students, some hanging out of the window to talk to their families, some fighting over seats. Harry pushed his trolley off down the platform in search of an empty seat. He passed a round-faced boy who was saying, 'Gran, I've lost my toad again.'

'Oh, *Neville*,' he heard the old woman sigh.

A boy with dreadlocks was surrounded by a small crowd.

'Give us a look, Lee, go on.'

The boy lifted the lid of a box in his arms and the people around him shrieked and yelled as something inside poked out a long, hairy leg.

Harry pressed on through the crowd until he found an empty compartment near the end of the train. He put Hedwig inside first and then started to shove and heave his trunk towards the train door. He tried to lift it up the steps but could hardly raise one end and twice he dropped it painfully on his foot.

'Want a hand?' It was one of the red-haired twins he'd followed through the ticket box.

'Yes, please,' Harry panted.

'Oy, Fred! C'mere and help!'

With the twins' help, Harry's trunk was at last tucked away in a corner of the compartment.

'Thanks,' said Harry, pushing his sweaty hair out of his eyes.

'What's that?' said one of the twins suddenly, pointing at Harry's lightning scar.

'Blimey,' said the other twin. 'Are you –?'

'He is,' said the first twin. 'Aren't you?' he added to Harry.

'What?' said Harry.

'*Harry Potter,*' chorused the twins.

'Oh, him,' said Harry. 'I mean, yes, I am.'

The two boys gawped at him and Harry felt himself going red. Then, to his relief, a voice came floating in through the train's open door.

'Fred? George? Are you there?'

'Coming, Mum.'

With a last look at Harry, the twins hopped off the train.

Harry sat down next to the window where, half-hidden, he could watch the red-haired family on the platform and hear what they were saying. Their mother had just taken out her handkerchief.

'Ron, you've got something on your nose.'

The youngest boy tried to jerk out of the way, but she grabbed him and began rubbing the end of his nose.

'*Mum* – geroff.' He wriggled free.

'Aaah, has ickle Ronnie got somefink on his nosie?' said one of the twins.

'Shut up,' said Ron.

'Where's Percy?' said their mother.

'He's coming now.'

The oldest boy came striding into sight. He had already changed into his billowing black Hogwarts robes and Harry noticed a shiny silver badge on his chest with the letter *P* on it.

'Can't stay long, Mother,' he said. 'I'm up front, the Prefects have got two compartments to themselves –'

'Oh, are you a *Prefect*, Percy?' said one of the twins, with an air of great surprise. 'You should have said something, we had no idea.'

'Hang on, I think I remember him saying something about it,' said the other twin. 'Once –'

'Or twice –'

'A minute –'

'All summer –'

'Oh, shut up,' said Percy the Prefect.

'How come Percy gets new robes, anyway?' said one of the twins.

'Because he's a *Prefect*,' said their mother fondly. 'All right, dear, well, have a good term – send me an owl when you get there.'

She kissed Percy on the cheek and he left. Then she turned to the twins.

'Now, you two – this year, you behave yourselves. If I get one more owl telling me you've – you've blown up a toilet or –'

'Blown up a toilet? We've never blown up a toilet.'

'Great idea though, thanks, Mum.'

'It's *not funny*. And look after Ron.'

'Don't worry, ickle Ronniekins is safe with us.'

'Shut up,' said Ron again. He was almost as tall

as the twins already and his nose was still pink where his mother had rubbed it.

'Hey, Mum, guess what? Guess who we just met on the train?'

Harry leant back quickly so they couldn't see him looking.

'You know that black-haired boy who was near us in the station? Know who he is?'

'Who?'

'*Harry Potter!*'

Harry heard the little girl's voice.

'Oh, Mum, can I go on the train and see him, Mum, oh please ...'

'You've already seen him, Ginny, and the poor boy isn't something you goggle at in a zoo. Is he really, Fred? How do you know?'

'Asked him. Saw his scar. It's really there – like lightning.'

'Poor *dear* – no wonder he was alone. I wondered. He was ever so polite when he asked how to get on to the platform.'

'Never mind that, do you think he remembers what You-Know-Who looks like?'

Their mother suddenly became very stern.

'I forbid you to ask him, Fred. No, don't you dare. As though he needs reminding of that on his first day at school.'

'All right, keep your hair on.'

A whistle sounded.

'Hurry up!' their mother said, and the three boys clambered on to the train. They leant out of the window for her to kiss them goodbye and their younger sister began to cry.

'Don't, Ginny, we'll send you loads of owls.'

'We'll send you a Hogwarts toilet seat.'

'*George!*'

'Only joking, Mum.'

The train began to move. Harry saw the boys' mother waving and their sister, half laughing, half crying, running to keep up with the train until it gathered too much speed; then she fell back and waved.

Harry watched the girl and her mother disappear as the train rounded the corner. Houses flashed past the window. Harry felt a great leap of excitement. He didn't know what he was going to – but it had to be better than what he was leaving behind.

The door of the compartment slid open and the youngest redheaded boy came in.

'Anyone sitting there?' he asked, pointing at the seat opposite Harry. 'Everywhere else is full.'

Harry shook his head and the boy sat down. He glanced at Harry and then looked quickly out of the window, pretending he hadn't looked. Harry saw he still had a black mark on his nose.

'Hey, Ron.'

The twins were back.

'Listen, we're going down the middle of the train – Lee Jordan's got a giant tarantula down there.'

'Right,' mumbled Ron.

'Harry,' said the other twin, 'did we introduce ourselves? Fred and George Weasley. And this is Ron, our brother. See you later, then.'

'Bye,' said Harry and Ron. The twins slid the compartment door shut behind them.

'Are you really Harry Potter?' Ron blurted out.

Harry nodded.

'Oh – well, I thought it might be one of Fred and George's jokes,' said Ron. 'And have you really got – you know ...'

He pointed at Harry's forehead.

Harry pulled back his fringe to show the lightning scar. Ron stared.

'So that's where You-Know-Who –?'

'Yes,' said Harry, 'but I can't remember it.'

'Nothing?' said Ron eagerly.

'Well – I remember a lot of green light, but nothing else.'

'Wow,' said Ron. He sat and stared at Harry for a few moments, then, as though he had suddenly realised what he was doing, he looked quickly out of the window again.

'Are all your family wizards?' asked Harry, who found Ron just as interesting as Ron found him.

'Er – yes, I think so,' said Ron. 'I think Mum's got a second cousin who's an accountant, but we never talk about him.'

'So you must know loads of magic already.'

The Weasleys were clearly one of those old wizarding families the pale boy in Diagon Alley had talked about.

'I heard you went to live with Muggles,' said Ron. 'What are they like?'

'Horrible – well, not all of them. My aunt and uncle and cousin are, though. Wish I'd had three wizard brothers.'

'Five,' said Ron. For some reason, he was looking gloomy. 'I'm the sixth in our family to go to Hogwarts. You could say I've got a lot to live up to.

Bill and Charlie have already left – Bill was Head Boy and Charlie was captain of Quidditch. Now Percy's a Prefect. Fred and George mess around a lot, but they still get really good marks and everyone thinks they're really funny. Everyone expects me to do as well as the others, but if I do, it's no big deal, because they did it first. You never get anything new, either, with five brothers. I've got Bill's old robes, Charlie's old wand and Percy's old rat.'

Ron reached inside his jacket and pulled out a fat grey rat, which was asleep.

'His name's Scabbers and he's useless, he hardly ever wakes up. Percy got an owl from my dad for being made a Prefect, but they couldn't aff– I mean, I got Scabbers instead.'

Ron's ears went pink. He seemed to think he'd said too much, because he went back to staring out of the window.

Harry didn't think there was anything wrong with not being able to afford an owl. After all, he'd never had any money in his life until a month ago, and he told Ron so, all about having to wear Dudley's old clothes and never getting proper birthday presents. This seemed to cheer Ron up.

'... and until Hagrid told me, I didn't know anything about being a wizard or about my parents or Voldemort –'

Ron gasped.

'What?' said Harry.

'*You said You-Know-Who's name!*' said Ron, sounding both shocked and impressed. 'I'd have thought you, of all people –'

'I'm not trying to be *brave* or anything, saying the

name,' said Harry. 'I just never knew you shouldn't. See what I mean? I've got loads to learn ... I bet,' he added, voicing for the first time something that had been worrying him a lot lately, 'I bet I'm the worst in the class.'

'You won't be. There's loads of people who come from Muggle families and they learn quick enough.'

While they had been talking, the train had carried them out of London. Now they were speeding past fields full of cows and sheep. They were quiet for a time, watching the fields and lanes flick past.

Around half past twelve there was a great clattering outside in the corridor and a smiling, dimpled woman slid back their door and said, 'Anything off the trolley, dears?'

Harry, who hadn't had any breakfast, leapt to his feet, but Ron's ears went pink again and he muttered that he'd brought sandwiches. Harry went out into the corridor.

He had never had any money for sweets with the Dursleys and now that he had pockets rattling with gold and silver he was ready to buy as many Mars Bars as he could carry – but the woman didn't have Mars Bars. What she did have were Bertie Bott's Every-Flavour Beans, Droobles Best Blowing Gum, Chocolate Frogs, Pumpkin Pasties, Cauldron Cakes, Liquorice Wands and a number of other strange things Harry had never seen in his life. Not wanting to miss anything, he got some of everything and paid the woman eleven silver Sickles and seven bronze Knuts.

Ron stared as Harry brought it all back into the compartment and tipped it on to an empty seat.

'Hungry, are you?'

'Starving,' said Harry, taking a large bite out of a pumpkin pasty.

Ron had taken out a lumpy package and unwrapped it. There were four sandwiches in there. He pulled one of them apart and said, 'She always forgets I don't like corned beef.'

'Swap you for one of these,' said Harry, holding up a pasty. 'Go on –'

'You don't want this, it's all dry,' said Ron. 'She hasn't got much time,' he added quickly, 'you know, with five of us.'

'Go on, have a pasty,' said Harry, who had never had anything to share before or, indeed, anyone to share it with. It was a nice feeling, sitting there with Ron, eating their way through all Harry's pasties and cakes (the sandwiches lay forgotten).

'What are these?' Harry asked Ron, holding up a pack of Chocolate Frogs. 'They're not *really* frogs, are they?' He was starting to feel that nothing would surprise him.

'No,' said Ron. 'But see what the card is, I'm missing Agrippa.'

'What?'

'Oh, of course, you wouldn't know – Chocolate Frogs have cards inside them, you know, to collect – Famous Witches and Wizards. I've got about five hundred, but I haven't got Agrippa or Ptolemy.'

Harry unwrapped his Chocolate Frog and picked up the card. It showed a man's face. He wore half-moon glasses, had a long crooked nose and flowing silver hair, beard and moustache. Underneath the picture was the name *Albus Dumbledore*.

'So *this* is Dumbledore!' said Harry.

'Don't tell me you'd never heard of Dumbledore!' said Ron. 'Can I have a frog? I might get Agrippa – thanks –'

Harry turned over his card and read:

> *Albus Dumbledore, currently Headmaster of*
> *Hogwarts*
> *Considered by many the greatest wizard of modern*
> *times, Professor Dumbledore is particularly famous for*
> *his defeat of the dark wizard Grindelwald in 1945,*
> *for the discovery of the twelve uses of dragon's*
> *blood and his work on alchemy with his partner,*
> *Nicolas Flamel. Professor Dumbledore enjoys*
> *chamber music and tenpin bowling.*

Harry turned the card back over and saw, to his astonishment, that Dumbledore's face had disappeared.

'He's gone!'

'Well, you can't expect him to hang around all day,' said Ron. 'He'll be back. No, I've got Morgana again and I've got about six of her ... do you want it? You can start collecting.'

Ron's eyes strayed to the pile of Chocolate Frogs waiting to be unwrapped.

'Help yourself,' said Harry. 'But in, you know, the Muggle world, people just stay put in photos.'

'Do they? What, they don't move at all?' Ron sounded amazed. '*Weird!*'

Harry stared as Dumbledore sidled back into the picture on his card and gave him a small smile. Ron was more interested in eating the frogs than looking at the Famous Witches and Wizards cards, but Harry couldn't keep his eyes off them. Soon he had not only Dumbledore and Morgana, but Hengist of Woodcroft, Alberic Grunnion, Circe, Paracelsus and Merlin. He finally tore his eyes away from the druidess Cliodna, who was scratching her nose, to open a bag of Bertie Bott's Every-Flavour Beans.

'You want to be careful with those,' Ron warned Harry. 'When they say every flavour, they *mean* every flavour – you know, you get all the ordinary ones like chocolate and peppermint and marmalade, but then you can get spinach and liver and tripe. George reckons he had a bogey-flavoured one once.'

Ron picked up a green bean, looked at it carefully and bit into a corner.

'Bleaaargh – see? Sprouts.'

They had a good time eating the Every-Flavour Beans. Harry got toast, coconut, baked bean, strawberry, curry, grass, coffee, sardine and was even brave enough to nibble the end off a funny grey one Ron wouldn't touch, which turned out to be pepper.

The countryside now flying past the window was becoming wilder. The neat fields had gone. Now there were woods, twisting rivers and dark green hills.

There was a knock on the door of their compartment and the round-faced boy Harry had passed on platform nine and three-quarters came in. He looked tearful.

'Sorry,' he said, 'but have you seen a toad at all?'

When they shook their heads, he wailed, 'I've lost him! He keeps getting away from me!'

'He'll turn up,' said Harry.

'Yes,' said the boy miserably. 'Well, if you see him ...'

He left.

'Don't know why he's so bothered,' said Ron. 'If I'd brought a toad I'd lose it as quick as I could. Mind you, I brought Scabbers, so I can't talk.'

The rat was still snoozing on Ron's lap.

'He might have died and you wouldn't know the difference,' said Ron in disgust. 'I tried to turn him yellow yesterday to make him more interesting, but the spell didn't work. I'll show you, look ...'

He rummaged around in his trunk and pulled out a very battered-looking wand. It was chipped in places and something white was glinting at the end.

'Unicorn hair's nearly poking out. Anyway –'

He had just raised his wand when the compartment door slid open again. The toadless boy was back, but this time he had a girl with him. She was already wearing her new Hogwarts robes.

'Has anyone seen a toad? Neville's lost one,' she said. She had a bossy sort of voice, lots of bushy brown hair and rather large front teeth.

'We've already told him we haven't seen it,' said Ron, but the girl wasn't listening, she was looking at the wand in his hand.

'Oh, are you doing magic? Let's see it, then.'

She sat down. Ron looked taken aback.

'Er – all right.'

He cleared his throat.

'Sunshine, daisies, butter mellow,
Turn this stupid, fat rat yellow.'

He waved his wand, but nothing happened. Scabbers stayed grey and fast asleep.

'Are you sure that's a real spell?' said the girl. 'Well, it's not very good, is it? I've tried a few simple spells just for practice and it's all worked for me. Nobody in my family's magic at all, it was ever such a surprise when I got my letter, but I was ever so pleased, of course, I mean, it's the very best school of witchcraft there is, I've heard – I've learnt all our set books off by heart, of course, I just hope it will be enough – I'm Hermione Granger, by the way, who are you?'

She said all this very fast.

Harry looked at Ron and was relieved to see by his stunned face that he hadn't learnt all the set books off by heart either.

'I'm Ron Weasley,' Ron muttered.

'Harry Potter,' said Harry.

'Are you really?' said Hermione. 'I know all about you, of course – I got a few extra books for background reading, and you're in *Modern Magical History* and *The Rise and Fall of the Dark Arts* and *Great Wizarding Events of the Twentieth Century*.'

'Am I?' said Harry, feeling dazed.

'Goodness, didn't you know, I'd have found out everything I could if it was me,' said Hermione. 'Do either of you know what house you'll be in? I've been asking around and I hope I'm in Gryffindor, it sounds by far the best, I hear Dumbledore himself was one, but I suppose Ravenclaw wouldn't be too bad ... Anyway, we'd better go and look for Neville's toad. You two had better change, you know, I expect we'll be there soon.'

And she left, taking the toadless boy with her.

'Whatever house I'm in, I hope she's not in it,' said Ron. He threw his wand back into his trunk. 'Stupid spell – George gave it to me, bet he knew it was a dud.'

'What house are your brothers in?' asked Harry.

'Gryffindor,' said Ron. Gloom seemed to be settling on him again. 'Mum and Dad were in it, too. I don't know what they'll say if I'm not. I don't suppose Ravenclaw *would* be too bad, but imagine if they put me in Slytherin.'

'That's the house Vol– I mean, You-Know-Who was in?'

'Yeah,' said Ron. He flopped back into his seat, looking depressed.

'You know, I think the ends of Scabbers's whiskers are a bit lighter,' said Harry, trying to take Ron's mind off houses. 'So what do your oldest brothers do now they've left, anyway?'

Harry was wondering what a wizard did once he'd finished school.

'Charlie's in Romania studying dragons and Bill's in Africa doing something for Gringotts,' said Ron. 'Did you hear about Gringotts? It's been all over the *Daily Prophet*, but I don't suppose you get that with the Muggles – someone tried to rob a high-security vault.'

Harry stared.

'Really? What happened to them?'

'Nothing, that's why it's such big news. They haven't been caught. My dad says it must've been a powerful Dark wizard to get round Gringotts, but they don't think they took anything, that's what's odd. 'Course, everyone gets scared when something like this happens in case You-Know-Who's behind it.'

Harry turned this news over in his mind. He was starting to get a prickle of fear every time You-Know-Who was mentioned. He supposed this was all part of entering the magical world, but it had been a lot more comfortable saying 'Voldemort' without worrying.

'What's your Quidditch team?' Ron asked.

'Er – I don't know any,' Harry confessed.

'What!' Ron looked dumbfounded. 'Oh, you wait, it's the best game in the world –' And he was off, explaining all about the four balls and the positions of the seven players, describing famous games he'd been to with his brothers and the broomstick he'd like to get if he had the money. He was just taking Harry through the finer points of the game when the compartment door slid open yet again, but it wasn't Neville the toadless boy or Hermione Granger this time.

Three boys entered and Harry recognised the middle one at once: it was the pale boy from Madam Malkin's robe shop. He was looking at Harry with a lot more interest than he'd shown back in Diagon Alley.

'Is it true?' he said. 'They're saying all down the train that Harry Potter's in this compartment. So it's you, is it?'

'Yes,' said Harry. He was looking at the other boys. Both of them were thickset and looked extremely mean. Standing either side of the pale boy they looked like bodyguards.

'Oh, this is Crabbe and this is Goyle,' said the pale boy carelessly, noticing where Harry was looking. 'And my name's Malfoy, Draco Malfoy.'

Ron gave a slight cough, which might have been hiding a snigger. Draco Malfoy looked at him.

'Think my name's funny, do you? No need to ask who you are. My father told me all the Weasleys have red hair, freckles and more children than they can afford.'

He turned back to Harry.

'You'll soon find out some wizarding families are much better than others, Potter. You don't want to go making friends with the wrong sort. I can help you there.'

He held out his hand to shake Harry's, but Harry didn't take it.

'I think I can tell who the wrong sort are for myself, thanks,' he said coolly.

Draco Malfoy didn't go red, but a pink tinge appeared in his pale cheeks.

'I'd be careful if I were you, Potter,' he said slowly. 'Unless you're a bit politer you'll go the same way as your parents. They didn't know what was good for them, either. You hang around with riff-raff like the Weasleys and that Hagrid and it'll rub off on you.'

Both Harry and Ron stood up. Ron's face was as red as his hair.

'Say that again,' he said.

'Oh, you're going to fight us, are you?' Malfoy sneered.

'Unless you get out now,' said Harry, more bravely than he felt, because Crabbe and Goyle were a lot bigger than him or Ron.

'But we don't feel like leaving, do we, boys? We've eaten all our food and you still seem to have some.'

Goyle reached towards the Chocolate Frogs next to Ron – Ron leapt forward, but before he'd so much as touched Goyle, Goyle let out a horrible yell.

Scabbers the rat was hanging off his finger, sharp little teeth sunk deep into Goyle's knuckle – Crabbe and Malfoy backed away as Goyle swung Scabbers round and round, howling, and when Scabbers finally flew off and hit the window, all three of them disappeared at once. Perhaps they thought there were more rats lurking among the sweets, or perhaps they'd heard footsteps, because a second later, Hermione Granger had come in.

'What *has* been going on?' she said, looking at the sweets all over the floor and Ron picking up Scabbers by his tail.

'I think he's been knocked out,' Ron said to Harry. He looked closer at Scabbers. 'No – I don't believe it – he's gone back to sleep.'

And so he had.

'You've met Malfoy before?'

Harry explained about their meeting in Diagon Alley.

'I've heard of his family,' said Ron darkly. 'They were some of the first to come back to our side after You-Know-Who disappeared. Said they'd been bewitched. My dad doesn't believe it. He says

Malfoy's father didn't need an excuse to go over to the Dark Side.' He turned to Hermione. 'Can we help you with something?'

'You'd better hurry up and put your robes on, I've just been up the front to ask the driver and he says we're nearly there. You haven't been fighting, have you? You'll be in trouble before we even get there!'

'Scabbers has been fighting, not us,' said Ron, scowling at her. 'Would you mind leaving while we change?'

'All right – I only came in here because people outside are behaving very childishly, racing up and down the corridors,' said Hermione in a sniffy voice. 'And you've got dirt on your nose, by the way, did you know?'

Ron glared at her as she left. Harry peered out of the window. It was getting dark. He could see mountains and forests under a deep-purple sky. The train did seem to be slowing down.

He and Ron took off their jackets and pulled on their long black robes. Ron's were a bit short for him, you could see his trainers underneath them.

A voice echoed through the train: 'We will be reaching Hogwarts in five minutes' time. Please leave your luggage on the train, it will be taken to the school separately.'

Harry's stomach lurched with nerves and Ron, he saw, looked pale under his freckles. They crammed their pockets with the last of the sweets and joined the crowd thronging the corridor.

The train slowed right down and finally stopped. People pushed their way towards the door and out on to a tiny, dark platform. Harry shivered in the cold night air. Then a lamp came bobbing over the heads of the students and Harry heard a familiar voice: 'Firs'-years! Firs'-years over here! All right there, Harry?'

Hagrid's big hairy face beamed over the sea of heads.

'C'mon, follow me – any more firs'-years? Mind yer step, now! Firs'-years follow me!'

Slipping and stumbling, they followed Hagrid down what seemed to be a steep, narrow path. It was so dark either side of them that Harry thought there must be thick trees there. Nobody spoke much. Neville, the boy who kept losing his toad, sniffed once or twice.

'Yeh'll get yer firs' sight o' Hogwarts in a sec,' Hagrid called over his shoulder, 'jus' round this bend here.'

There was a loud 'Ooooooh!'

The narrow path had opened suddenly on to the edge of a great black lake. Perched atop a high mountain on the other side, its windows sparkling in the starry sky, was a vast castle with many turrets and towers.

'No more'n four to a boat!' Hagrid called, pointing to a fleet of little boats sitting in the water by the shore. Harry and Ron were followed into their boat by Neville and Hermione.

'Everyone in?' shouted Hagrid, who had a boat to himself. 'Right then – FORWARD!'

And the fleet of little boats moved off all at once, gliding across the lake, which was as smooth as glass. Everyone was silent, staring up at the great castle overhead. It towered over them as they sailed nearer and nearer to the cliff on which it stood.

'Heads down!' yelled Hagrid as the first boats reached the cliff; they all bent their heads and the little boats carried them through a curtain of ivy which hid a wide opening in the cliff face. They were carried along a dark tunnel, which seemed to be taking them right underneath the castle, until they reached a kind of underground harbour, where they clambered out on to rocks and pebbles.

'Oy, you there! Is this your toad?' said Hagrid, who was checking the boats as people climbed out of them.

'Trevor!' cried Neville blissfully, holding out his hands. Then they clambered up a passageway in the rock after Hagrid's lamp, coming out at last on to smooth, damp grass right in the shadow of the castle.

They walked up a flight of stone steps and crowded around the huge, oak front door.

'Everyone here? You there, still got yer toad?'

Hagrid raised a gigantic fist and knocked three times on the castle door.

— CHAPTER SEVEN —

The Sorting Hat

The door swung open at once. A tall, black-haired witch in emerald-green robes stood there. She had a very stern face and Harry's first thought was that this was not someone to cross.

'The firs'-years, Professor McGonagall,' said Hagrid.

'Thank you, Hagrid. I will take them from here.'

She pulled the door wide. The Entrance Hall was so big you could have fitted the whole of the Dursleys' house in it. The stone walls were lit with flaming torches like the ones at Gringotts, the ceiling was too high to make out, and a magnificent marble staircase facing them led to the upper floors.

They followed Professor McGonagall across the flagged stone floor. Harry could hear the drone of hundreds of voices from a doorway to the right – the rest of the school must already be here – but Professor McGonagall showed the first-years into a small empty chamber off the hall. They crowded in, standing rather closer together than they would usually have done, peering about nervously.

'Welcome to Hogwarts,' said Professor McGonagall. 'The start-of-term banquet will begin shortly, but before you take your seats in the Great Hall, you will be sorted into your houses. The Sorting is a very important ceremony because, while you are here, your house will be something like your family within Hogwarts. You will have classes with the rest of your house, sleep in your house dormitory and spend free time in your house common room.

'The four houses are called Gryffindor, Hufflepuff, Ravenclaw and Slytherin. Each house has its own noble history and each has produced outstanding witches and wizards. While you are at Hogwarts, your triumphs will earn your house points, while any rule-breaking will lose house points. At the end of the year, the house with the most points is awarded the House Cup, a great honour. I hope each of you will be a credit to whichever house becomes yours.

'The Sorting Ceremony will take place in a few minutes in front of the rest of the school. I suggest you all smarten yourselves up as much as you can while you are waiting.'

Her eyes lingered for a moment on Neville's cloak, which was fastened under his left ear, and on Ron's smudged nose. Harry nervously tried to flatten his hair.

'I shall return when we are ready for you,' said Professor McGonagall. 'Please wait quietly.'

She left the chamber. Harry swallowed.

'How exactly do they sort us into houses?' he asked Ron.

'Some sort of test, I think. Fred said it hurts a lot, but I think he was joking.'

Harry's heart gave a horrible jolt. A test? In front of the whole school? But he didn't know any magic yet – what on earth would he have to do? He hadn't expected something like this the moment they arrived. He looked around anxiously and saw that everyone else looked terrified too. No one was talking much except Hermione Granger, who was whispering very fast about all the spells she'd learnt and wondering which one she'd need. Harry tried hard not to listen to her. He'd never been more nervous, never, not even when he'd had to take a school report home to the Dursleys saying that he'd somehow turned his teacher's wig blue. He kept his eyes fixed on the door. Any second now, Professor McGonagall would come back and lead him to his doom.

Then something happened which made him jump about a foot in the air – several people behind him screamed.

'What the –?'

He gasped. So did the people around him. About twenty ghosts had just streamed through the back wall. Pearly-white and slightly transparent, they glided across the room talking to each other and hardly glancing at the first-years. They seemed to be arguing. What looked like a fat little monk was saying, 'Forgive and forget, I say, we ought to give him a second chance –'

'My dear Friar, haven't we given Peeves all the chances he deserves? He gives us all a bad name and you know, he's not really even a ghost – I say, what are you all doing here?'

A ghost wearing a ruff and tights had suddenly noticed the first-years.

Nobody answered.

'New students!' said the Fat Friar, smiling around at them. 'About to be sorted, I suppose?'

A few people nodded mutely.

'Hope to see you in Hufflepuff!' said the Friar. 'My old house, you know.'

'Move along now,' said a sharp voice. 'The Sorting Ceremony's about to start.'

Professor McGonagall had returned. One by one, the ghosts floated away through the opposite wall.

'Now, form a line,' Professor McGonagall told the first-years, 'and follow me.'

Feeling oddly as though his legs had turned to lead, Harry got into line behind a boy with sandy hair, with Ron behind him, and they walked out of the chamber, back across the hall and through a pair of double doors into the Great Hall.

Harry had never even imagined such a strange and splendid place. It was lit by thousands and thousands of candles which were floating in mid-air over four long tables, where the rest of the students were sitting. These tables were laid with glittering golden plates and goblets. At the top of the Hall was another long table where the teachers were sitting. Professor McGonagall led the first-years up here, so that they came to a halt in a line facing the other students, with the teachers behind them. The hundreds of faces staring at them looked like pale lanterns in the flickering candlelight. Dotted here and there among the students, the ghosts shone misty silver. Mainly to avoid all the staring eyes, Harry looked upwards and saw a velvety black ceiling dotted with stars. He heard Hermione whisper, 'It's bewitched to look like the sky outside, I read about it in *Hogwarts: A History*.'

It was hard to believe there was a ceiling there at all, and that the Great Hall didn't simply open on to the heavens.

Harry quickly looked down again as Professor McGonagall silently placed a four-legged stool in front of the first-years. On top of the stool she put a pointed wizard's hat. This hat was patched and frayed and extremely dirty. Aunt Petunia wouldn't have let it in the house.

Maybe they had to try and get a rabbit out of it, Harry thought wildly, that seemed the sort of thing – noticing that everyone in the Hall was now staring at the hat, he stared at it too. For a few seconds, there was complete silence. Then the hat twitched. A rip near the brim opened wide like a mouth – and the hat began to sing:

> '*Oh, you may not think I'm pretty,*
> *But don't judge on what you see,*
> *I'll eat myself if you can find*
> *A smarter hat than me.*
> *You can keep your bowlers black,*
> *Your top hats sleek and tall,*
> *For I'm the Hogwarts Sorting Hat*
> *And I can cap them all.*
> *There's nothing hidden in your head*
> *The Sorting Hat can't see,*
> *So try me on and I will tell you*
> *Where you ought to be.*

You might belong in Gryffindor,
Where dwell the brave at heart,
Their daring, nerve and chivalry
Set Gryffindors apart;
You might belong in Hufflepuff,
Where they are just and loyal,
Those patient Hufflepuffs are true
And unafraid of toil;
Or yet in wise old Ravenclaw,
If you've a ready mind,
Where those of wit and learning,
Will always find their kind;
Or perhaps in Slytherin
You'll make your real friends,
Those cunning folk use any means
To achieve their ends.
So put me on! Don't be afraid!
And don't get in a flap!
You're in safe hands (though I have none)
For I'm a Thinking Cap!'

The whole Hall burst into applause as the hat finished its song. It bowed to each of the four tables and then became quite still again.

'So we've just got to try on the hat!' Ron whispered to Harry. 'I'll kill Fred, he was going on about wrestling a troll.'

Harry smiled weakly. Yes, trying on the hat was a lot better than having to do a spell, but he did wish they could have tried it on without everyone watching. The hat seemed to be asking rather a lot; Harry didn't feel brave or quick-witted or any of it at the moment. If only the hat had mentioned a house for people who felt a bit queasy, that would have been the one for him.

Professor McGonagall now stepped forward holding a long roll of parchment.

'When I call your name, you will put on the hat and sit on the stool to be sorted,' she said. 'Abbott, Hannah!'

A pink-faced girl with blonde pigtails stumbled out of line, put on the hat, which fell right down over her eyes, and sat down. A moment's pause –

'HUFFLEPUFF!' shouted the hat.

The table on the right cheered and clapped as Hannah went to sit down at the Hufflepuff table. Harry saw the ghost of the Fat Friar waving merrily at her.

'Bones, Susan!'

'HUFFLEPUFF!' shouted the hat again, and Susan scuttled off to sit next to Hannah.

'Boot, Terry!'

'RAVENCLAW!'

The table second from the left clapped this time; several Ravenclaws stood up to shake hands with Terry as he joined them.

'Brocklehurst, Mandy' went to Ravenclaw too, but 'Brown, Lavender' became the first new Gryffindor and the table on the far left exploded with cheers; Harry could see Ron's twin brothers catcalling.

'Bulstrode, Millicent' then became a Slytherin. Perhaps it was Harry's imagination, after all he'd heard about Slytherin, but he thought they looked an unpleasant lot.

He was starting to feel definitely sick now. He

remembered being picked for teams during sports lessons at his old school. He had always been last to be chosen, not because he was no good, but because no one wanted Dudley to think they liked him.

'Finch-Fletchley, Justin!'

'HUFFLEPUFF!'

Sometimes, Harry noticed, the hat shouted out the house at once, but at others it took a little while to decide. 'Finnigan, Seamus', the sandy-haired boy next to Harry in the line, sat on the stool for almost a whole minute before the hat declared him a Gryffindor.

'Granger, Hermione!'

Hermione almost ran to the stool and jammed the hat eagerly on her head.

'GRYFFINDOR!' shouted the hat. Ron groaned.

A horrible thought struck Harry, as horrible thoughts always do when you're very nervous. What if he wasn't chosen at all? What if he just sat there with the hat over his eyes for ages, until Professor McGonagall jerked it off his head and said there had obviously been a mistake and he'd better get back on the train?

When Neville Longbottom, the boy who kept losing his toad, was called, he fell over on his way to the stool. The hat took a long time to decide with Neville. When it finally shouted 'GRYFFIN-DOR', Neville ran off still wearing it, and had to jog back amid gales of laughter to give it to 'MacDougal, Morag'.

Malfoy swaggered forward when his name was called and got his wish at once: the hat had barely touched his head when it screamed, 'SLYTHERIN!'

Malfoy went to join his friends Crabbe and Goyle, looking pleased with himself.

There weren't many people left now.

'Moon' ... 'Nott' ... 'Parkinson' ... then a pair of twin girls, 'Patil' and 'Patil' ... then 'Perks, Sally-Anne' ... and then, at last –

'Potter, Harry!'

As Harry stepped forward, whispers suddenly broke out like little hissing fires all over the hall.

'*Potter*, did she say?'

'*The* Harry Potter?'

The last thing Harry saw before the hat dropped over his eyes was the Hall full of people craning to get a good look at him. Next second he was looking at the black inside of the hat. He waited.

'Hmm,' said a small voice in his ear. 'Difficult. Very difficult. Plenty of courage, I see. Not a bad mind, either. There's talent, oh my goodness, yes – and a nice thirst to prove yourself, now that's interesting ... So where shall I put you?'

Harry gripped the edges of the stool and thought, 'Not Slytherin, not Slytherin.'

'Not Slytherin, eh?' said the small voice. 'Are you sure? You could be great, you know, it's all here in your head, and Slytherin will help you on the way to greatness, no doubt about that – no? Well, if you're sure – better be GRYFFINDOR!'

Harry heard the hat shout the last word to the whole Hall. He took off the hat and walked shakily towards the Gryffindor table. He was so relieved to have been chosen and not put in Slytherin, he hardly noticed that he was getting the loudest cheer yet. Percy the Prefect got up and shook his hand vigorously, while the Weasley twins yelled, 'We got Potter! We got Potter!' Harry sat down opposite the ghost in the ruff he'd seen earlier. The ghost patted his arm, giving Harry the sudden, horrible feeling he'd just plunged it into a bucket of ice-cold water.

He could see the High Table properly now. At the end nearest him sat Hagrid, who caught his eye and gave him the thumbs-up. Harry grinned back. And there, in the centre of the High Table, in a large gold chair, sat Albus Dumbledore. Harry recognised him at once from the card he'd got out of the Chocolate Frog on the train. Dumbledore's silver hair was the only thing in the whole Hall that shone as brightly as the ghosts. Harry spotted Professor Quirrell, too, the nervous young man from the Leaky Cauldron. He was looking very peculiar in a large purple turban.

And now there were only three people left to be sorted. 'Turpin, Lisa' became a Ravenclaw and then it was Ron's turn. He was pale green by now. Harry crossed his fingers under the table and a second later the hat had shouted, 'GRYFFINDOR!'

Harry clapped loudly with the rest as Ron collapsed into the chair next to him.

'Well done, Ron, excellent,' said Percy Weasley pompously across Harry as 'Zabini, Blaise' was made a Slytherin. Professor McGonagall rolled up her scroll and took the Sorting Hat away.

Harry looked down at his empty gold plate. He had only just realised how hungry he was. The pumpkin pasties seemed ages ago.

Albus Dumbledore had got to his feet. He was beaming at the students, his arms opened wide, as if nothing could have pleased him more than to see them all there.

'Welcome!' he said. 'Welcome to a new year at Hogwarts! Before we begin our banquet, I would like to say a few words. And here they are: Nitwit! Blubber! Oddment! Tweak!

'Thank you!'

He sat back down. Everybody clapped and cheered. Harry didn't know whether to laugh or not.

'Is he – a bit mad?' he asked Percy uncertainly.

'Mad?' said Percy airily. 'He's a genius! Best wizard in the world! But he is a bit mad, yes. Potatoes, Harry?'

Harry's mouth fell open. The dishes in front of him were now piled with food. He had never seen so many things he liked to eat on one table: roast beef, roast chicken, pork chops and lamb chops, sausages, bacon and steak, boiled potatoes, roast potatoes, chips, Yorkshire pudding, peas, carrots, gravy, ketchup and, for some strange reason, mint humbugs.

The Dursleys had never exactly starved Harry, but he'd never been allowed to eat as much as he liked. Dudley had always taken anything that Harry really wanted, even if it made him sick. Harry piled his plate with a bit of everything except the humbugs and began to eat. It was all delicious.

'That does look good,' said the ghost in the ruff sadly, watching Harry cut up his steak.

'Can't you –?'

'I haven't eaten for nearly five hundred years,' said the ghost. 'I don't need to, of course, but one does miss it. I don't think I've introduced myself? Sir Nicholas de Mimsy-Porpington at your service. Resident ghost of Gryffindor Tower.'

'I know who you are!' said Ron suddenly. 'My brothers told me about you – you're Nearly Headless Nick!'

'I would *prefer* you to call me Sir Nicholas de Mimsy –' the ghost began stiffly, but sandy-haired Seamus Finnigan interrupted.

'*Nearly* Headless? How can you be *nearly* headless?'

Sir Nicholas looked extremely miffed, as if their little chat wasn't going at all the way he wanted.

'Like *this*,' he said irritably. He seized his left ear and pulled. His whole head swung off his neck and fell on to his shoulder as if it was on a hinge. Someone had obviously tried to behead him, but not done it properly. Looking pleased at the stunned looks on their faces, Nearly Headless Nick flipped his head back on to his neck, coughed and said, 'So – new Gryffindors! I hope you're going to help us win the House Championship this year? Gryffindor have never gone so long without winning. Slytherin have got the cup six years in a row! The Bloody Baron's becoming almost unbearable – he's the Slytherin ghost.'

Harry looked over at the Slytherin table and saw a horrible ghost sitting there, with blank staring eyes, a gaunt face and robes stained with silver blood. He was right next to Malfoy who, Harry was pleased to see, didn't look too pleased with the seating arrangements.

'How did he get covered in blood?' asked Seamus with great interest.

'I've never asked,' said Nearly Headless Nick delicately.

When everyone had eaten as much as they could, the remains of the food faded from the plates, leaving them sparkling clean as before. A moment later the puddings appeared. Blocks of ice-cream in every flavour you could think of, apple pies, treacle tarts, chocolate éclairs and jam doughnuts, trifle, strawberries, jelly, rice pudding ...

As Harry helped himself to a treacle tart, the talk turned to their families.

'I'm half and half,' said Seamus. 'Me dad's a Muggle. Mam didn't tell him she was a witch 'til after they were married. Bit of a nasty shock for him.'

The others laughed.

'What about you, Neville?' said Ron.

'Well, my gran brought me up and she's a witch,' said Neville, 'but the family thought I was all Muggle for ages. My great-uncle Algie kept trying to catch me off my guard and force some magic out of me – he pushed me off the end of Blackpool pier once, I nearly drowned – but nothing happened until I was eight. Great-uncle Algie came round for tea and he was hanging me out of an upstairs window by the ankles when my great-auntie Enid offered him a meringue and he accidentally let go. But I bounced – all the way down the garden and into the road. They were all really pleased. Gran was crying, she was so happy. And you should have seen their faces when I got in here – they thought I might not be magic enough to come, you see. Great-uncle Algie was so pleased he bought me my toad.'

On Harry's other side, Percy Weasley and Hermione were talking about lessons ('I *do* hope they start straight away, there's so much to learn, I'm particularly interested in Transfiguration, you know, turning something into something else, of course, it's supposed to be very difficult –'; 'You'll be starting small, just matches into needles and that sort of thing –').

Harry, who was starting to feel warm and sleepy, looked up at the High Table again. Hagrid was drinking deeply from his goblet. Professor McGonagall was talking to Professor Dumbledore. Professor Quirrell, in his absurd turban, was talking to a teacher with greasy black hair, a hooked nose and sallow skin.

It happened very suddenly. The hook-nosed teacher looked past Quirrell's turban straight into Harry's eyes – and a sharp, hot pain shot across the scar on Harry's forehead.

'Ouch!' Harry clapped a hand to his head.

'What is it?' asked Percy.

'N-nothing.'

The pain had gone as quickly as it had come. Harder to shake off was the feeling Harry had got from the teacher's look – a feeling that he didn't like Harry at all.

'Who's that teacher talking to Professor Quirrell?' he asked Percy.

'Oh, you know Quirrell already, do you? No

wonder he's looking so nervous, that's Professor Snape. He teaches Potions, but he doesn't want to – everyone knows he's after Quirrell's job. Knows an awful lot about the Dark Arts, Snape.'

Harry watched Snape for a while but Snape didn't look at him again.

At last, the puddings too disappeared and Professor Dumbledore got to his feet again. The Hall fell silent.

'Ahem – just a few more words now we are all fed and watered. I have a few start-of-term notices to give you.

'First-years should note that the forest in the grounds is forbidden to all pupils. And a few of our older students would do well to remember that as well.'

Dumbledore's twinkling eyes flashed in the direction of the Weasley twins.

'I have also been asked by Mr Filch, the caretaker, to remind you all that no magic should be used between classes in the corridors.

'Quidditch trials will be held in the second week of term. Anyone interested in playing for their house teams should contact Madam Hooch.

'And finally, I must tell you that this year, the third-floor corridor on the right-hand side is out of bounds to everyone who does not wish to die a very painful death.'

Harry laughed, but he was one of the few who did.

'He's not serious?' he muttered to Percy.

'Must be,' said Percy, frowning at Dumbledore. 'It's odd, because he usually gives us a reason why we're not allowed to go somewhere – the forest's full of dangerous beasts, everyone knows that. I do think he might have told us Prefects, at least.'

'And now, before we go to bed, let us sing the school song!' cried Dumbledore. Harry noticed that the other teachers' smiles had become rather fixed.

Dumbledore gave his wand a little flick as if he was trying to get a fly off the end and a long golden ribbon flew out of it, which rose high above the tables and twisted itself snake-like into words.

'Everyone pick their favourite tune,' said Dumbledore, 'and off we go!'

And the school bellowed:

> *'Hogwarts, Hogwarts, Hoggy Warty Hogwarts,*
> *Teach us something please,*
> *Whether we be old and bald*
> *Or young with scabby knees,*
> *Our heads could do with filling*
> *With some interesting stuff,*
> *For now they're bare and full of air,*
> *Dead flies and bits of fluff,*
> *So teach us things worth knowing,*
> *Bring back what we've forgot,*
> *Just do your best, we'll do the rest,*
> *And learn until our brains all rot.'*

Everybody finished the song at different times. At last, only the Weasley twins were left singing along to a very slow funeral march. Dumbledore conducted their last few lines with his wand, and when they had finished, he was one of those who clapped loudest.

'Ah, music,' he said, wiping his eyes. 'A magic beyond all we do here! And now, bedtime. Off you trot!'

The Gryffindor first-years followed Percy through the chattering crowds, out of the Great Hall and up the marble staircase. Harry's legs were like lead again, but only because he was so tired and full of food. He was too sleepy even to be surprised that the people in the portraits along the corridors whispered and pointed as they passed, or that twice Percy led them through doorways hidden behind sliding panels and hanging tapestries. They climbed more staircases, yawning and dragging their feet, and Harry was just wondering how much further they had to go when they came to a sudden halt.

A bundle of walking sticks was floating in mid-air ahead of them and as Percy took a step towards them they started throwing themselves at him.

'Peeves,' Percy whispered to the first-years. 'A poltergeist.' He raised his voice, 'Peeves – show yourself.'

A loud, rude sound, like the air being let out of a balloon, answered.

'Do you want me to go to the Bloody Baron?'

There was a *pop* and a little man with wicked dark eyes and a wide mouth appeared, floating cross-legged in the air, clutching the walking sticks.

'Ooooooooh!' he said, with an evil cackle. 'Ickle firsties! What fun!'

He swooped suddenly at them. They all ducked.

'Go away, Peeves, or the Baron'll hear about this,

I mean it!' barked Percy.

Peeves stuck out his tongue and vanished, dropping the walking sticks on Neville's head. They heard him zooming away, rattling coats of armour as he passed.

'You want to watch out for Peeves,' said Percy, as they set off again. 'The Bloody Baron's the only one who can control him, he won't even listen to us Prefects. Here we are.'

At the very end of the corridor hung a portrait of a very fat woman in a pink silk dress.

'Password?' she said.

'*Caput Draconis*,' said Percy, and the portrait swung forward to reveal a round hole in the wall. They all scrambled through it – Neville needed a leg up – and found themselves in the Gryffindor common room, a cosy, round room full of squashy armchairs.

Percy directed the girls through one door to their dormitory and the boys through another. At the top of a spiral staircase – they were obviously in one of the towers – they found their beds at last: five four-posters hung with deep-red velvet curtains. Their trunks had already been brought up. Too tired to talk much, they pulled on their pyjamas and fell into bed.

'Great food, isn't it?' Ron muttered to Harry through the hangings. 'Get *off*, Scabbers! He's chewing my sheets.'

Harry was going to ask Ron if he'd had any of the treacle tart, but he fell asleep almost at once.

Perhaps Harry had eaten a bit too much, because he had a very strange dream. He was wearing

Professor Quirrell's turban, which kept talking to him, telling him he must transfer to Slytherin at once, because it was his destiny. Harry told the turban he didn't want to be in Slytherin; it got heavier and heavier; he tried to pull it off but it tightened painfully – and there was Malfoy, laughing at him as he struggled with it – then Malfoy turned into the hook-nosed teacher, Snape, whose laugh became high and cold – there was a burst of green light and Harry woke, sweating and shaking.

He rolled over and fell asleep again, and when he woke next day, he didn't remember the dream at all.

— CHAPTER EIGHT —

The Potions Master

'There, look.'

'Where?'

'Next to the tall kid with the red hair.'

'Wearing the glasses?'

'Did you see his face?'

'Did you see his scar?'

Whispers followed Harry from the moment he left his dormitory next day. People queuing outside classrooms stood on tiptoe to get a look at him, or doubled back to pass him in the corridors again, staring. Harry wished they wouldn't, because he was trying to concentrate on finding his way to classes.

There were a hundred and forty-two staircases at Hogwarts: wide, sweeping ones; narrow, rickety ones; some that led somewhere different on a Friday; some with a vanishing step halfway up that you had to remember to jump. Then there were doors that wouldn't open unless you asked politely, or tickled them in exactly the right place, and doors that weren't really doors at all, but solid walls just pretending. It was also very hard to remember where anything was, because it all seemed to move around a lot. The people in the portraits kept going to visit each other and Harry was sure the coats of armour could walk.

The ghosts didn't help, either. It was always a nasty shock when one of them glided suddenly through a door you were trying to open. Nearly Headless Nick was always happy to point new Gryffindors in the right direction, but Peeves the poltergeist was worth two locked doors and a trick staircase if you met him when you were late for class. He would drop waste-paper baskets on your head, pull rugs from under your feet, pelt you with bits of chalk or sneak up behind you, invisible, grab your nose and screech, 'GOT YOUR CONK!'

Even worse than Peeves, if that was possible, was the caretaker, Argus Filch. Harry and Ron managed to get on the wrong side of him on their very first morning. Filch found them trying to force their way through a door which unluckily turned out to be the entrance to the out-of-bounds corridor on the third floor. He wouldn't believe they were lost, was sure they were trying to break into it on purpose and was threatening to lock them in the dungeons when they were rescued by Professor Quirrell, who was passing.

Filch owned a cat called Mrs Norris, a scrawny, dust-coloured creature with bulging, lamp-like eyes just like Filch's. She patrolled the corridors alone. Break a rule in front of her, put just one toe out of line, and she'd whisk off for Filch, who'd appear, wheezing, two seconds later. Filch knew the secret passageways of the school better than anyone (except perhaps the Weasley twins) and could pop up as suddenly as any of the ghosts. The students all hated him and it was the dearest ambition of many to give Mrs Norris a good kick.

And then, once you had managed to find them, there were the lessons themselves. There was a lot more to magic, as Harry quickly found out, than waving your wand and saying a few funny words.

They had to study the night skies through their telescopes every Wednesday at midnight and learn the names of different stars and the movements of the planets. Three times a week they went out to the greenhouses behind the castle to study Herbology, with a dumpy little witch called Professor Sprout, where they learnt how to take care of all the strange plants and fungi and found out what they were used for.

Easily the most boring lesson was History of Magic, which was the only class taught by a ghost. Professor Binns had been very old indeed when he had fallen asleep in front of the staff-room fire and got up next morning to teach, leaving his body behind him. Binns droned on and on while they scribbled down names and dates and got Emeric the Evil and Uric the Oddball mixed up.

Professor Flitwick, the Charms teacher, was a tiny little wizard who had to stand on a pile of books to see over his desk. At the start of their first lesson he took the register, and when he reached Harry's name he gave an excited squeak and toppled out of sight.

Professor McGonagall was again different. Harry had been quite right to think she wasn't a teacher to cross. Strict and clever, she gave them a talking-to the moment they had sat down in her first class.

'Transfiguration is some of the most complex and dangerous magic you will learn at Hogwarts,' she said. 'Anyone messing around in my class will leave and not come back. You have been warned.'

Then she changed her desk into a pig and back again. They were all very impressed and couldn't wait to get started, but soon realised they weren't going to be changing the furniture into animals for a long time. After making a lot of complicated notes, they were each given a match and started trying to turn it into a needle. By the end of the lesson, only Hermione Granger had made any difference to her match; Professor McGonagall showed the class how it had gone all silver and pointy and gave Hermione a rare smile.

The class everyone had really been looking for-ward to was Defence Against the Dark Arts, but Quirrell's lessons turned out to be a bit of a joke. His classroom smelled strongly of garlic, which everyone said was to ward off a vampire he'd met in Romania and was afraid would be coming back to get him one of these days. His turban, he told them, had been given to him by an African prince as a thank-you for getting rid of a troublesome zombie, but they weren't sure they believed this story. For one thing, when Seamus Finnigan asked eagerly to hear how Quirrell had fought off the zombie, Quirrell went pink and started talking about the weather; for another, they had noticed that a funny smell hung around the turban, and the Weasley twins insisted that it was stuffed full of garlic as well, so that Quirrell was protected wherever he went.

Harry was very relieved to find out that he wasn't miles behind everyone else. Lots of people had come from Muggle families and, like him, hadn't had any idea that they were witches and wizards. There was so much to learn that even people like Ron didn't have much of a head start.

Friday was an important day for Harry and Ron. They finally managed to find their way down to the Great Hall for breakfast without getting lost once.

'What have we got today?' Harry asked Ron as he poured sugar on his porridge.

'Double Potions with the Slytherins,' said Ron. 'Snape's Head of Slytherin house. They say he always favours them – we'll be able to see if it's true.'

'Wish McGonagall favoured us,' said Harry. Professor McGonagall was head of Gryffindor house, but it hadn't stopped her giving them a huge pile of homework the day before.

Just then, the post arrived. Harry had got used to this by now, but it had given him a bit of a shock on the first morning, when about a hundred owls had suddenly streamed into the Great Hall during breakfast, circling the tables until they saw their owners and dropping letters and packages on to their laps.

Hedwig hadn't brought Harry anything so far. She sometimes flew in to nibble his ear and have a bit of toast before going off to sleep in the owlery with the other school owls. This morning, however, she fluttered down between the marmalade and the sugar bowl and dropped a note on to Harry's plate. Harry tore it open at once.

Dear Harry, (it said, in a very untidy scrawl)
   I know you get Friday afternoons off, so would you like to come and have a cup of tea with me around three? I want to hear all about your first week. Send us an answer back with Hedwig.
Hagrid

Harry borrowed Ron's quill, scribbled *'Yes, please, see you later'* on the back of the note and sent Hedwig off again.

It was lucky that Harry had tea with Hagrid to look forward to, because the Potions lesson turned out to be the worst thing that had happened to him so far.

At the start-of-term banquet, Harry had got the idea that Professor Snape disliked him. By the end of the first Potions lesson, he knew he'd been wrong. Snape didn't dislike Harry – he *hated* him.

Potions lessons took place down in one of the dungeons. It was colder here than up in the main castle and would have been quite creepy enough without the pickled animals floating in glass jars all around the walls.

Snape, like Flitwick, started the class by taking the register, and like Flitwick, he paused at Harry's name.

'Ah, yes,' he said softly, 'Harry Potter. Our new – *celebrity.*'

Draco Malfoy and his friends Crabbe and Goyle

sniggered behind their hands. Snape finished calling the names and looked up at the class. His eyes
were black like Hagrid's, but they had none of
Hagrid's warmth. They were cold and empty and
made you think of dark tunnels.

'You are here to learn the subtle science and
exact art of potion-making,' he began. He spoke in
barely more than a whisper, but they caught every
word – like Professor McGonagall, Snape had the
gift of keeping a class silent without effort. 'As
there is little foolish wand-waving here, many of
you will hardly believe this is magic. I don't expect
you will really understand the beauty of the softly
simmering cauldron with its shimmering fumes,
the delicate power of liquids that creep through
human veins, bewitching the mind, ensnaring the
senses ... I can teach you how to bottle fame, brew
glory, even stopper death – if you aren't as big a
bunch of dunderheads as I usually have to teach.'

More silence followed this little speech. Harry
and Ron exchanged looks with raised eyebrows.
Hermione Granger was on the edge of her seat and
looked desperate to start proving that she wasn't a
dunderhead.

'Potter!' said Snape suddenly. 'What would I get
if I added powdered root of asphodel to an infusion
of wormwood?'

Powdered root of what to an infusion of what?
Harry glanced at Ron, who looked as stumped as
he was; Hermione's hand had shot into the air.

'I don't know, sir,' said Harry.

Snape's lips curled into a sneer.

'Tut, tut – fame clearly isn't everything.'

He ignored Hermione's hand.

'Let's try again. Potter, where would you look if I told you to find me a bezoar?'

Hermione stretched her hand as high into the air as it would go without her leaving her seat, but Harry didn't have the faintest idea what a bezoar was. He tried not to look at Malfoy, Crabbe and Goyle, who were shaking with laughter.

'I don't know, sir.'

'Thought you wouldn't open a book before coming, eh, Potter?'

Harry forced himself to keep looking straight into those cold eyes. He *had* looked through his books at the Dursleys', but did Snape expect him to remember everything in *One Thousand Magical Herbs and Fungi*?

Snape was still ignoring Hermione's quivering hand.

'What is the difference, Potter, between monkshood and wolfsbane?'

At this, Hermione stood up, her hand stretching towards the dungeon ceiling.

'I don't know,' said Harry quietly. 'I think Hermione does, though, why don't you try her?'

A few people laughed; Harry caught Seamus's eye and Seamus winked. Snape, however, was not pleased.

'Sit down,' he snapped at Hermione. 'For your information, Potter, asphodel and wormwood make a sleeping potion so powerful it is known as the Draught of Living Death. A bezoar is a stone taken from the stomach of a goat and it will save you from most poisons. As for monkshood and wolfsbane, they are the same plant, which also goes by the name of aconite. Well? Why aren't you all copying that down?'

There was a sudden rummaging for quills and parchment. Over the noise, Snape said, 'And a point will be taken from Gryffindor house for your cheek, Potter.'

Things didn't improve for the Gryffindors as the Potions lesson continued. Snape put them all into pairs and set them to mixing up a simple potion to cure boils. He swept around in his long black cloak, watching them weigh dried nettles and crush snake fangs, criticising almost everyone except Malfoy, whom he seemed to like. He was just telling everyone to look at the perfect way Malfoy had stewed his horned slugs when clouds of acid green smoke and a loud hissing filled the dungeon. Neville had somehow managed to melt Seamus's cauldron into a twisted blob and their potion was seeping across the stone floor, burning holes in people's shoes. Within seconds, the whole class were standing on their stools while Neville, who had been drenched in the potion when the cauldron collapsed, moaned in pain as angry red boils sprang up all over his arms and legs.

'Idiot boy!' snarled Snape, clearing the spilled potion away with one wave of his wand. 'I suppose you added the porcupine quills before taking the cauldron off the fire?'

Neville whimpered as boils started to pop up all over his nose.

'Take him up to the hospital wing,' Snape spat at Seamus. Then he rounded on Harry and Ron, who had been working next to Neville.

'You – Potter – why didn't you tell him not to add the quills? Thought he'd make you look good if he got it wrong, did you? That's another point you've lost for Gryffindor.'

This was so unfair that Harry opened his mouth to argue, but Ron kicked him behind their cauldron.

'Don't push it,' he muttered. 'I've heard Snape can turn very nasty.'

As they climbed the steps out of the dungeon an hour later, Harry's mind was racing and his spirits were low. He'd lost two points for Gryffindor in his very first week – *why* did Snape hate him so much?

'Cheer up,' said Ron. 'Snape's always taking points off Fred and George. Can I come and meet Hagrid with you?'

At five to three they left the castle and made their way across the grounds. Hagrid lived in a small wooden house on the edge of the Forbidden Forest. A crossbow and a pair of galoshes were outside the front door.

When Harry knocked they heard a frantic scrabbling from inside and several booming barks. Then Hagrid's voice rang out, saying, '*Back*, Fang – *back*.'

Hagrid's big hairy face appeared in the crack as he pulled the door open.

'Hang on,' he said. '*Back*, Fang.'

He let them in, struggling to keep a hold on the collar of an enormous black boarhound.

There was only one room inside. Hams and pheasants were hanging from the ceiling, a copper kettle was boiling on the open fire and in a corner stood a massive bed with a patchwork quilt over it.

'Make yerselves at home,' said Hagrid, letting go of Fang, who bounded straight at Ron and started licking his ears. Like Hagrid, Fang was clearly not as fierce as he looked.

'This is Ron,' Harry told Hagrid, who was pouring boiling water into a large teapot and putting rock cakes on to a plate.

'Another Weasley, eh?' said Hagrid, glancing at Ron's freckles. 'I spent half me life chasin' yer twin brothers away from the Forest.'

The rock cakes almost broke their teeth, but Harry and Ron pretended to be enjoying them as they told Hagrid all about their first lessons. Fang rested his head on Harry's knee and drooled all over his robes.

Harry and Ron were delighted to hear Hagrid call Filch 'that old git'.

'An' as fer that cat, Mrs Norris, I'd like ter introduce her to Fang some time. D'yeh know, every time I go up ter the school, she follows me everywhere? Can't get rid of her – Filch puts her up to it.'

Harry told Hagrid about Snape's lesson. Hagrid, like Ron, told Harry not to worry about it, that Snape liked hardly any of the students.

'But he seemed to really *hate* me.'

'Rubbish!' said Hagrid. 'Why should he?'

Yet Harry couldn't help thinking that Hagrid didn't quite meet his eyes when he said that.

'How's yer brother Charlie?' Hagrid asked Ron. 'I liked him a lot – great with animals.'

Harry wondered if Hagrid had changed the subject on purpose. While Ron told Hagrid all about Charlie's work with dragons, Harry picked up a piece of paper that was lying on the table under the tea cosy. It was a cutting from the *Daily Prophet*:

GRINGOTTS BREAK-IN LATEST

Investigations continue into the break-in at Gringotts on 31 July, widely believed to be the work of dark wizards or witches unknown.

Gringotts' goblins today insisted that nothing had been taken. The vault that was searched had in fact been emptied the same day.

'But we're not telling you what was in there, so keep your noses out if you know what's good for you,' said a Gringotts spokesgoblin this afternoon.

Harry remembered Ron telling him on the train that someone had tried to rob Gringotts, but Ron hadn't mentioned the date.

'Hagrid!' said Harry. 'That Gringotts break-in happened on my birthday! It might've been happening while we were there!'

There was no doubt about it, Hagrid definitely didn't meet Harry's eyes this time. He grunted and offered him another rock cake. Harry read the story again. *The vault that was searched had in fact been emptied earlier that same day.* Hagrid had emptied vault seven hundred and thirteen, if you could call it emptying, taking out that grubby little package. Had that been what the thieves were looking for?

As Harry and Ron walked back to the castle for dinner, their pockets weighed down with rock cakes they'd been too polite to refuse, Harry thought that none of the lessons he'd had so far had given him as much to think about as tea with Hagrid. Had Hagrid collected that package just in time? Where was it now? And did Hagrid know something about Snape that he didn't want to tell Harry?

— CHAPTER NINE —

The Midnight Duel

Harry had never believed he would meet a boy he hated more than Dudley, but that was before he met Draco Malfoy. Still, first-year Gryffindors only had Potions with the Slytherins, so they didn't have to put up with Malfoy much. Or at least, they didn't until they spotted a notice pinned up in the Gryffindor common room which made them all groan. Flying lessons would be starting on Thursday – and Gryffindor and Slytherin would be learning together.

'Typical,' said Harry darkly. 'Just what I always wanted. To make a fool of myself on a broomstick in front of Malfoy.'

He had been looking forward to learning to fly more than anything else.

'You don't know you'll make a fool of yourself,' said Ron reasonably. 'Anyway, I know Malfoy's always going on about how good he is at Quidditch, but I bet that's all talk.'

Malfoy certainly did talk about flying a lot. He complained loudly about first-years never getting in the house Quidditch teams and told long, boastful stories which always seemed to end with him narrowly escaping Muggles in helicopters. He wasn't the only one, though: the way Seamus Finnigan told it, he'd spent most of his childhood zooming around the countryside on his broomstick. Even Ron would tell anyone who'd listen about the time he'd almost hit a hang-glider on Charlie's old broom. Everyone from wizarding families talked about Quidditch constantly. Ron had already had a big argument with Dean Thomas, who shared their dormitory, about football. Ron couldn't see what was exciting about a game with only one ball where no one was allowed to fly. Harry had caught Ron prodding Dean's poster of West Ham football team, trying to make the players move.

Neville had never been on a broomstick in his life, because his grandmother had never let him near one. Privately, Harry felt she'd had good reason, because Neville managed to have an extraordinary number of accidents even with both feet on the ground.

Hermione Granger was almost as nervous about flying as Neville was. This was something you couldn't learn by heart out of a book – not that she hadn't tried. At breakfast on Thursday she bored them all stupid with flying tips she'd got out of a library book called *Quidditch through the Ages*. Neville was hanging on to her every word, desperate for anything that might help him hang on to his broomstick later, but everybody else was very pleased when Hermione's lecture was interrupted by the arrival of the post.

Harry hadn't had a single letter since Hagrid's note, something that Malfoy had been quick to notice, of course. Malfoy's eagle owl was always bringing him packages of sweets from home, which he opened gloatingly at the Slytherin table.

A barn owl brought Neville a small package from his grandmother. He opened it excitedly and showed them a glass ball the size of a large marble, which seemed to be full of white smoke.

'It's a Remembrall!' he explained. 'Gran knows I forget things – this tells you if there's something you've forgotten to do. Look, you hold it tight like this and if it turns red – oh ...' His face fell, because the Remembrall had suddenly glowed scarlet, '... you've forgotten something ...'

Neville was trying to remember what he'd forgotten when Draco Malfoy, who was passing the Gryffindor table, snatched the Remembrall out of his hand.

Harry and Ron jumped to their feet. They were half hoping for a reason to fight Malfoy, but Professor McGonagall, who could spot trouble quicker than any teacher in the school, was there in a flash.

'What's going on?'

'Malfoy's got my Remembrall, Professor.'

Scowling, Malfoy quickly dropped the Remembrall back on the table.

'Just looking,' he said, and he sloped away with Crabbe and Goyle behind him.

*

At three-thirty that afternoon, Harry, Ron and the other Gryffindors hurried down the front steps into the grounds for their first flying lesson. It was a clear, breezy day and the grass rippled under their feet as they marched down the sloping lawns towards a smooth lawn on the opposite side of the grounds to the Forbidden Forest, whose trees were swaying darkly in the distance.

The Slytherins were already there, and so were twenty broomsticks lying in neat lines on the ground. Harry had heard Fred and George Weasley complain about the school brooms, saying that some of them started to vibrate if you flew too high, or always flew slightly to the left.

Their teacher, Madam Hooch, arrived. She had short, grey hair and yellow eyes like a hawk.

'Well, what are you all waiting for?' she barked. 'Everyone stand by a broomstick. Come on, hurry up.'

Harry glanced down at his broom. It was old and some of the twigs stuck out at odd angles.

'Stick out your right hand over your broom,' called Madam Hooch at the front, 'and say, "Up!"'

'UP!' everyone shouted.

Harry's broom jumped into his hand at once, but it was one of the few that did. Hermione Granger's had simply rolled over on the ground and Neville's hadn't moved at all. Perhaps brooms, like horses, could tell when you were afraid, thought Harry; there was a quaver in Neville's voice that said only too clearly that he wanted to keep his feet on the ground.

Madam Hooch then showed them how to mount their brooms without sliding off the end, and walked up and down the rows, correcting their grips. Harry and Ron were delighted when she told Malfoy he'd been doing it wrong for years.

'Now, when I blow my whistle, you kick off from the ground, hard,' said Madam Hooch. 'Keep your brooms steady, rise a few feet and then come straight back down by leaning forwards slightly. On my whistle – three – two –'

But Neville, nervous and jumpy and frightened of being left on the ground, pushed off hard before the whistle had touched Madam Hooch's lips.

'Come back, boy!' she shouted, but Neville was rising straight up like a cork shot out of a bottle – twelve feet – twenty feet. Harry saw his scared white face look down at the ground falling away, saw him gasp, slip sideways off the broom and –

WHAM – a thud and a nasty crack and Neville lay, face down, on the grass in a heap. His broomstick was still rising higher and higher and started to drift lazily towards the Forbidden Forest and out of sight.

Madam Hooch was bending over Neville, her face as white as his.

'Broken wrist,' Harry heard her mutter. 'Come on, boy – it's all right, up you get.'

She turned to the rest of the class.

'None of you is to move while I take this boy to the hospital wing! You leave those brooms where they are or you'll be out of Hogwarts before you can say "Quidditch". Come on, dear.'

Neville, his face tear-streaked, clutching his wrist, hobbled off with Madam Hooch, who had her arm around him.

No sooner were they out of earshot than Malfoy burst into laughter.

'Did you see his face, the great lump?'

The other Slytherins joined in.

'Shut up, Malfoy,' snapped Parvati Patil.

'Ooh, sticking up for Longbottom?' said Pansy Parkinson, a hard-faced Slytherin girl. 'Never thought *you'd* like fat little cry babies, Parvati.'

'Look!' said Malfoy, darting forward and snatching something out of the grass. 'It's that stupid thing Longbottom's gran sent him.'

The Remembrall glittered in the sun as he held it up.

'Give that here, Malfoy,' said Harry quietly. Everyone stopped talking to watch.

Malfoy smiled nastily.

'I think I'll leave it somewhere for Longbottom to collect – how about – up a tree?'

'Give it *here*!' Harry yelled, but Malfoy had leapt on to his broomstick and taken off. He hadn't been lying, he *could* fly well – hovering level with the topmost branches of an oak he called, 'Come and get it, Potter!'

Harry grabbed his broom.

'*No!*' shouted Hermione Granger. 'Madam Hooch told us not to move – you'll get us all into trouble.'

Harry ignored her. Blood was pounding in his ears. He mounted the broom and kicked hard against the ground and up, up he soared, air rushed through his hair and his robes whipped out behind him – and in a rush of fierce joy he realised he'd found something he could do without being taught – this was easy, this was *wonderful*. He pulled his broomstick up a little to take it even higher and heard screams and gasps of girls back on the ground and an admiring whoop from Ron.

He turned his broomstick sharply to face Malfoy in mid-air. Malfoy looked stunned.

'Give it here,' Harry called, 'or I'll knock you off that broom!'

'Oh, yeah?' said Malfoy, trying to sneer, but looking worried.

Harry knew, somehow, what to do. He leant forward and grasped the broom tightly in both hands and it shot towards Malfoy like a javelin. Malfoy only just got out of the way in time; Harry made a sharp about turn and held the broom steady. A few people below were clapping.

'No Crabbe and Goyle up here to save your neck, Malfoy,' Harry called.

The same thought seemed to have struck Malfoy.

'Catch it if you can, then!' he shouted, and he threw the glass ball high into the air and streaked back towards the ground.

Harry saw, as though in slow motion, the ball rise up in the air and then start to fall. He leant forward and pointed his broom handle down – next second he was gathering speed in a steep dive, racing the ball – wind whistled in his ears, mingled with the screams of people watching – he stretched out his hand – a foot from the ground he caught it, just in time to pull his broom straight, and he toppled gently on to the grass with the Remembrall clutched safely in his fist.

'HARRY POTTER!'

His heart sank faster than he'd just dived. Professor McGonagall was running towards them. He got to his feet, trembling.

'*Never* – in all my time at Hogwarts –'

Professor McGonagall was almost speechless with shock, and her glasses flashed furiously, '– how *dare* you – might have broken your neck –'

'It wasn't his fault, Professor –'

'Be quiet, Miss Patil –'

'But Malfoy –'

'That's *enough*, Mr Weasley. Potter, follow me, now.'

Harry caught sight of Malfoy, Crabbe and Goyle's triumphant faces as he left, walking numbly in Professor McGonagall's wake as she strode towards the castle. He was going to be expelled, he just knew it. He wanted to say something to defend himself, but there seemed to be something wrong with his voice. Professor McGonagall was sweeping along without even looking at him; he had to jog to keep up. Now he'd done it. He hadn't even lasted two weeks. He'd be packing his bags in ten minutes. What would the Dursleys say when he turned up on the doorstep?

Up the front steps, up the marble staircase inside, and still Professor McGonagall didn't say a word to him. She wrenched open doors and marched along corridors with Harry trotting miserably behind her. Maybe she was taking him to Dumbledore. He thought of Hagrid, expelled but allowed to stay on as gamekeeper. Perhaps he could be Hagrid's assistant. His stomach twisted as he imagined it, watching Ron and the others becoming wizards while he stumped around the grounds, carrying Hagrid's bag.

Professor McGonagall stopped outside a classroom. She opened the door and poked her head inside.

'Excuse me, Professor Flitwick, could I borrow

Wood for a moment?'

Wood? thought Harry, bewildered; was Wood a cane she was going to use on him?

But Wood turned out to be a person, a burly fifth-year boy who came out of Flitwick's class looking confused.

'Follow me, you two,' said Professor McGonagall, and they marched on up the corridor, Wood looking curiously at Harry.

'In here.'

Professor McGonagall pointed them into a classroom which was empty except for Peeves, who was busy writing rude words on the blackboard.

'Out, Peeves!' she barked. Peeves threw the chalk into a bin, which clanged loudly, and he swooped out cursing. Professor McGonagall slammed the door behind him and turned to face the two boys.

'Potter, this is Oliver Wood. Wood – I've found you a Seeker.'

Wood's expression changed from puzzlement to delight.

'Are you serious, Professor?'

'Absolutely,' said Professor McGonagall crisply. 'The boy's a natural. I've never seen anything like it. Was that your first time on a broomstick, Potter?'

Harry nodded silently. He didn't have a clue what was going on, but he didn't seem to be being expelled, and some of the feeling started coming back to his legs.

'He caught that thing in his hand after a fifty-foot dive,' Professor McGonagall told Wood. 'Didn't even scratch himself. Charlie Weasley couldn't have done it.'

Wood was now looking as though all his dreams had come true at once.

'Ever seen a game of Quidditch, Potter?' he asked excitedly.

'Wood's captain of the Gryffindor team,' Professor McGonagall explained.

'He's just the build for a Seeker, too,' said Wood, now walking around Harry and staring at him. 'Light – speedy – we'll have to get him a decent broom, Professor – a Nimbus Two Thousand or a Cleansweep Seven, I'd say.'

'I shall speak to Professor Dumbledore and see if we can't bend the first-year rule. Heaven knows, we need a better team than last year. *Flattened* in that last match by Slytherin, I couldn't look Severus Snape in the face for weeks ...'

Professor McGonagall peered sternly over her glasses at Harry.

'I want to hear you're training hard, Potter, or I may change my mind about punishing you.'

Then she suddenly smiled.

'Your father would have been proud,' she said. 'He was an excellent Quidditch player himself.'

*

'You're *joking*.'

It was dinner time. Harry had just finished telling Ron what had happened when he'd left the grounds with Professor McGonagall. Ron had a piece of steak-and-kidney pie halfway to his mouth, but he'd forgotten all about it.

'*Seeker*?' he said. 'But first-years *never* – you must be the youngest house player in about –'

'– a century,' said Harry, shovelling pie into his

mouth. He felt particularly hungry after the excitement of the afternoon. 'Wood told me.'

Ron was so amazed, so impressed, he just sat and gaped at Harry.

'I start training next week,' said Harry. 'Only don't tell anyone, Wood wants to keep it a secret.'

Fred and George Weasley now came into the hall, spotted Harry and hurried over.

'Well done,' said George in a low voice. 'Wood told us. We're on the team too – Beaters.'

'I tell you, we're going to win that Quidditch Cup for sure this year,' said Fred. 'We haven't won since Charlie left, but this year's team is going to be brilliant. You must be good, Harry, Wood was almost skipping when he told us.'

'Anyway, we've got to go, Lee Jordan reckons he's found a new secret passageway out of the school.'

'Bet it's that one behind the statue of Gregory the Smarmy that we found in our first week. See you.'

Fred and George had hardly disappeared when someone far less welcome turned up: Malfoy, flanked by Crabbe and Goyle.

'Having a last meal, Potter? When are you getting the train back to the Muggles?'

'You're a lot braver now you're back on the ground and you've got your little friends with you,' said Harry coolly. There was of course nothing at all little about Crabbe and Goyle, but as the High Table was full of teachers, neither of them could do more than crack their knuckles and scowl.

'I'd take you on any time on my own,' said Malfoy. 'Tonight, if you want. Wizard's duel. Wands only – no contact. What's the matter? Never heard of a wizard's duel before, I suppose?'

'Of course he has,' said Ron, wheeling round. 'I'm his second, who's yours?'

Malfoy looked at Crabbe and Goyle, sizing them up.

'Crabbe,' he said. 'Midnight all right? We'll meet you in the trophy room, that's always unlocked.'

When Malfoy had gone, Ron and Harry looked at each other.

'What *is* a wizard's duel?' said Harry. 'And what do you mean, you're my second?'

'Well, a second's there to take over if you die,' said Ron casually, getting started at last on his cold pie. Catching the look on Harry's face, he added quickly, 'but people only die in proper duels, you know, with real wizards. The most you and Malfoy'll be able to do is send sparks at each other. Neither of you knows enough magic to do any real damage. I bet he expected you to refuse, anyway.'

'And what if I wave my wand and nothing happens?'

'Throw it away and punch him on the nose,' Ron suggested.

'Excuse me.'

They both looked up. It was Hermione Granger.

'Can't a person eat in peace in this place?' said Ron.

Hermione ignored him and spoke to Harry.

'I couldn't help overhearing what you and Malfoy were saying –'

'Bet you could,' Ron muttered.

'– and you *mustn't* go wandering around the school at night, think of the points you'll lose

Gryffindor if you're caught, and you're bound to be. It's really very selfish of you.'

'And it's really none of your business,' said Harry.

'Goodbye,' said Ron.

*

All the same, it wasn't what you'd call the perfect end to the day, Harry thought, as he lay awake much later listening to Dean and Seamus falling asleep (Neville wasn't back from the hospital wing). Ron had spent all evening giving him advice such as 'If he tries to curse you, you'd better dodge it, because I can't remember how to block them'. There was a very good chance they were going to get caught by Filch or Mrs Norris, and Harry felt he was pushing his luck, breaking another school rule today. On the other hand, Malfoy's sneering face kept looming up out of the darkness – this was his big chance to beat Malfoy, face to face. He couldn't miss it.

'Half past eleven,' Ron muttered at last. 'We'd better go.'

They pulled on their dressing-gowns, picked up their wands and crept across the tower room, down the spiral staircase and into the Gryffindor common room. A few embers were still glowing in the fireplace, turning all the armchairs into hunched black shadows. They had almost reached the portrait hole when a voice spoke from the chair nearest them: 'I can't believe you're going to do this, Harry.'

A lamp flickered on. It was Hermione Granger, wearing a pink dressing-gown and a frown.

'*You!*' said Ron furiously. 'Go back to bed!'

'I almost told your brother,' Hermione snapped. 'Percy – he's a Prefect, he'd put a stop to this.'

Harry couldn't believe anyone could be so interfering.

'Come on,' he said to Ron. He pushed open the portrait of the Fat Lady and climbed through the hole.

Hermione wasn't going to give up that easily. She followed Ron through the portrait hole, hissing at them like an angry goose.

'Don't you *care* about Gryffindor, do you *only* care about yourselves, *I* don't want Slytherin to win the House Cup and you'll lose all the points I got from Professor McGonagall for knowing about Switching Spells.'

'Go away.'

'All right, but I warned you, you just remember what I said when you're on the train home tomorrow, you're so –'

But what they were, they didn't find out. Hermione had turned to the portrait of the Fat Lady to get back inside and found herself facing an empty painting. The Fat Lady had gone on a night-time visit and Hermione was locked out of Gryffindor Tower.

'Now what am I going to do?' she asked shrilly.

'That's your problem,' said Ron. 'We've got to go, we're going to be late.'

They hadn't even reached the end of the corridor when Hermione caught up with them.

'I'm coming with you,' she said.

'You are *not*.'

'D'you think I'm going to stand out here and wait

for Filch to catch me? If he finds all three of us I'll tell him the truth, that I was trying to stop you and you can back me up.'

'You've got some nerve –' said Ron loudly.

'Shut up, both of you!' said Harry sharply. 'I heard something.'

It was a sort of snuffling.

'Mrs Norris?' breathed Ron, squinting through the dark.

It wasn't Mrs Norris. It was Neville. He was curled up on the floor, fast asleep, but jerked suddenly awake as they crept nearer.

'Thank goodness you found me! I've been out here for hours. I couldn't remember the new password to get in to bed.'

'Keep your voice down, Neville. The password's "Pig snout" but it won't help you now, the Fat Lady's gone off somewhere.'

'How's your arm?' said Harry.

'Fine,' said Neville, showing them. 'Madam Pomfrey mended it in about a minute.'

'Good – well, look, Neville, we've got to be somewhere, we'll see you later –'

'Don't leave me!' said Neville, scrambling to his feet. 'I don't want to stay here alone, the Bloody Baron's been past twice already.'

Ron looked at his watch and then glared furiously at Hermione and Neville.

'If either of you get us caught, I'll never rest until I've learnt that Curse of the Bogies Quirrell told us about and used it on you.'

Hermione opened her mouth, perhaps to tell Ron exactly how to use the Curse of the Bogies, but

Harry hissed at her to be quiet and beckoned them all forward.

They flitted along corridors striped with bars of moonlight from the high windows. At every turn Harry expected to run into Filch or Mrs Norris, but they were lucky. They sped up a staircase to the third floor and tiptoed towards the trophy room.

Malfoy and Crabbe weren't there yet. The crystal trophy cases glimmered where the moonlight caught them. Cups, shields, plates and statues winked silver and gold in the darkness. They edged along the walls, keeping their eyes on the doors at either end of the room. Harry took out his wand in case Malfoy leapt in and started at once. The minutes crept by.

'He's late, maybe he's chickened out,' Ron whispered.

Then a noise in the next room made them jump. Harry had only just raised his wand when they heard someone speak – and it wasn't Malfoy.

'Sniff around, my sweet, they might be lurking in a corner.'

It was Filch speaking to Mrs Norris. Horror-struck, Harry waved madly at the other three to follow him as quickly as possible; they scurried silently towards the door away from Filch's voice. Neville's robes had barely whipped round the corner when they heard Filch enter the trophy room.

'They're in here somewhere,' they heard him mutter, 'probably hiding.'

'This way!' Harry mouthed to the others and, petrified, they began to creep down a long gallery full of suits of armour. They could hear Filch getting nearer. Neville suddenly let out a frightened squeak and broke into a run – he tripped, grabbed Ron around the waist and the pair of them toppled right into a suit of armour.

The clanging and crashing were enough to wake the whole castle.

'RUN!' Harry yelled and the four of them sprinted down the gallery, not looking back to see whether Filch was following – they swung around the doorpost and galloped down one corridor then another, Harry in the lead without any idea where they were or where they were going. They ripped through a tapestry and found themselves in a hidden passageway, hurtled along it and came out near their Charms classroom, which they knew was miles from the trophy room.

'I think we've lost him,' Harry panted, leaning against the cold wall and wiping his forehead. Neville was bent double, wheezing and spluttering.

'I – told – you,' Hermione gasped, clutching at the stitch in her chest. 'I – told – you.'

'We've got to get back to Gryffindor Tower,' said Ron, 'quickly as possible.'

'Malfoy tricked you,' Hermione said to Harry. 'You realise that, don't you? He was never going to meet you – Filch knew someone was going to be in the trophy room, Malfoy must have tipped him off.'

Harry thought she was probably right, but he wasn't going to tell her that.

'Let's go.'

It wasn't going to be that simple. They hadn't gone more than a dozen paces when a doorknob rattled and something came shooting out of a classroom in front of them.

It was Peeves. He caught sight of them and gave a squeal of delight.

'Shut up, Peeves – please – you'll get us thrown out.'

Peeves cackled.

'Wandering around at midnight, ickle firsties? Tut, tut, tut. Naughty, naughty, you'll get caught.'

'Not if you don't give us away, Peeves, please.'

'Should tell Filch, I should,' said Peeves in a saintly voice, but his eyes glittered wickedly. 'It's for your own good, you know.'

'Get out of the way,' snapped Ron, taking a swipe at Peeves – this was a big mistake.

'STUDENTS OUT OF BED!' Peeves bellowed. 'STUDENTS OUT OF BED DOWN THE CHARMS CORRIDOR!'

Ducking under Peeves they ran for their lives, right to the end of the corridor, where they slammed into a door – and it was locked.

'This is it!' Ron moaned, as they pushed helplessly at the door. 'We're done for! This is the end!'

They could hear footsteps, Filch running as fast as he could towards Peeves's shouts.

'Oh, move over,' Hermione snarled. She grabbed Harry's wand, tapped the lock and whispered, 'Alohomora!'

The lock clicked and the door swung open – they piled through it, shut it quickly and pressed their ears against it, listening.

'Which way did they go, Peeves?' Filch was saying. 'Quick, tell me.'

'Say "please".'

'Don't mess me about, Peeves, now *where did they go?*'

'Shan't say nothing if you don't say please,' said Peeves in his annoying sing-song voice.

'All right – *please.*'

'NOTHING! Ha haaa! Told you I wouldn't say nothing if you didn't say please! Ha ha! Haaaaaa!' And they heard the sound of Peeves whooshing away and Filch cursing in rage.

'He thinks this door is locked,' Harry whispered. 'I think we'll be OK – get *off*, Neville!' For Neville had been tugging on the sleeve of Harry's dressing-gown for the last minute. '*What?*'

Harry turned around – and saw, quite clearly, what. For a moment, he was sure he'd walked into a nightmare – this was too much, on top of everything that had happened so far.

They weren't in a room, as he had supposed. They were in a corridor. The forbidden corridor on the third floor. And now they knew why it was forbidden.

They were looking straight into the eyes of a monstrous dog, a dog which filled the whole space between ceiling and floor. It had three heads. Three pairs of rolling, mad eyes; three noses, twitching and quivering in their direction; three drooling mouths, saliva hanging in slippery ropes from yellowish fangs.

It was standing quite still, all six eyes staring at them, and Harry knew that the only reason they weren't already dead was that their sudden appearance had taken it by surprise, but it was quickly getting over that, there was no mistaking what those thunderous growls meant.

Harry groped for the doorknob – between Filch and death, he'd take Filch.

They fell backwards – Harry slammed the door shut, and they ran, they almost flew, back down the corridor. Filch must have hurried off to look for them somewhere else because they didn't see him anywhere, but they hardly cared – all they wanted to do was put as much space as possible between them and that monster. They didn't stop running until they reached the portrait of the Fat Lady on the seventh floor.

'Where on earth have you all been?' she asked, looking at their dressing-gowns hanging off their shoulders and their flushed, sweaty faces.

'Never mind that – pig snout, pig snout,' panted Harry, and the portrait swung forward. They scrambled into the common room and collapsed, trembling into armchairs.

It was a while before any of them said anything. Neville, indeed, looked as if he'd never speak again.

'What do they think they're doing, keeping a thing like that locked up in a school?' said Ron finally. 'If any dog needs exercise, that one does.'

Hermione had got both her breath and her bad temper back again.

'You don't use your eyes, any of you, do you?' she snapped. 'Didn't you see what it was standing on?'

'The floor?' Harry suggested. 'I wasn't looking at its feet, I was too busy with its heads.'

'No, *not* the floor. It was standing on a trapdoor. It's obviously guarding something.'

She stood up, glaring at them.

'I hope you're pleased with yourselves. We could all have been killed – or worse, expelled. Now, if you don't mind, I'm going to bed.'

Ron stared after her, his mouth open.

'No, we don't mind,' he said. 'You'd think we dragged her along, wouldn't you?'

But Hermione had given Harry something else to think about as he climbed back into bed. The dog was guarding something ... What had Hagrid said? Gringotts was the safest place in the world for something you wanted to hide – except perhaps Hogwarts.

It looked as though Harry had found out where the grubby little package from vault seven hundred and thirteen was.

— CHAPTER TEN —

Hallowe'en

Malfoy couldn't believe his eyes when he saw that Harry and Ron were still at Hogwarts next day, looking tired but perfectly cheerful. Indeed, by next morning Harry and Ron thought that meeting the three-headed dog had been an excellent adventure and they were quite keen to have another one. In the meantime, Harry filled Ron in about the package that seemed to have been moved from Gringotts to Hogwarts, and they spent a lot of time wondering what could possibly need such heavy protection.

'It's either really valuable or really dangerous,' said Ron.

'Or both,' said Harry.

But as all they knew for sure about the mysterious object was that it was about two inches long, they didn't have much chance of guessing what it was without further clues.

Neither Neville or Hermione showed the slightest interest in what lay underneath the dog and the trapdoor. All Neville cared about was never going near the dog again.

Hermione was now refusing to speak to Harry

and Ron, but she was such a bossy know-it-all that they saw this as an added bonus. All they really wanted now was a way of getting back at Malfoy, and to their great delight, just such a thing arrived with the post about a week later.

As the owls flooded into the Great Hall as usual, everyone's attention was caught at once by a long thin package carried by six large screech owls. Harry was just as interested as everyone else to see what was in this large parcel and was amazed when the owls soared down and dropped it right in front of him, knocking his bacon to the floor. They had hardly fluttered out of the way when another owl dropped a letter on top of the parcel.

Harry ripped open the letter first, which was lucky, because it said:

DO NOT OPEN THE PARCEL AT THE TABLE.
It contains your new Nimbus Two Thousand,
but I don't want everybody knowing you've
got a broomstick or they'll all want one.
Oliver Wood will meet you tonight on the
Quidditch pitch at seven o'clock for your
first training session.
         Professor M. McGonagall

Harry had difficulty hiding his glee as he handed the note to Ron to read.

'A Nimbus Two Thousand!' Ron moaned enviously. 'I've never even *touched* one.'

They left the Hall quickly, wanting to unwrap the broomstick in private before their first lesson, but halfway across the Entrance Hall they found the way upstairs barred by Crabbe and Goyle. Malfoy seized the package from Harry and felt it.

'That's a broomstick,' he said, throwing it back to Harry with a mixture of jealousy and spite on his face. 'You'll be for it this time, Potter, first-years aren't allowed them.'

Ron couldn't resist it.

'It's not any old broomstick,' he said, 'it's a Nimbus Two Thousand. What did you say you've got at home, Malfoy, a Comet Two Sixty?' Ron grinned at Harry. 'Comets look flashy, but they're not in the same league as the Nimbus.'

'What would you know about it, Weasley, you couldn't afford half the handle,' Malfoy snapped back. 'I suppose you and your brothers have to save up, twig by twig.'

Before Ron could answer, Professor Flitwick appeared at Malfoy's elbow.

'Not arguing, I hope, boys?' he squeaked.

'Potter's been sent a broomstick, Professor,' said Malfoy quickly.

'Yes, yes, that's right,' said Professor Flitwick, beaming at Harry. 'Professor McGonagall told me all about the special circumstances, Potter. And what model is it?'

'A Nimbus Two Thousand, sir,' said Harry, fighting not to laugh at the look of horror on Malfoy's face. 'And it's really thanks to Malfoy here that I've got it,' he added.

Harry and Ron headed upstairs, smothering their laughter at Malfoy's obvious rage and confusion.

'Well, it's true,' Harry chortled as they reached the top of the marble staircase. 'If he hadn't stolen

Neville's Remembrall I wouldn't be in the team ...'

'So I suppose you think that's a reward for breaking rules?' came an angry voice from just behind them. Hermione was stomping up the stairs looking disapprovingly at the package in Harry's hand.

'I thought you weren't speaking to us?' said Harry.

'Yes, don't stop now,' said Ron, 'it's doing us so much good.'

Hermione marched away with her nose in the air.

Harry had a lot of trouble keeping his mind on his lessons that day. It kept wandering up to the dormitory, where his new broomstick was lying under his bed, or straying off to the Quidditch pitch where he'd be learning to play that night. He bolted his dinner that evening without noticing what he was eating and then rushed upstairs with Ron to unwrap the Nimbus Two Thousand at last.

'Wow,' Ron sighed, as the broomstick rolled on to Harry's bedspread.

Even Harry, who knew nothing about the different brooms, thought it looked wonderful. Sleek and shiny, with a mahogany handle, it had a long tail of neat, straight twigs and *Nimbus Two Thousand* written in gold near the top.

As seven o'clock drew nearer, Harry left the castle and set off towards the Quidditch pitch in the dusk. He'd never been inside the stadium before. Hundreds of seats were raised in stands around the pitch so that the spectators were high enough to see what was going on. At either end of the pitch were three golden poles with hoops on the end.

They reminded Harry of the little plastic sticks Muggle children blew bubbles through, except that they were fifty feet high.

Too eager to fly again to wait for Wood, Harry mounted his broomstick and kicked off from the ground. What a feeling – he swooped in and out of the goalposts and then sped up and down the pitch. The Nimbus Two Thousand turned wherever he wanted at his lightest touch.

'Hey, Potter, come down!'

Oliver Wood had arrived. He was carrying a large wooden crate under his arm. Harry landed next to him.

'Very nice,' said Wood, his eyes glinting. 'I see what McGonagall meant ... you really are a natural. I'm just going to teach you the rules this evening, then you'll be joining team practice three times a week.'

He opened the crate. Inside were four different-sized balls.

'Right,' said Wood. 'Now, Quidditch is easy enough to understand, even if it's not too easy to play. There are seven players on each side. Three of them are called Chasers.'

'Three Chasers,' Harry repeated, as Wood took out a bright red ball about the size of a football.

'This ball's called the Quaffle,' said Wood. 'The Chasers throw the Quaffle to each other and try and get it through one of the hoops to score a goal. Ten points every time the Quaffle goes through one of the hoops. Follow me?'

'The Chasers throw the Quaffle and put it through the hoops to score,' Harry recited. 'So –

that's sort of like basketball on broomsticks with six hoops, isn't it?'

'What's basketball?' said Wood curiously.

'Never mind,' said Harry quickly.

'Now, there's another player on each side who's called the Keeper – I'm Keeper for Gryffindor. I have to fly around our hoops and stop the other team from scoring.'

'Three Chasers, one Keeper,' said Harry, who was determined to remember it all. 'And they play with the Quaffle. OK, got that. So what are they for?' He pointed at the three balls left inside the box.

'I'll show you now,' said Wood. 'Take this.'

He handed Harry a small club, a bit like a rounders bat.

'I'm going to show you what the Bludgers do,' Wood said. 'These two are the Bludgers.'

He showed Harry two identical balls, jet black and slightly smaller than the red Quaffle. Harry noticed that they seemed to be straining to escape the straps holding them inside the box.

'Stand back,' Wood warned Harry. He bent down and freed one of the Bludgers.

At once, the black ball rose high in the air and then pelted straight at Harry's face. Harry swung at it with the bat to stop it breaking his nose and sent it zig-zagging away into the air – it zoomed around their heads and then shot at Wood, who dived on top of it and managed to pin it to the ground.

'See?' Wood panted, forcing the struggling Bludger back into the crate and strapping it down safely. 'The Bludgers rocket around trying to knock players off their brooms. That's why you have two

Beaters on each team. The Weasley twins are ours –
it's their job to protect their side from the Bludgers
and try and knock them towards the other team. So
– think you've got all that?'

'Three Chasers try and score with the Quaffle;
the Keeper guards the goalposts; the Beaters keep
the Bludgers away from their team,' Harry reeled
off.

'Very good,' said Wood.

'Er – have the Bludgers ever killed anyone?'
Harry asked, hoping he sounded offhand.

'Never at Hogwarts. We've had a couple of broken jaws but nothing worse than that. Now, the last
member of the team is the Seeker. That's you. And
you don't have to worry about the Quaffle or the
Bludgers –'

'– unless they crack my head open.'

'Don't worry, the Weasleys are more than a match
for the Bludgers – I mean, they're like a pair of
human Bludgers themselves.'

Wood reached into the crate and took out the
fourth and last ball. Compared with the Quaffle
and the Bludgers, it was tiny, about the size of a
large walnut. It was bright gold and had little fluttering silver wings.

'*This*,' said Wood, 'is the Golden Snitch, and it's
the most important ball of the lot. It's very hard to
catch because it's so fast and difficult to see. It's the
Seeker's job to catch it. You've got to weave in and
out of the Chasers, Beaters, Bludgers and Quaffle to
get it before the other team's Seeker, because
whichever Seeker catches the Snitch wins his team
an extra hundred and fifty points, so they nearly

always win. That's why Seekers get fouled so much. A game of Quidditch only ends when the Snitch is caught, so it can go on for ages – I think the record is three months, they had to keep bringing on substitutes so the players could get some sleep.

'Well, that's it – any questions?'

Harry shook his head. He understood what he had to do all right, it was doing it that was going to be the problem.

'We won't practise with the Snitch yet,' said Wood, carefully shutting it back inside the crate. 'It's too dark, we might lose it. Let's try you out with a few of these.'

He pulled a bag of ordinary golf balls out of his pocket, and a few minutes later, he and Harry were up in the air, Wood throwing the golf balls as hard as he could in every direction for Harry to catch.

Harry didn't miss a single one, and Wood was delighted. After half an hour, night had really fallen and they couldn't carry on.

'That Quidditch Cup'll have our name on it this year,' said Wood happily as they trudged back up to the castle. 'I wouldn't be surprised if you turn out better than Charlie Weasley, and he could have played for England if he hadn't gone off chasing dragons.'

*

Perhaps it was because he was now so busy, what with Quidditch practice three evenings a week on top of all his homework, but Harry could hardly believe it when he realised that he'd already been at Hogwarts two months. The castle felt more like home than Privet Drive had ever done. His lessons, too, were becoming more and more interesting now that they had mastered the basics.

On Hallowe'en morning they woke to the delicious smell of baking pumpkin wafting through the corridors. Even better, Professor Flitwick announced in Charms that he thought they were ready to start making objects fly, something they had all been dying to try since they'd seen him make Neville's toad zoom around the classroom. Professor Flitwick put the class into pairs to practise. Harry's partner was Seamus Finnigan (which was a relief, because Neville had been trying to catch his eye). Ron, however, was to be working with Hermione Granger. It was hard to tell whether Ron or Hermione was angrier about this. She hadn't spoken to either of them since the day Harry's broomstick had arrived.

'Now, don't forget that nice wrist movement we've been practising!' squeaked Professor Flitwick, perched on top of his pile of books as usual. 'Swish and flick, remember, swish and flick. And saying the magic words properly is very important, too – never forget Wizard Baruffio, who said 's' instead of 'f' and found himself on the floor with a buffalo on his chest.'

It was very difficult. Harry and Seamus swished and flicked, but the feather they were supposed to be sending skywards just lay on the desktop. Seamus got so impatient that he prodded it with his wand and set fire to it – Harry had to put it out with his hat.

Ron, at the next table, wasn't having much more luck.

'*Wingardium Leviosa!*' he shouted, waving his long arms like a windmill.

'You're saying it wrong,' Harry heard Hermione snap. 'It's Wing-*gar*-dium Levi-*o*-sa, make the "gar" nice and long.'

'You do it, then, if you're so clever,' Ron snarled.

Hermione rolled up the sleeves of her gown, flicked her wand and said, '*Wingardium Leviosa!*'

Their feather rose off the desk and hovered about four feet above their heads.

'Oh, well done!' cried Professor Flitwick, clapping. 'Everyone see here, Miss Granger's done it!'

Ron was in a very bad temper by the end of the class.

'It's no wonder no one can stand her,' he said to Harry as they pushed their way into the crowded corridor. 'She's a nightmare, honestly.'

Someone knocked into Harry as they hurried past him. It was Hermione. Harry caught a glimpse of her face – and was startled to see that she was in tears.

'I think she heard you.'

'So?' said Ron, but he looked a bit uncomfortable. 'She must've noticed she's got no friends.'

Hermione didn't turn up for the next class and wasn't seen all afternoon. On their way down to the Great Hall for the Hallowe'en feast, Harry and Ron overheard Parvati Patil telling her friend Lavender that Hermione was crying in the girls' toilets and wanted to be left alone. Ron looked still more awkward at this, but a moment later they had entered the Great Hall, where the Hallowe'en decorations put Hermione out of their minds.

A thousand live bats fluttered from the walls and ceiling while a thousand more swooped over the tables in low black clouds, making the candles in the pumpkins stutter. The feast appeared suddenly on the golden plates, as it had at the start-of-term banquet.

Harry was just helping himself to a jacket potato when Professor Quirrell came sprinting into the Hall, his turban askew and terror on his face. Everyone stared as he reached Professor Dumbledore's chair, slumped against the table and gasped, 'Troll – in the dungeons – thought you ought to know.'

He then sank to the floor in a dead faint.

There was uproar. It took several purple fire-crackers exploding from the end of Professor Dumbledore's wand to bring silence.

'Prefects,' he rumbled, 'lead your houses back to the dormitories immediately!'

Percy was in his element.

'Follow me! Stick together, first-years! No need to fear the troll if you follow my orders! Stay close behind me, now. Make way, first-years coming through! Excuse me, I'm a Prefect!'

'How could a troll get in?' Harry asked as they climbed the stairs.

'Don't ask me, they're supposed to be really stupid,' said Ron. 'Maybe Peeves let it in for a Hallowe'en joke.'

They passed different groups of people hurrying in different directions. As they jostled their way through a crowd of confused Hufflepuffs, Harry suddenly grabbed Ron's arm.

'I've just thought – Hermione.'

'What about her?'

'She doesn't know about the troll.'

Ron bit his lip.

'Oh, all right,' he snapped. 'But Percy'd better not see us.'

Ducking down, they joined the Hufflepuffs going the other way, slipped down a deserted side corridor and hurried off towards the girls' toilets. They had just turned the corner when they heard quick footsteps behind them.

'Percy!' hissed Ron, pulling Harry behind a large stone griffin.

Peering around it, however, they saw not Percy but Snape. He crossed the corridor and disappeared from view.

'What's he doing?' Harry whispered. 'Why isn't he down in the dungeons with the rest of the teachers?'

'Search me.'

Quietly as possible, they crept along the next corridor after Snape's fading footsteps.

'He's heading for the third floor,' Harry said, but Ron held up his hand.

'Can you smell something?'

Harry sniffed and a foul stench reached his nostrils, a mixture of old socks and the kind of public toilet no one seems to clean.

And then they heard it – a low grunting and the shuffling footfalls of gigantic feet. Ron pointed: at the end of a passage to the left, something huge was moving towards them. They shrank into the shadows and watched as it emerged into a patch of moonlight.

It was a horrible sight. Twelve feet tall, its skin was a dull, granite grey, its great lumpy body like a boulder with its small bald head perched on top like a coconut. It had short legs thick as tree trunks with flat, horny feet. The smell coming from it was incredible. It was holding a huge wooden club, which dragged along the floor because its arms were so long.

The troll stopped next to a doorway and peered inside. It waggled its long ears, making up its tiny mind, then slouched slowly into the room.

'The key's in the lock,' Harry muttered. 'We could lock it in.'

'Good idea,' said Ron nervously.

They edged towards the open door, mouths dry, praying the troll wasn't about to come out of it. With one great leap, Harry managed to grab the key, slam the door and lock it.

'*Yes!*'

Flushed with their victory they started to run back up the passage, but as they reached the corner they heard something that made their hearts stop – a high, petrified scream – and it was coming from the chamber they'd just locked up.

'Oh, no,' said Ron, pale as the Bloody Baron.

'It's the girls' toilets!' Harry gasped.

'*Hermione!*' they said together.

It was the last thing they wanted to do, but what choice did they have? Wheeling around they sprinted back to the door and turned the key, fumbling in their panic – Harry pulled the door open – they ran inside.

Hermione Granger was shrinking against the

wall opposite, looking as if she was about to faint.
The troll was advancing on her, knocking the sinks
off the walls as it went.

'Confuse it!' Harry said desperately to Ron, and
seizing a tap he threw it as hard as he could against
the wall.

The troll stopped a few feet from Hermione. It
lumbered around, blinking stupidly, to see what
had made the noise. Its mean little eyes saw Harry.
It hesitated, then made for him instead, lifting its
club as it went.

'Oy, pea-brain!' yelled Ron from the other side of
the chamber, and he threw a metal pipe at it. The
troll didn't even seem to notice the pipe hitting its
shoulder, but it heard the yell and paused again,
turning its ugly snout towards Ron instead, giving
Harry time to run around it.

'Come on, run, *run*!' Harry yelled at Hermione,
trying to pull her towards the door, but she couldn't
move, she was still flat against the wall, her mouth
open with terror.

The shouting and the echoes seemed to be driving
the troll berserk. It roared again and started towards
Ron, who was nearest and had no way to escape.

Harry then did something that was both very
brave and very stupid: he took a great running
jump and managed to fasten his arms around the
troll's neck from behind. The troll couldn't feel
Harry hanging there, but even a troll will notice if
you stick a long bit of wood up its nose, and
Harry's wand had still been in his hand when he'd
jumped – it had gone straight up one of the troll's
nostrils.

Howling with pain, the troll twisted and flailed its club, with Harry clinging on for dear life; any second, the troll was going to rip him off or catch him a terrible blow with the club.

Hermione had sunk to the floor in fright; Ron pulled out his own wand – not knowing what he was going to do he heard himself cry the first spell that came into his head: 'Wingardium Leviosa!'

The club flew suddenly out of the troll's hand, rose high, high up into the air, turned slowly over – and dropped, with a sickening crack, on to its owner's head. The troll swayed on the spot and then fell flat on its face, with a thud that made the whole room tremble.

Harry got to his feet. He was shaking and out of breath. Ron was standing there with his wand still raised, staring at what he had done.

It was Hermione who spoke first.

'Is it – dead?'

'I don't think so,' said Harry. 'I think it's just been knocked out.'

He bent down and pulled his wand out of the troll's nose. It was covered in what looked like lumpy grey glue.

'Urgh – troll bogies.'

He wiped it on the troll's trousers.

A sudden slamming and loud footsteps made the three of them look up. They hadn't realised what a racket they had been making, but of course, some-one downstairs must have heard the crashes and the troll's roars. A moment later, Professor McGonagall had come bursting into the room, closely followed by Snape, with Quirrell bringing up the rear. Quirrell took one look at the troll, let out a faint whimper and sat quickly down on a toilet, clutching his heart.

Snape bent over the troll. Professor McGonagall was looking at Ron and Harry. Harry had never seen her look so angry. Her lips were white. Hopes of winning fifty points for Gryffindor faded quickly from Harry's mind.

'What on earth were you thinking of?' said Professor McGonagall, with cold fury in her voice. Harry looked at Ron, who was still standing with his wand in the air. 'You're lucky you weren't killed. Why aren't you in your dormitory?'

Snape gave Harry a swift, piercing look. Harry looked at the floor. He wished Ron would put his wand down.

Then a small voice came out of the shadows.

'Please, Professor McGonagall – they were looking for me.'

'Miss Granger!'

Hermione had managed to get to her feet at last.

'I went looking for the troll because I – I thought I could deal with it on my own – you know, because I've read all about them.'

Ron dropped his wand. Hermione Granger, telling a downright lie to a teacher?

'If they hadn't found me, I'd be dead now. Harry stuck his wand up its nose and Ron knocked it out with its own club. They didn't have time to come and fetch anyone. It was about to finish me off when they arrived.'

Harry and Ron tried to look as though this story wasn't new to them.

'Well – in that case ...' said Professor McGonagall, staring at the three of them. 'Miss Granger,
you foolish girl, how could you think of tackling a
mountain troll on your own?'

Hermione hung her head. Harry was speechless.
Hermione was the last person to do anything
against the rules, and here she was, pretending she
had, to get them out of trouble. It was as if Snape
had started handing out sweets.

'Miss Granger, five points will be taken from
Gryffindor for this,' said Professor McGonagall. 'I'm
very disappointed in you. If you're not hurt at all,
you'd better get off to Gryffindor Tower. Students
are finishing the feast in their houses.'

Hermione left.

Professor McGonagall turned to Harry and Ron.

'Well, I still say you were lucky, but not many
first-years could have taken on a full-grown mountain troll. You each win Gryffindor five points.
Professor Dumbledore will be informed of this. You
may go.'

They hurried out of the chamber and didn't
speak at all until they had climbed two floors up. It
was a relief to be away from the smell of the troll,
quite apart from anything else.

'We should have got more than ten points,' Ron
grumbled.

'Five, you mean, once she's taken off Hermione's.'

'Good of her to get us out of trouble like that,'
Ron admitted. 'Mind you, we *did* save her.'

'She might not have needed saving if we hadn't
locked the thing in with her,' Harry reminded him.

They had reached the portrait of the Fat Lady.

'Pig snout,' they said and entered.

The common room was packed and noisy. Everyone was eating the food that had been sent up. Hermione, however, stood alone by the door, waiting for them. There was a very embarrassed pause. Then, none of them looking at each other, they all said 'Thanks', and hurried off to get plates.

But from that moment on, Hermione Granger became their friend. There are some things you can't share without ending up liking each other, and knocking out a twelve-foot mountain troll is one of them.

— CHAPTER ELEVEN —

Quidditch

As they entered November, the weather turned very cold. The mountains around the school became icy grey and the lake like chilled steel. Every morning the ground was covered in frost. Hagrid could be seen from the upstairs windows, defrosting broomsticks on the Quidditch pitch, bundled up in a long moleskin overcoat, rabbit-fur gloves and enormous beaverskin boots.

The Quidditch season had begun. On Saturday, Harry would be playing in his first match after weeks of training: Gryffindor versus Slytherin. If Gryffindor won, they would move up into second place in the House Championship.

Hardly anyone had seen Harry play because Wood had decided that, as their secret weapon, Harry should be kept, well, secret. But the news that he was playing Seeker had leaked out somehow, and Harry didn't know which was worse – people telling him he'd be brilliant or people telling him they'd be running around underneath him, holding a mattress.

It was really lucky that Harry now had Hermione as a friend. He didn't know how he'd have got through all his homework without her, what with all the last-minute Quidditch practice Wood was making them do. She had also lent him *Quidditch through the Ages*, which turned out to be a very interesting read.

Harry learnt that there were seven hundred ways of committing a Quidditch foul and that all of them had happened during a World Cup match in 1473; that Seekers were usually the smallest and fastest players and that most serious Quidditch accidents seemed to happen to them; that although people rarely died playing Quidditch, referees had been known to vanish and turn up months later in the Sahara Desert.

Hermione had become a bit more relaxed about breaking rules since Harry and Ron had saved her from the mountain troll and she was much nicer for it. The day before Harry's first Quidditch match the three of them were out in the freezing court-yard during break, and she had conjured them up a bright blue fire which could be carried around in a jam jar. They were standing with their backs to it, getting warm, when Snape crossed the yard. Harry noticed at once that Snape was limping. Harry, Ron and Hermione moved closer together to block the fire from view; they were sure it wouldn't be allowed. Unfortunately, something about their guilty faces caught Snape's eye. He limped over. He hadn't seen the fire, but he seemed to be looking for a reason to tell them off anyway.

'What's that you've got there, Potter?'

It was *Quidditch through the Ages*. Harry showed him.

'Library books are not to be taken outside the

school,' said Snape. 'Give it to me. Five points from Gryffindor.'

'He's just made that rule up,' Harry muttered angrily as Snape limped away. 'Wonder what's wrong with his leg?'

'Dunno, but I hope it's really hurting him,' said Ron bitterly.

*

The Gryffindor common room was very noisy that evening. Harry, Ron and Hermione sat together next to a window. Hermione was checking Harry and Ron's Charms homework for them. She would never let them copy ('How will you learn?'), but by asking her to read it through, they got the right answers anyway.

Harry felt restless. He wanted *Quidditch through the Ages* back, to take his mind off his nerves about tomorrow. Why should he be afraid of Snape? Getting up, he told Ron and Hermione he was going to ask Snape if he could have it.

'Rather you than me,' they said together, but Harry had an idea that Snape wouldn't refuse if there were other teachers listening.

He made his way down to the staff room and knocked. There was no answer. He knocked again. Nothing.

Perhaps Snape had left the book in there? It was worth a try. He pushed the door ajar and peered inside – and a horrible scene met his eyes.

Snape and Filch were inside, alone. Snape was holding his robes above his knees. One of his legs was bloody and mangled. Filch was handing Snape bandages.

'Blasted thing,' Snape was saying. 'How are you supposed to keep your eyes on all three heads at once?'

Harry tried to shut the door quietly, but –

'POTTER!'

Snape's face was twisted with fury as he dropped his robes quickly to hide his leg. Harry gulped.

'I just wondered if I could have my book back.'

'GET OUT! *OUT!*'

Harry left, before Snape could take any more points from Gryffindor. He sprinted back upstairs.

'Did you get it?' Ron asked as Harry joined them. 'What's the matter?'

In a low whisper, Harry told them what he'd seen.

'You know what this means?' he finished breathlessly. 'He tried to get past that three-headed dog at Hallowe'en! That's where he was going when we saw him – he's after whatever it's guarding! And I'd bet my broomstick *he* let that troll in, to create a diversion!'

Hermione's eyes were wide.

'No – he wouldn't,' she said. 'I know he's not very nice, but he wouldn't try and steal something Dumbledore was keeping safe.'

'Honestly, Hermione, you think all teachers are saints or something,' snapped Ron. 'I'm with Harry. I wouldn't put anything past Snape. But what's he after? What's that dog guarding?'

Harry went to bed with his head buzzing with the same question. Neville was snoring loudly, but Harry couldn't sleep. He tried to empty his mind – he needed to sleep, he had to, he had his first

Quidditch match in a few hours – but the expression on Snape's face when Harry had seen his leg wasn't easy to forget.

*

The next morning dawned very bright and cold. The Great Hall was full of the delicious smell of fried sausages and the cheerful chatter of everyone looking forward to a good Quidditch match.

'You've got to eat some breakfast.'

'I don't want anything.'

'Just a bit of toast,' wheedled Hermione.

'I'm not hungry.'

Harry felt terrible. In an hour's time he'd be walking on to the pitch.

'Harry, you need your strength,' said Seamus Finnigan. 'Seekers are always the ones who get nobbled by the other team.'

'Thanks, Seamus,' said Harry, watching Seamus pile ketchup on his sausages.

*

By eleven o'clock the whole school seemed to be out in the stands around the Quidditch pitch. Many students had binoculars. The seats might be raised high in the air but it was still difficult to see what was going on sometimes.

Ron and Hermione joined Neville, Seamus and Dean the West Ham fan up in the top row. As a surprise for Harry, they had painted a large banner on one of the sheets Scabbers had ruined. It said *Potter for President* and Dean, who was good at drawing, had done a large Gryffindor lion underneath. Then Hermione had performed a tricky little charm so that the paint flashed different colours.

Meanwhile, in the changing rooms, Harry and the rest of the team were changing into their scarlet Quidditch robes (Slytherin would be playing in green).

Wood cleared his throat for silence.

'OK, men,' he said.

'And women,' said Chaser Angelina Johnson.

'And women,' Wood agreed. 'This is it.'

'The big one,' said Fred Weasley.

'The one we've all been waiting for,' said George.

'We know Oliver's speech by heart,' Fred told Harry. 'We were in the team last year.'

'Shut up, you two,' said Wood. 'This is the best team Gryffindor's had in years. We're going to win. I know it.'

He glared at them all as if to say, 'Or else.'

'Right. It's time. Good luck, all of you.'

Harry followed Fred and George out of the changing room and, hoping his knees weren't going to give way, walked on to the pitch to loud cheers.

Madam Hooch was refereeing. She stood in the middle of the pitch, waiting for the two teams, her broom in her hand.

'Now, I want a nice fair game, all of you,' she said, once they were all gathered around her. Harry noticed that she seemed to be speaking particularly to the Slytherin captain, Marcus Flint, a fifth-year. Harry thought Flint looked as if he had some troll blood in him. Out of the corner of his eye he saw the fluttering banner high above, flashing *Potter for President* over the crowd. His heart skipped. He felt braver.

'Mount your brooms, please.'

Harry clambered on to his Nimbus Two Thousand.

Madam Hooch gave a loud blast on her silver whistle.

Fifteen brooms rose up, high, high into the air. They were off.

'And the Quaffle is taken immediately by Angelina Johnson of Gryffindor – what an excellent Chaser that girl is, and rather attractive, too –'

'JORDAN!'

'Sorry, Professor.'

The Weasley twins' friend, Lee Jordan, was doing the commentary for the match, closely watched by Professor McGonagall.

'And she's really belting along up there, a neat pass to Alicia Spinnet, a good find of Oliver Wood's, last year only a reserve – back to Johnson and – no, Slytherin have taken the Quaffle, Slytherin captain Marcus Flint gains the Quaffle and off he goes – Flint flying like an eagle up there – he's going to sc– no, stopped by an excellent move by Gryffindor Keeper Wood and Gryffindor take the Quaffle – that's Chaser Katie Bell of Gryffindor there, nice dive around Flint, off up the field and – OUCH – that must have hurt, hit in the back of the head by a Bludger – Quaffle taken by Slytherin – that's Adrian Pucey speeding off towards the goalposts, but he's blocked by a second Bludger – sent his way by Fred or George Weasley, can't tell which – nice play by the Gryffindor Beater, anyway, and Johnson back in possession of the Quaffle, a clear field ahead and off she goes – she's really flying – dodges a speeding Bludger – the goalposts are ahead – come on, now, Angelina –

Keeper Bletchley dives – misses – GRYFFINDOR SCORE!'

Gryffindor cheers filled the cold air, with howls and moans from the Slytherins.

'Budge up there, move along.'

'Hagrid!'

Ron and Hermione squeezed together to give Hagrid enough space to join them.

'Bin watchin' from me hut,' said Hagrid, patting a large pair of binoculars round his neck. 'But it isn't the same as bein' in the crowd. No sign of the Snitch yet, eh?'

'Nope,' said Ron. 'Harry hasn't had much to do yet.'

'Kept outta trouble, though, that's somethin',' said Hagrid, raising his binoculars and peering sky-wards at the speck that was Harry.

Way up above them, Harry was gliding over the game, squinting about for some sign of the Snitch. This was part of his and Wood's game plan.

'Keep out of the way until you catch sight of the Snitch,' Wood had said. 'We don't want you attacked before you have to be.'

When Angelina had scored, Harry had done a couple of loop-the-loops to let out his feelings. Now he was back to staring around for the Snitch. Once he caught sight of a flash of gold but it was just a reflection from one of the Weasleys' wristwatches, and once a Bludger decided to come pelting his way, more like a cannon ball than anything, but Harry dodged it and Fred Weasley came chasing after it.

'All right there, Harry?' he had time to yell, as he beat the Bludger furiously towards Marcus Flint.

'Slytherin in possession,' Lee Jordan was saying. 'Chaser Pucey ducks two Bludgers, two Weasleys and Chaser Bell and speeds towards the – wait a moment – was that the Snitch?'

A murmur ran through the crowd as Adrian Pucey dropped the Quaffle, too busy looking over his shoulder at the flash of gold that had passed his left ear.

Harry saw it. In a great rush of excitement he dived downwards after the streak of gold. Slytherin Seeker Terence Higgs had seen it, too. Neck and neck they hurtled towards the Snitch – all the Chasers seemed to have forgotten what they were supposed to be doing as they hung in mid-air to watch.

Harry was faster than Higgs – he could see the little round ball, wings fluttering, darting up ahead – he put on an extra spurt of speed –

WHAM! A roar of rage echoed from the Gryffindors below – Marcus Flint had blocked Harry on purpose and Harry's broom span off course, Harry holding on for dear life.

'Foul!' screamed the Gryffindors.

Madam Hooch spoke angrily to Flint and then ordered a free shot at the goalposts for Gryffindor. But in all the confusion, of course, the Golden Snitch had disappeared from sight again.

Down in the stands, Dean Thomas was yelling, 'Send him off, ref! Red card!'

'This isn't football, Dean,' Ron reminded him. 'You can't send people off in Quidditch – and what's a red card?'

But Hagrid was on Dean's side.

'They oughta change the rules, Flint coulda knocked Harry outta the air.'

Lee Jordan was finding it difficult not to take sides.

'So – after that obvious and disgusting bit of cheating –'

'Jordan!' growled Professor McGonagall.

'I mean, after that open and revolting foul –'

'Jordan, I'm warning you –'

'All right, all right. Flint nearly kills the Gryffindor Seeker, which could happen to anyone, I'm sure, so a penalty to Gryffindor, taken by Spinnet, who puts it away, no trouble, and we continue play, Gryffindor still in possession.'

It was as Harry dodged another Bludger which went spinning dangerously past his head that it happened. His broom gave a sudden, frightening lurch. For a split second, he thought he was going to fall. He gripped the broom tightly with both his hands and knees. He'd never felt anything like that.

It happened again. It was as though the broom was trying to buck him off. But Nimbus Two Thousands did not suddenly decide to buck their riders off. Harry tried to turn back towards the Gryffindor goalposts; he had half a mind to ask Wood to call time out – and then he realised that his broom was completely out of his control. He couldn't turn it. He couldn't direct it at all. It was zig-zagging through the air and every now and then making violent swishing movements which almost unseated him.

Lee was still commentating.

'Slytherin in possession – Flint with the Quaffle –

passes Spinnet – passes Bell – hit hard in the face by a Bludger, hope it broke his nose – only joking, Professor – Slytherin score – oh no ...'

The Slytherins were cheering. No one seemed to have noticed that Harry's broom was behaving strangely. It was carrying him slowly higher, away from the game, jerking and twitching as it went.

'Dunno what Harry thinks he's doing,' Hagrid mumbled. He stared through his binoculars. 'If I didn' know better, I'd say he'd lost control of his broom ... but he can't have ...'

Suddenly, people were pointing up at Harry all over the stands. His broom had started to roll over and over, with him only just managing to hold on. Then the whole crowd gasped. Harry's broom had given a wild jerk and Harry swung off it. He was now dangling from it, holding on with only one hand.

'Did something happen to it when Flint blocked him?' Seamus whispered.

'Can't have,' Hagrid said, his voice shaking. 'Can't nothing interfere with a broomstick except powerful Dark Magic – no kid could do that to a Nimbus Two Thousand.'

At these words, Hermione seized Hagrid's binoculars, but instead of looking up at Harry, she started looking frantically at the crowd.

'What are you doing?' moaned Ron, grey-faced.

'I knew it,' Hermione gasped. 'Snape – look.'

Ron grabbed the binoculars. Snape was in the middle of the stands opposite them. He had his eyes fixed on Harry and was muttering non-stop under his breath.

'He's doing something – jinxing the broom,' said Hermione.

'What should we do?'

'Leave it to me.'

Before Ron could say another word, Hermione had disappeared. Ron turned the binoculars back on Harry. His broom was vibrating so hard, it was almost impossible for him to hang on much longer. The whole crowd were on their feet, watching, terrified, as the Weasleys flew up to try and pull Harry safely on to one of their brooms, but it was no good – every time they got near him, the broom would jump higher still. They dropped lower and circled beneath him, obviously hoping to catch him if he fell. Marcus Flint seized the Quaffle and scored five times without anyone noticing.

'Come on, Hermione,' Ron muttered desperately.

Hermione had fought her way across to the stand where Snape stood and was now racing along the row behind him; she didn't even stop to say sorry as she knocked Professor Quirrell headfirst into the row in front. Reaching Snape, she crouched down, pulled out her wand and whispered a few, well chosen words. Bright blue flames shot from her wand on to the hem of Snape's robes.

It took perhaps thirty seconds for Snape to realise that he was on fire. A sudden yelp told her she had done her job. Scooping the fire off him into a little jar in her pocket she scrambled back along the row – Snape would never know what had happened.

It was enough. Up in the air, Harry was suddenly able to clamber back on to his broom.

'Neville, you can look!' Ron said. Neville had

been sobbing into Hagrid's jacket for the last five minutes.

Harry was speeding towards the ground when the crowd saw him clap his hand to his mouth as though he was about to be sick – he hit the pitch on all fours – coughed – and something gold fell into his hand.

'I've got the Snitch!' he shouted, waving it above his head, and the game ended in complete confusion.

'He didn't *catch* it, he nearly *swallowed* it,' Flint was still howling twenty minutes later, but it made no difference – Harry hadn't broken any rules and Lee Jordan was still happily shouting the result – Gryffindor had won by one hundred and seventy points to sixty. Harry heard none of this, though. He was being made a cup of strong tea back in Hagrid's hut, with Ron and Hermione.

'It was Snape,' Ron was explaining. 'Hermione and I saw him. He was cursing your broomstick, muttering, he wouldn't take his eyes off you.'

'Rubbish,' said Hagrid, who hadn't heard a word of what had gone on next to him in the stands. 'Why would Snape do somethin' like that?'

Harry, Ron and Hermione looked at each other, wondering what to tell him. Harry decided on the truth.

'I found out something about him,' he told Hagrid. 'He tried to get past that three-headed dog at Hallowe'en. It bit him. We think he was trying to steal whatever it's guarding.'

Hagrid dropped the teapot.

'How do you know about Fluffy?' he said.

'Fluffy?'

'Yeah – he's mine – bought him off a Greek chappie I met in the pub las' year – I lent him to Dumbledore to guard the –'

'Yes?' said Harry eagerly.

'Now, don't ask me any more,' said Hagrid gruffly. 'That's top secret, that is.'

'But Snape's trying to *steal* it.'

'Rubbish,' said Hagrid again. 'Snape's a Hogwarts teacher, he'd do nothin' of the sort.'

'So why did he just try and kill Harry?' cried Hermione.

The afternoon's events certainly seemed to have changed her mind about Snape.

'I know a jinx when I see one, Hagrid, I've read all about them! You've got to keep eye contact, and Snape wasn't blinking at all, I saw him!'

'I'm tellin' yeh, yer wrong!' said Hagrid hotly. 'I don' know why Harry's broom acted like that, but Snape wouldn' try an' kill a student! Now, listen to me, all three of yeh – yer meddlin' in things that don' concern yeh. It's dangerous. You forget that dog, an' you forget what it's guardin', that's between Professor Dumbledore an' Nicolas Flamel –'

'Aha!' said Harry. 'So there's someone called Nicolas Flamel involved, is there?'

Hagrid looked furious with himself.

— CHAPTER TWELVE —

The Mirror of Erised

Christmas was coming. One morning in mid-December, Hogwarts woke to find itself covered in several feet of snow. The lake froze solid and the Weasley twins were punished for bewitching several snowballs so that they followed Quirrell around, bouncing off the back of his turban. The few owls that managed to battle their way through the stormy sky to deliver post had to be nursed back to health by Hagrid before they could fly off again.

No one could wait for the holidays to start. While the Gryffindor common room and the Great Hall had roaring fires, the draughty corridors had become icy and a bitter wind rattled the windows in the classrooms. Worst of all were Professor Snape's classes down in the dungeons, where their breath rose in a mist before them and they kept as close as possible to their hot cauldrons.

'I do feel so sorry,' said Draco Malfoy, one Potions class, 'for all those people who have to stay at Hogwarts for Christmas because they're not wanted at home.'

He was looking over at Harry as he spoke. Crabbe and Goyle chuckled. Harry, who was measuring out powdered spine of lionfish, ignored them. Malfoy had been even more unpleasant than usual since the Quidditch match. Disgusted that Slytherin had lost, he had tried to get everyone laughing at how a wide-mouthed tree frog would be replacing Harry as Seeker next. Then he'd realised that nobody found this funny, because they were all so impressed at the way Harry had managed to stay on his bucking broomstick. So Malfoy, jealous and angry, had gone back to taunting Harry about having no proper family.

It was true that Harry wasn't going back to Privet Drive for Christmas. Professor McGonagall had come round the week before, making a list of students who would be staying for the holidays, and Harry had signed up at once. He didn't feel sorry for himself at all; this would probably be the best Christmas he'd ever had. Ron and his brothers were staying too, because Mr and Mrs Weasley were going to Romania to visit Charlie.

When they left the dungeons at the end of Potions, they found a large fir tree blocking the corridor ahead. Two enormous feet sticking out at the bottom and a loud puffing sound told them that Hagrid was behind it.

'Hi, Hagrid, want any help?' Ron asked, sticking his head through the branches.

'Nah, I'm all right, thanks, Ron.'

'Would you mind moving out of the way?' came Malfoy's cold drawl from behind them. 'Are you trying to earn some extra money, Weasley? Hoping to be gamekeeper yourself when you leave Hogwarts, I suppose – that hut of Hagrid's must seem like a palace compared to what your family's used to.'

Ron dived at Malfoy just as Snape came up the stairs.

'WEASLEY!'

Ron let go of the front of Malfoy's robes.

'He was provoked, Professor Snape,' said Hagrid, sticking his huge hairy face out from behind the tree. 'Malfoy was insultin' his family.'

'Be that as it may, fighting is against Hogwarts rules, Hagrid,' said Snape silkily. 'Five points from Gryffindor, Weasley, and be grateful it isn't more. Move along, all of you.'

Malfoy, Crabbe and Goyle pushed roughly past the tree, scattering needles everywhere and smirking.

'I'll get him,' said Ron, grinding his teeth at Malfoy's back, 'one of these days, I'll get him –'

'I hate them both,' said Harry, 'Malfoy and Snape.'

'Come on, cheer up, it's nearly Christmas,' said Hagrid. 'Tell yeh what, come with me an' see the Great Hall, looks a treat.'

So Harry, Ron and Hermione followed Hagrid and his tree off to the Great Hall, where Professor McGonagall and Professor Flitwick were busy with the Christmas decorations.

'Ah, Hagrid, the last tree – put it in the far corner, would you?'

The Hall looked spectacular. Festoons of holly and mistletoe hung all around the walls and no fewer than twelve towering Christmas trees stood around the room, some sparkling with tiny icicles, some glittering with hundreds of candles.

'How many days you got left until yer holidays?' Hagrid asked.

'Just one,' said Hermione. 'And that reminds me – Harry, Ron, we've got half an hour before lunch, we should be in the library.'

'Oh yeah, you're right,' said Ron, tearing his eyes away from Professor Flitwick, who had golden bubbles blossoming out of his wand and was trailing them over the branches of the new tree.

'The library?' said Hagrid, following them out of the Hall. 'Just before the holidays? Bit keen, aren't yeh?'

'Oh, we're not working,' Harry told him brightly. 'Ever since you mentioned Nicolas Flamel we've been trying to find out who he is.'

'You *what*?' Hagrid looked shocked. 'Listen here – I've told yeh – drop it. It's nothin' to you what that dog's guardin'.'

'We just want to know who Nicolas Flamel is, that's all,' said Hermione.

'Unless you'd like to tell us and save us the trouble?' Harry added. 'We must've been through hundreds of books already and we can't find him anywhere – just give us a hint – I know I've read his name somewhere.'

'I'm sayin' nothin',' said Hagrid flatly.

'Just have to find out for ourselves, then,' said Ron, and they left Hagrid looking disgruntled and hurried off to the library.

They had indeed been searching books for Flamel's name ever since Hagrid had let it slip, because how else were they going to find out what

Snape was trying to steal? The trouble was, it was very hard to know where to begin, not knowing what Flamel might have done to get himself into a book. He wasn't in *Great Wizards of the Twentieth Century*, or *Notable Magical Names of Our Time*; he was missing, too, from *Important Modern Magical Discoveries*, and *A Study of Recent Developments in Wizardry*. And then, of course, there was the sheer size of the library; tens of thousands of books; thousands of shelves; hundreds of narrow rows.

Hermione took out a list of subjects and titles she had decided to search while Ron strode off down a row of books and started pulling them off the shelves at random. Harry wandered over to the Restricted Section. He had been wondering for a while if Flamel wasn't somewhere in there. Unfortunately, you needed a specially signed note from one of the teachers to look in any of the restricted books and he knew he'd never get one. These were the books containing powerful Dark Magic never taught at Hogwarts and only read by older students studying advanced Defence Against the Dark Arts.

'What are you looking for, boy?'

'Nothing,' said Harry.

Madam Pince the librarian brandished a feather duster at him.

'You'd better get out, then. Go on – out!'

Wishing he'd been a bit quicker at thinking up some story, Harry left the library. He, Ron and Hermione had already agreed they'd better not ask Madam Pince where they could find Flamel. They were sure she'd be able to tell them, but they couldn't risk Snape hearing what they were up to.

Harry waited outside in the corridor to see if the other two had found anything, but he wasn't very hopeful. They had been looking for a fortnight, after all, but as they only had odd moments between lessons it wasn't surprising they'd found nothing. What they really needed was a nice long search without Madam Pince breathing down their necks.

Five minutes later, Ron and Hermione joined him, shaking their heads. They went off to lunch.

'You will keep looking while I'm away, won't you?' said Hermione. 'And send me an owl if you find anything.'

'And you could ask your parents if they know who Flamel is,' said Ron. 'It'd be safe to ask them.'

'Very safe, as they're both dentists,' said Hermione.

*

Once the holidays had started, Ron and Harry were having too good a time to think much about Flamel. They had the dormitory to themselves and the common room was far emptier than usual, so they were able to get the good armchairs by the fire. They sat by the hour eating anything they could spear on a toasting fork – bread, crumpets, marshmallows – and plotting ways of getting Malfoy expelled, which were fun to talk about even if they wouldn't work.

Ron also started teaching Harry wizard chess. This was exactly like Muggle chess except that the figures were alive, which made it a lot like directing troops in battle. Ron's set was very old and battered. Like everything else he owned, it had once belonged to someone else in his family – in this case, his grandfather. However, old chessmen weren't a drawback at all. Ron knew them so well he never had trouble getting them to do what he wanted.

Harry played with chessmen Seamus Finnigan had lent him and they didn't trust him at all. He wasn't a very good player yet and they kept shouting different bits of advice at him, which was confusing: 'Don't send me there, can't you see his knight? Send *him*, we can afford to lose *him*.'

On Christmas Eve, Harry went to bed looking forward to the next day for the food and the fun, but not expecting any presents at all. When he woke early next morning, however, the first thing he saw was a small pile of packages at the foot of his bed.

'Happy Christmas,' said Ron sleepily as Harry scrambled out of bed and pulled on his dressing-gown.

'You too,' said Harry. 'Will you look at this? I've got some presents!'

'What did you expect, turnips?' said Ron, turning to his own pile, which was a lot bigger than Harry's.

Harry picked up the top parcel. It was wrapped in thick brown paper and scrawled across it was *To Harry, from Hagrid*. Inside was a roughly cut wooden flute. Hagrid had obviously whittled it himself. Harry blew it – it sounded a bit like an owl.

A second, very small parcel contained a note.

We received your message and enclose your Christmas present. From Uncle Vernon and Aunt

Petunia. Sellotaped to the note was a fifty-pence piece.

'That's friendly,' said Harry.

Ron was fascinated by the fifty pence.

'*Weird!*' he said. 'What a shape! This is *money*?'

'You can keep it,' said Harry, laughing at how pleased Ron was. 'Hagrid and my aunt and uncle – so who sent these?'

'I think I know who that one's from,' said Ron, going a bit pink and pointing to a very lumpy parcel. 'My mum. I told her you didn't expect any presents and – oh, no,' he groaned, 'she's made you a Weasley jumper.'

Harry had torn open the parcel to find a thick, hand-knitted sweater in emerald green and a large box of home-made fudge.

'Every year she makes us a jumper,' said Ron, unwrapping his own, 'and mine's *always* maroon.'

'That's really nice of her,' said Harry, trying the fudge, which was very tasty.

His next present also contained sweets – a large box of Chocolate Frogs from Hermione.

This left only one parcel. Harry picked it up and felt it. It was very light. He unwrapped it.

Something fluid and silvery grey went slithering to the floor, where it lay in gleaming folds. Ron gasped.

'I've heard of those,' he said in a hushed voice, dropping the box of Every-Flavour Beans he'd got from Hermione. 'If that's what I think it is – they're really rare, and *really* valuable.'

'What is it?'

Harry picked the shining, silvery cloth off the

floor. It was strange to the touch, like water woven into material.

'It's an Invisibility Cloak,' said Ron, a look of awe on his face. 'I'm sure it is – try it on.'

Harry threw the Cloak around his shoulders and Ron gave a yell.

'It *is*! Look down!'

Harry looked down at his feet, but they had gone. He dashed to the mirror. Sure enough, his reflection looked back at him, just his head suspended in mid-air, his body completely invisible. He pulled the Cloak over his head and his reflection vanished completely.

'There's a note!' said Ron suddenly. 'A note fell out of it!'

Harry pulled off the Cloak and seized the letter. Written in narrow, loopy writing he had never seen before were the following words:

Your father left this in my possession before he died.
It is time it was returned to you.
Use it well.
A Very Merry Christmas to you.

There was no signature. Harry stared at the note. Ron was admiring the Cloak.

'I'd give *anything* for one of these,' he said. '*Anything*. What's the matter?'

'Nothing,' said Harry. He felt very strange. Who had sent the Cloak? Had it really once belonged to his father?

Before he could say or think anything else, the dormitory door was flung open and Fred and

George Weasley bounded in. Harry stuffed the Cloak quickly out of sight. He didn't feel like sharing it with anyone else yet.

'Merry Christmas!'

'Hey, look – Harry's got a Weasley jumper, too!'

Fred and George were wearing blue jumpers, one with a large yellow F on it, the other with a large yellow G.

'Harry's is better than ours, though,' said Fred, holding up Harry's jumper. 'She obviously makes more of an effort if you're not family.'

'Why aren't you wearing yours, Ron?' George demanded. 'Come on, get it on, they're lovely and warm.'

'I hate maroon,' Ron moaned half-heartedly as he pulled it over his head.

'You haven't got a letter on yours,' George observed. 'I suppose she thinks you don't forget your name. But we're not stupid – we know we're called Gred and Forge.'

'What's all this noise?'

Percy Weasley stuck his head through the door, looking disapproving. He had clearly come halfway through unwrapping his presents as he, too, carried a lumpy jumper over his arm, which Fred seized.

'P for prefect! Get it on, Percy, come on, we're all wearing ours, even Harry got one.'

'I – don't – want –' said Percy thickly, as the twins forced the jumper over his head, knocking his glasses askew.

'And you're not sitting with the Prefects today, either,' said George. 'Christmas is a time for family.'

They frog-marched Percy from the room, his arms pinned to his sides by his jumper.

*

Harry had never in all his life had such a Christmas dinner. A hundred fat, roast turkeys, mountains of roast and boiled potatoes, platters of fat chipolatas, tureens of buttered peas, silver boats of thick, rich gravy and cranberry sauce – and stacks of wizard crackers every few feet along the table. These fantastic crackers were nothing like the feeble Muggle ones the Dursleys usually bought, with their little plastic toys and their flimsy paper hats. Harry pulled a wizard cracker with Fred and it didn't just bang, it went off with a blast like a cannon and engulfed them all in a cloud of blue smoke, while from the inside exploded a rear-admiral's hat and several live, white mice. Up on the High Table, Dumbledore had swapped his pointed wizard's hat for a flowered bonnet and was chuckling merrily at a joke Professor Flitwick had just read him.

Flaming Christmas puddings followed the turkey. Percy nearly broke his teeth on a silver Sickle embedded in his slice. Harry watched Hagrid getting redder and redder in the face as he called for more wine, finally kissing Professor McGonagall on the cheek, who, to Harry's amazement, giggled and blushed, her top hat lop-sided.

When Harry finally left the table, he was laden down with a stack of things out of the crackers, including a pack of non-explodable, luminous balloons, a grow-your-own-warts kit and his own new wizard chess set. The white mice had disappeared and Harry had a nasty feeling they were going to end up as Mrs Norris' Christmas dinner.

Harry and the Weasleys spent a happy afternoon having a furious snowball fight in the grounds. Then, cold, wet and gasping for breath, they returned to the fire in the Gryffindor common room, where Harry broke in his new chess set by losing spectacularly to Ron. He suspected he wouldn't have lost so badly if Percy hadn't tried to help him so much.

After a tea of turkey sandwiches, crumpets, trifle and Christmas cake, everyone felt too full and sleepy to do much before bed except sit and watch Percy chase Fred and George all over Gryffindor Tower because they'd stolen his prefect badge.

It had been Harry's best Christmas day ever. Yet something had been nagging at the back of his mind all day. Not until he climbed into bed was he free to think about it: the Invisibility Cloak and whoever had sent it.

Ron, full of turkey and cake and with nothing mysterious to bother him, fell asleep almost as soon as he'd drawn the curtains of his four-poster. Harry leant over the side of his own bed and pulled the Cloak out from under it.

His father's ... this had been his father's. He let the material flow over his hands, smoother than silk, light as air. *Use it well*, the note had said.

He had to try it, now. He slipped out of bed and wrapped the Cloak around himself. Looking down at his legs, he saw only moonlight and shadows. It was a very funny feeling.

Use it well.

Suddenly, Harry felt wide awake. The whole of Hogwarts was open to him in this Cloak. Excitement flooded through him as he stood there in the dark and silence. He could go anywhere in this, anywhere, and Filch would never know.

Ron grunted in his sleep. Should Harry wake him? Something held him back – his father's Cloak – he felt that this time – the first time – he wanted to use it alone.

He crept out of the dormitory, down the stairs, across the common room and climbed through the portrait hole.

'Who's there?' squawked the Fat Lady. Harry said nothing. He walked quickly down the corridor.

Where should he go? He stopped, his heart racing, and thought. And then it came to him. The Restricted Section in the library. He'd be able to read as long as he liked, as long as it took to find out who Flamel was. He set off, drawing the Invisibility Cloak tight around him as he walked.

The library was pitch black and very eerie. Harry lit a lamp to see his way along the rows of books. The lamp looked as if it was floating along in mid-air, and even though Harry could feel his arm supporting it, the sight gave him the creeps.

The Restricted Section was right at the back of the library. Stepping carefully over the rope which separated these books from the rest of the library, he held up his lamp to read the titles.

They didn't tell him much. Their peeling, faded gold letters spelled words in languages Harry couldn't understand. Some had no title at all. One book had a dark stain on it that looked horribly like blood. The hairs on the back of Harry's neck prickled. Maybe he was imagining it, maybe not, but he thought a faint whispering was coming from the books, as though they knew someone was there who shouldn't be.

He had to start somewhere. Setting the lamp down carefully on the floor, he looked along the bottom shelf for an interesting-looking book. A large black and silver volume caught his eye. He pulled it out with difficulty, because it was very heavy, and, balancing it on his knee, let it fall open.

A piercing, blood-curdling shriek split the silence – the book was screaming! Harry snapped it shut, but the shriek went on and on, one high, unbroken, ear-splitting note. He stumbled backwards and knocked over his lamp, which went out at once. Panicking, he heard footsteps coming down the corridor outside – stuffing the shrieking book back on the shelf, he ran for it. He passed Filch almost in the doorway; Filch's pale, wild eyes looked straight through him and Harry slipped under Filch's outstretched arm and streaked off up the corridor, the book's shrieks still ringing in his ears.

He came to a sudden halt in front of a tall suit of armour. He had been so busy getting away from the library, he hadn't paid attention to where he was going. Perhaps because it was dark, he didn't recognise where he was at all. There was a suit of armour near the kitchens, he knew, but he must be five floors above there.

'You asked me to come directly to you, Professor,

if anyone was wandering around at night, and somebody's been in the library – Restricted Section.'

Harry felt the blood drain out of his face. Wherever he was, Filch must know a short cut, because his soft, greasy voice was getting nearer, and to his horror, it was Snape who replied.

'The Restricted Section? Well, they can't be far, we'll catch them.'

Harry stood rooted to the spot as Filch and Snape came around the corner ahead. They couldn't see him, of course, but it was a narrow corridor and if they came much nearer they'd knock right into him – the Cloak didn't stop him being solid.

He backed away as quietly as he could. A door stood ajar to his left. It was his only hope. He squeezed through it, holding his breath, trying not to move it, and to his relief he managed to get inside the room without their noticing anything. They walked straight past and Harry leant against the wall, breathing deeply, listening to their footsteps dying away. That had been close, very close. It was a few seconds before he noticed anything about the room he had hidden in.

It looked like a disused classroom. The dark shapes of desks and chairs were piled against the walls and there was an upturned waste-paper basket – but propped against the wall facing him was something that didn't look as if it belonged there, something that looked as if someone had just put it there to keep it out of the way.

It was a magnificent mirror, as high as the ceiling, with an ornate gold frame, standing on two clawed feet. There was an inscription carved around the top: *Erised stra ehru oyt ube cafru oyt on wohsi*.

His panic fading now that there was no sound of Filch and Snape, Harry moved nearer to the mirror, wanting to look at himself but see no reflection again. He stepped in front of it.

He had to clap his hands to his mouth to stop himself screaming. He whirled around. His heart was pounding far more furiously than when the book had screamed – for he had seen not only himself in the mirror, but a whole crowd of people standing right behind him.

But the room was empty. Breathing very fast, he turned slowly back to the mirror.

There he was, reflected in it, white and scared-looking, and there, reflected behind him, were at least ten others. Harry looked over his shoulder – but, still, no one was there. Or were they all invisible, too? Was he in fact in a room full of invisible people and this mirror's trick was that it reflected them, invisible or not?

He looked in the mirror again. A woman standing right behind his reflection was smiling at him and waving. He reached out a hand and felt the air behind him. If she was really there, he'd touch her, their reflections were so close together, but he felt only air – she and the others existed only in the mirror.

She was a very pretty woman. She had dark red hair and her eyes – her eyes are just like mine, Harry thought, edging a little closer to the glass. Bright green – exactly the same shape, but then he noticed that she was crying; smiling, but crying at

the same time. The tall, thin, black-haired man
standing next to her put his arm around her. He
wore glasses, and his hair was very untidy. It stuck
up at the back, just like Harry's did.

Harry was so close to the mirror now that his
nose was nearly touching that of his reflection.

'Mum?' he whispered. 'Dad?'

They just looked at him, smiling. And slowly,
Harry looked into the faces of the other people in
the mirror and saw other pairs of green eyes like
his, other noses like his, even a little old man who
looked as though he had Harry's knobbly knees –
Harry was looking at his family, for the first time in
his life.

The Potters smiled and waved at Harry and he
stared hungrily back at them, his hands pressed flat
against the glass as though he was hoping to fall
right through it and reach them. He had a powerful
kind of ache inside him, half joy, half terrible
sadness.

How long he stood there, he didn't know. The
reflections did not fade and he looked and looked
until a distant noise brought him back to his senses. He couldn't stay here, he had to find his way
back to bed. He tore his eyes away from his mother's face, whispered, 'I'll come back,' and hurried
from the room.

                              *

'You could have woken me up,' said Ron, crossly.

'You can come tonight, I'm going back, I want to
show you the mirror.'

'I'd like to see your mum and dad,' Ron said
eagerly.

'And I want to see all your family, all the Weasleys, you'll be able to show me your other brothers and everyone.'

'You can see them any old time,' said Ron. 'Just come round my house this summer. Anyway, maybe it only shows dead people. Shame about not finding Flamel, though. Have some bacon or something, why aren't you eating anything?'

Harry couldn't eat. He had seen his parents and would be seeing them again tonight. He had almost forgotten about Flamel. It didn't seem very important any more. Who cared what the three-headed dog was guarding? What did it matter if Snape stole it, really?

'Are you all right?' said Ron. 'You look odd.'

*

What Harry feared most was that he might not be able to find the mirror room again. With Ron covered in the Cloak too, they had to walk much more slowly next night. They tried retracing Harry's route from the library, wandering around the dark passageways for nearly an hour.

'I'm freezing,' said Ron. 'Let's forget it and go back.'

'No!' Harry hissed. 'I know it's here somewhere.'

They passed the ghost of a tall witch gliding in the opposite direction, but saw no one else. Just as Ron started moaning that his feet were dead with cold, Harry spotted the suit of armour.

'It's here – just here – yes!'

They pushed the door open. Harry dropped the Cloak from round his shoulders and ran to the mirror.

There they were. His mother and father beamed at the sight of him.

'See?' Harry whispered.

'I can't see anything.'

'Look! Look at them all ... there are loads of them ...'

'I can only see you.'

'Look in it properly, go on, stand where I am.'

Harry stepped aside, but with Ron in front of the mirror, he couldn't see his family any more, just Ron in his paisley pyjamas.

Ron, though, was staring transfixed at his image.

'Look at me!' he said.

'Can you see all your family standing around you?'

'No – I'm alone – but I'm different – I look older – and I'm Head Boy!'

'*What?*'

'I am – I'm wearing the badge like Bill used to – and I'm holding the House Cup and the Quidditch Cup – I'm Quidditch captain, too!'

Ron tore his eyes away from this splendid sight to look excitedly at Harry.

'Do you think this mirror shows the future?'

'How can it? All my family are dead – let me have another look –'

'You had it to yourself all last night, give me a bit more time.'

'You're only holding the Quidditch Cup, what's interesting about that? I want to see my parents.'

'Don't push me –'

A sudden noise outside in the corridor put an end to their discussion. They hadn't realised how loudly they had been talking.

'Quick!'

Ron threw the Cloak back over them as the luminous eyes of Mrs Norris came round the door. Ron and Harry stood quite still, both thinking the same thing – did the Cloak work on cats? After what seemed an age, she turned and left.

'This isn't safe – she might have gone for Filch, I bet she heard us. Come on.'

And Ron pulled Harry out of the room.

*

The snow still hadn't melted next morning.

'Want to play chess, Harry?' said Ron.

'No.'

'Why don't we go down and visit Hagrid?'

'No ... you go ...'

'I know what you're thinking about, Harry, that mirror. Don't go back tonight.'

'Why not?'

'I dunno, I've just got a bad feeling about it – and anyway, you've had too many close shaves already. Filch, Snape and Mrs Norris are wandering around. So what if they can't see you? What if they walk into you? What if you knock something over?'

'You sound like Hermione.'

'I'm serious, Harry, don't go.'

But Harry only had one thought in his head, which was to get back in front of the mirror, and Ron wasn't going to stop him.

*

That third night he found his way more quickly than before. He was walking so fast he knew he was making more noise than was wise, but he didn't meet anyone.

And there were his mother and father smiling at him again, and one of his grandfathers nodding happily. Harry sank down to sit on the floor in front of the mirror. There was nothing to stop him staying here all night with his family. Nothing at all.

Except –

'So – back again, Harry?'

Harry felt as though his insides had turned to ice. He looked behind him. Sitting on one of the desks by the wall was none other than Albus Dumbledore. Harry must have walked straight past him, so desperate to get to the mirror he hadn't noticed him.

'I – I didn't see you, sir.'

'Strange how short-sighted being invisible can make you,' said Dumbledore, and Harry was relieved to see that he was smiling.

'So,' said Dumbledore, slipping off the desk to sit on the floor with Harry, 'you, like hundreds before you, have discovered the delights of the Mirror of Erised.'

'I didn't know it was called that, sir.'

'But I expect you've realised by now what it does?'

'It – well – it shows me my family –'

'And it showed your friend Ron himself as Head Boy.'

'How did you know –?'

'I don't need a cloak to become invisible,' said Dumbledore gently. 'Now, can you think what the Mirror of Erised shows us all?'

Harry shook his head.

'Let me explain. The happiest man on earth would be able to use the Mirror of Erised like a normal mirror, that is, he would look into it and see himself exactly as he is. Does that help?'

Harry thought. Then he said slowly, 'It shows us what we want ... whatever we want ...'

'Yes and no,' said Dumbledore quietly. 'It shows us nothing more or less than the deepest, most desperate desire of our hearts. You, who have never known your family, see them standing around you. Ronald Weasley, who has always been overshadowed by his brothers, sees himself standing alone, the best of all of them. However, this mirror will give us neither knowledge or truth. Men have wasted away before it, entranced by what they have seen, or been driven mad, not knowing if what it shows is real or even possible.

'The Mirror will be moved to a new home tomorrow, Harry, and I ask you not to go looking for it again. If you ever *do* run across it, you will now be prepared. It does not do to dwell on dreams and forget to live, remember that. Now, why don't you put that admirable Cloak back on and get off to bed?'

Harry stood up.

'Sir – Professor Dumbledore? Can I ask you something?'

'Obviously, you've just done so,' Dumbledore smiled. 'You may ask me one more thing, however.'

'What do you see when you look in the Mirror?'

'I? I see myself holding a pair of thick, woollen socks.'

Harry stared.

'One can never have enough socks,' said Dumbledore. 'Another Christmas has come and gone and I didn't get a single pair. People will insist on giving me books.'

It was only when he was back in bed that it struck Harry that Dumbledore might not have been quite truthful. But then, he thought, as he shoved Scabbers off his pillow, it had been quite a personal question.

— CHAPTER THIRTEEN —

Nicolas Flamel

Dumbledore had convinced Harry not to go looking for the Mirror of Erised again and for the rest of the Christmas holidays the Invisibility Cloak stayed folded at the bottom of his trunk. Harry wished he could forget what he'd seen in the Mirror as easily, but he couldn't. He started having nightmares. Over and over again he dreamed about his parents disappearing in a flash of green light while a high voice cackled with laughter.

'You see, Dumbledore was right, that mirror could drive you mad,' said Ron, when Harry told him about these dreams.

Hermione, who came back the day before term started, took a different view of things. She was torn between horror at the idea of Harry being out of bed, roaming the school three nights in a row ('If Filch had caught you!') and disappointment that he hadn't at least found out who Nicolas Flamel was.

They had almost given up hope of ever finding Flamel in a library book, even though Harry was still sure he'd read the name somewhere. Once term had started, they were back to skimming through books for ten minutes during their breaks.

Harry had even less time than the other two, because Quidditch practice had started again.

Wood was working the team harder than ever. Even the endless rain that had replaced the snow couldn't dampen his spirits. The Weasleys complained that Wood was becoming a fanatic, but Harry was on Wood's side. If they won their next match, against Hufflepuff, they would overtake Slytherin in the House Championship for the first time in seven years. Quite apart from wanting to win, Harry found that he had fewer nightmares when he was tired out after training.

Then, during one particularly wet and muddy practice session, Wood gave the team a bit of bad news. He'd just got very angry with the Weasleys, who kept dive-bombing each other and pretending to fall off their brooms.

'Will you stop messing around!' he yelled. 'That's exactly the sort of thing that'll lose us the match! Snape's refereeing this time, and he'll be looking for any excuse to knock points off Gryffindor!'

George Weasley really did fall off his broom at these words.

'*Snape's* refereeing?' he spluttered through a mouthful of mud. 'When's he ever refereed a Quidditch match? He's not going to be fair if we might overtake Slytherin.'

The rest of the team landed next to George to complain, too.

'It's not *my* fault,' said Wood. 'We've just got to make sure we play a clean game, so Snape hasn't got an excuse to pick on us.'

Which was all very well, thought Harry, but he

had another reason for not wanting Snape near him while he was playing Quidditch ...

The rest of the team hung back to talk to each other as usual at the end of practice, but Harry headed straight back to the Gryffindor common room, where he found Ron and Hermione playing chess. Chess was the only thing Hermione ever lost at, something Harry and Ron thought was very good for her.

'Don't talk to me for a moment,' said Ron when Harry sat down next to him. 'I need to concen–' He caught sight of Harry's face. 'What's the matter with you? You look terrible.'

Speaking quietly so that no one else would hear, Harry told the other two about Snape's sudden, sinister desire to be a Quidditch referee.

'Don't play,' said Hermione at once.

'Say you're ill,' said Ron.

'Pretend to break your leg,' Hermione suggested.

'*Really* break your leg,' said Ron.

'I can't,' said Harry. 'There isn't a reserve Seeker. If I back out, Gryffindor can't play at all.'

At that moment Neville toppled into the common room. How he had managed to climb through the portrait hole was anyone's guess, because his legs had been stuck together with what they recognised at once as the Leg-Locker Curse. He must have had to bunny hop all the way up to Gryffindor Tower.

Everyone fell about laughing except Hermione, who leapt up and performed the counter-curse. Neville's legs sprang apart and he got to his feet, trembling.

'What happened?' Hermione asked him, leading him over to sit with Harry and Ron.

'Malfoy,' said Neville shakily. 'I met him outside the library. He said he'd been looking for someone to practise that on.'

'Go to Professor McGonagall!' Hermione urged Neville. 'Report him!'

Neville shook his head.

'I don't want more trouble,' he mumbled.

'You've got to stand up to him, Neville!' said Ron. 'He's used to walking all over people, but that's no reason to lie down in front of him and make it easier.'

'There's no need to tell me I'm not brave enough to be in Gryffindor, Malfoy's already done that,' Neville choked.

Harry felt in the pocket of his robes and pulled out a Chocolate Frog, the very last one from the box Hermione had given him for Christmas. He gave it to Neville, who looked as though he might cry.

'You're worth twelve of Malfoy,' Harry said. 'The Sorting Hat chose you for Gryffindor, didn't it? And where's Malfoy? In stinking Slytherin.'

Neville's lips twitched in a weak smile as he unwrapped the Frog.

'Thanks, Harry ... I think I'll go to bed ... D'you want the card, you collect them, don't you?'

As Neville walked away Harry looked at the Famous Wizard card.

'Dumbledore again,' he said. 'He was the first one I ever –'

He gasped. He stared at the back of the card. Then he looked up at Ron and Hermione.

'*I've found him!*' he whispered. '*I've found Flamel!* I *told* you I'd read the name somewhere before, I read it on the train coming here – listen to this: "Professor Dumbledore is particularly famous for his defeat of the dark wizard Grindelwald in 1945, for the discovery of the twelve uses of dragon's blood *and his work on alchemy with his partner, Nicolas Flamel*"!'

Hermione jumped to her feet. She hadn't looked so excited since they'd got back the marks for their very first piece of homework.

'Stay there!' she said, and she sprinted up the stairs to the girls' dormitories. Harry and Ron barely had time to exchange mystified looks before she was dashing back, an enormous old book in her arms.

'I never thought to look in here!' she whispered excitedly. 'I got this out of the library weeks ago for a bit of light reading.'

'*Light?*' said Ron, but Hermione told him to be quiet until she'd looked something up, and started flicking frantically through the pages, muttering to herself.

At last she found what she was looking for.

'I knew it! I *knew* it!'

'Are we allowed to speak yet?' said Ron grumpily. Hermione ignored him.

'Nicolas Flamel,' she whispered dramatically, 'is the *only known maker of the Philosopher's Stone*!'

This didn't have quite the effect she'd expected.

'The what?' said Harry and Ron.

'Oh, *honestly*, don't you two read? Look – read that, there.'

She pushed the book towards them, and Harry and Ron read:

The ancient study of alchemy is concerned with making the Philosopher's Stone, a legendary substance with astonishing powers. The Stone will transform any metal into pure gold. It also produces the Elixir of Life, which will make the drinker immortal.

There have been many reports of the Philosopher's Stone over the centuries, but the only Stone currently in existence belongs to Mr Nicolas Flamel, the noted alchemist and opera-lover. Mr Flamel, who celebrated his six hundred and sixty-fifth birthday last year, enjoys a quiet life in Devon with his wife, Perenelle (six hundred and fifty-eight).

'See?' said Hermione, when Harry and Ron had finished. 'The dog must be guarding Flamel's Philosopher's Stone! I bet he asked Dumbledore to keep it safe for him, because they're friends and he knew someone was after it. That's why he wanted the Stone moved out of Gringotts!'

'A stone that makes gold and stops you ever dying!' said Harry. 'No wonder Snape's after it! *Anyone* would want it.'

'And no wonder we couldn't find Flamel in that *Study of Recent Developments in Wizardry*,' said Ron. 'He's not exactly recent if he's six hundred and sixty-five, is he?'

*

Next morning in Defence Against the Dark Arts,

while copying down different ways of treating werewolf bites, Harry and Ron were still discussing what they'd do with a Philosopher's Stone if they had one. It wasn't until Ron said he'd buy his own Quidditch team that Harry remembered about Snape and the coming match.

'I'm going to play,' he told Ron and Hermione. 'If I don't, all the Slytherins will think I'm just too scared to face Snape. I'll show them ... it'll really wipe the smiles off their faces if we win.'

'Just as long as we're not wiping you off the pitch,' said Hermione.

*

As the match drew nearer, however, Harry became more and more nervous, whatever he told Ron and Hermione. The rest of the team weren't too calm, either. The idea of overtaking Slytherin in the House Championship was wonderful, no one had done it for nearly seven years, but would they be allowed to, with such a biased referee?

Harry didn't know whether he was imagining it or not, but he seemed to keep running into Snape wherever he went. At times, he even wondered whether Snape was following him, trying to catch him on his own. Potions lessons were turning into a sort of weekly torture, Snape was so horrible to Harry. Could Snape possibly know they'd found out about the Philosopher's Stone? Harry didn't see how he could – yet he sometimes had the horrible feeling that Snape could read minds.

*

Harry knew, when they wished him good luck outside the changing rooms next afternoon, that Ron and Hermione were wondering whether they'd ever see him alive again. This wasn't what you'd call comforting. Harry hardly heard a word of Wood's pep talk as he pulled on his Quidditch robes and picked up his Nimbus Two Thousand.

Ron and Hermione, meanwhile, had found a place in the stands next to Neville, who couldn't understand why they looked so grim and worried, or why they had both brought their wands to the match. Little did Harry know that Ron and Hermione had been secretly practising the Leg-Locker Curse. They'd got the idea from Malfoy using it on Neville, and were ready to use it on Snape if he showed any sign of wanting to hurt Harry.

'Now, don't forget, it's *Locomotor Mortis*,' Hermione muttered as Ron slipped his wand up his sleeve.

'I *know*,' Ron snapped. 'Don't nag.'

Back in the changing room, Wood had taken Harry aside.

'Don't want to pressure you, Potter, but if we ever need an early capture of the Snitch it's now. Finish the game before Snape can favour Hufflepuff too much.'

'The whole school's out there!' said Fred Weasley, peering out of the door. 'Even – blimey – Dumbledore's come to watch!'

Harry's heart did a somersault.

'*Dumbledore?*' he said, dashing to the door to make sure. Fred was right. There was no mistaking that silver beard.

Harry could have laughed out loud with relief. He was safe. There was simply no way that Snape would dare to try and hurt him if Dumbledore was watching.

Perhaps that was why Snape was looking so angry as the teams marched on to the pitch, something that Ron noticed, too.

'I've never seen Snape look so mean,' he told Hermione. 'Look – they're off. Ouch!'

Someone had poked Ron in the back of the head. It was Malfoy.

'Oh, sorry, Weasley, didn't see you there.'

Malfoy grinned broadly at Crabbe and Goyle.

'Wonder how long Potter's going to stay on his broom this time? Anyone want a bet? What about you, Weasley?'

Ron didn't answer; Snape had just awarded Hufflepuff a penalty because George Weasley had hit a Bludger at him. Hermione, who had all her fingers crossed in her lap, was squinting fixedly at Harry, who was circling the game like a hawk, looking for the Snitch.

'You know how I think they choose people for the Gryffindor team?' said Malfoy loudly a few minutes later, as Snape awarded Hufflepuff another penalty for no reason at all. 'It's people they feel sorry for. See, there's Potter, who's got no parents, then there's the Weasleys, who've got no money – you should be on the team, Longbottom, you've got no brains.'

Neville went bright red but turned in his seat to face Malfoy.

'I'm worth twelve of you, Malfoy,' he stammered.

Malfoy, Crabbe and Goyle howled with laughter, but Ron, still not daring to take his eyes from the game, said, 'You tell him, Neville.'

'Longbottom, if brains were gold you'd be poorer than Weasley, and that's saying something.'

Ron's nerves were already stretched to breaking point with anxiety about Harry.

'I'm warning you, Malfoy – one more word –'

'Ron!' said Hermione suddenly. 'Harry –!'

'What? Where?'

Harry had suddenly gone into a spectacular dive, which drew gasps and cheers from the crowd. Hermione stood up, her crossed fingers in her mouth, as Harry streaked towards the ground like a bullet.

'You're in luck, Weasley, Potter's obviously spotted some money on the ground!' said Malfoy.

Ron snapped. Before Malfoy knew what was happening, Ron was on top of him, wrestling him to the ground. Neville hesitated, then clambered over the back of his seat to help.

'Come on, Harry!' Hermione screamed, leaping on to her seat to watch as Harry sped straight at Snape – she didn't even notice Malfoy and Ron rolling around under her seat, or the scuffles and yelps coming from the whirl of fists that was Neville, Crabbe and Goyle.

Up in the air, Snape turned on his broomstick just in time to see something scarlet shoot past him, missing him by inches – next second, Harry had pulled out of the dive, his arm raised in triumph, the Snitch clasped in his hand.

The stands erupted; it had to be a record, no one could ever remember the Snitch being caught so quickly.

'Ron! Ron! Where are you? The game's over! Harry's won! We've won! Gryffindor are in the lead!' shrieked Hermione, dancing up and down on her seat and hugging Parvati Patil in the row in front.

Harry jumped off his broom, a foot from the ground. He couldn't believe it. He'd done it – the game was over; it had barely lasted five minutes. As Gryffindors came spilling on to the pitch, he saw Snape land nearby, white-faced and tight-lipped – then Harry felt a hand on his shoulder and looked up into Dumbledore's smiling face.

'Well done,' said Dumbledore quietly, so that only Harry could hear. 'Nice to see you haven't been brooding about that mirror ... been keeping busy ... excellent ...'

Snape spat bitterly on the ground.

*

Harry left the changing room alone some time later, to take his Nimbus Two Thousand back to the broomshed. He couldn't ever remember feeling happier. He'd really done something to be proud of now – no one could say he was just a famous name any more. The evening air had never smelled so sweet. He walked over the damp grass, reliving the last hour in his head, which was a happy blur: Gryffindors running to lift him on to their shoulders; Ron and Hermione in the distance, jumping up and down, Ron cheering through a heavy nosebleed.

Harry had reached the shed. He leant against the wooden door and looked up at Hogwarts, with its windows glowing red in the setting sun. Gryffindor in the lead. He'd done it, he'd shown Snape ...

And speaking of Snape ...

A hooded figure came swiftly down the front steps of the castle. Clearly not wanting to be seen, it walked as fast as possible towards the Forbidden Forest. Harry's victory faded from his mind as he watched. He recognised the figure's prowling walk. Snape, sneaking into the Forest while everyone else was at dinner – what was going on?

Harry jumped back on his Nimbus Two Thousand and took off. Gliding silently over the castle he saw Snape enter the Forest at a run. He followed.

The trees were so thick he couldn't see where Snape had gone. He flew in circles, lower and lower, brushing the top branches of trees until he heard voices. He glided towards them and landed noiselessly in a towering beech tree.

He climbed carefully along one of the branches, holding tight to his broomstick, trying to see through the leaves.

Below, in a shadowy clearing, stood Snape, but he wasn't alone. Quirrell was there, too. Harry couldn't make out the look on his face, but he was stuttering worse than ever. Harry strained to catch what they were saying.

'... d-don't know why you wanted t-t-to meet here of all p-places, Severus ...'

'Oh, I thought we'd keep this private,' said Snape, his voice icy. 'Students aren't supposed to know about the Philosopher's Stone, after all.'

Harry leant forward. Quirrell was mumbling

something. Snape interrupted him.

'Have you found out how to get past that beast of Hagrid's yet?'

'B-b-but Severus, I –'

'You don't want me as your enemy, Quirrell,' said Snape, taking a step towards him.

'I-I don-t know what you –'

'You know perfectly well what I mean.'

An owl hooted loudly and Harry nearly fell out of the tree. He steadied himself in time to hear Snape say, '– your little bit of hocus pocus. I'm waiting.'

'B-but I d-d-don't –'

'Very well,' Snape cut in. 'We'll have another little chat soon, when you've had time to think things over and decided where your loyalties lie.'

He threw his cloak over his head and strode out of the clearing. It was almost dark now, but Harry could see Quirrell, standing quite still as though he was petrified.

*

'Harry, where have you *been*?' Hermione squeaked.

'We won! You won! We won!' shouted Ron, thumping Harry on the back. 'And I gave Malfoy a black eye and Neville tried to take on Crabbe and Goyle single-handed! He's still out cold but Madam Pomfrey says he'll be all right – talk about showing Slytherin! Everyone's waiting for you in the common room, we're having a party, Fred and George stole some cakes and stuff from the kitchens.'

'Never mind that now,' said Harry breathlessly. 'Let's find an empty room, you wait 'til you hear this ...'

He made sure Peeves wasn't inside before shutting the door behind them, then he told them what
he'd seen and heard.

'So we were right, it *is* the Philosopher's Stone,
and Snape's trying to force Quirrell to help him get
it. He asked if he knew how to get past Fluffy – and
he said something about Quirrell's "hocus-pocus" –
I reckon there are other things guarding the stone
apart from Fluffy, loads of enchantments, probably,
and Quirrell would have done some anti-Dark Arts
spell which Snape needs to break through –'

'So you mean the Stone's only safe as long as
Quirrell stands up to Snape?' said Hermione in
alarm.

'It'll be gone by next Tuesday,' said Ron.

— CHAPTER FOURTEEN —

Norbert the Norwegian Ridgeback

Quirrell, however, must have been braver than they'd thought. In the weeks that followed he did seem to be getting paler and thinner, but it didn't look as though he'd cracked yet.

Every time they passed the third-floor corridor, Harry, Ron and Hermione would press their ears to the door to check that Fluffy was still growling inside. Snape was sweeping about in his usual bad temper, which surely meant that the Stone was still safe. Whenever Harry passed Quirrell these days he gave him an encouraging sort of smile, and Ron had started telling people off for laughing at Quirrell's stutter.

Hermione, however, had more on her mind than the Philosopher's Stone. She had started drawing up revision timetables and colour-coding all her notes. Harry and Ron wouldn't have minded, but she kept nagging them to do the same.

'Hermione, the exams are ages away.'

'Ten weeks,' Hermione snapped. 'That's not ages, that's like a second to Nicolas Flamel.'

'But we're not six hundred years old,' Ron reminded her. 'Anyway, what are you revising for, you already know it all.'

'What am I revising for? Are you mad? You realise we need to pass these exams to get into the second year? They're very important, I should have started studying a month ago, I don't know what's got into me ...'

Unfortunately, the teachers seemed to be thinking along the same lines as Hermione. They piled so much homework on them that the Easter holidays weren't nearly as much fun as the Christmas ones. It was hard to relax with Hermione next to you reciting the twelve uses of dragon's blood or practising wand movements. Moaning and yawning, Harry and Ron spent most of their free time in the library with her, trying to get through all their extra work.

'I'll never remember this,' Ron burst out one afternoon, throwing down his quill and looking longingly out of the library window. It was the first really fine day they'd had in months. The sky was a clear, forget-me-not blue and there was a feeling in the air of summer coming.

Harry, who was looking up 'Dittany' in *One Thousand Magical Herbs and Fungi*, didn't look up until he heard Ron say, 'Hagrid! What are you doing in the library?'

Hagrid shuffled into view, hiding something behind his back. He looked very out of place in his moleskin overcoat.

'Jus' lookin',' he said, in a shifty voice that got their interest at once. 'An' what're you lot up ter?'

He looked suddenly suspicious. 'Yer not still lookin' fer Nicolas Flamel, are yeh?'

'Oh, we found out who he is ages ago,' said Ron impressively. '*And* we know what that dog's guarding, it's a Philosopher's St—"

'*Shhhh!*' Hagrid looked around quickly to see if anyone was listening. 'Don' go shoutin' about it, what's the matter with yeh?'

'There are a few things we wanted to ask you, as a matter of fact,' said Harry, 'about what's guarding the Stone apart from Fluffy —'

'SHHHH!' said Hagrid again. 'Listen — come an' see me later, I'm not promisin' I'll tell yeh anythin', mind, but don' go rabbitin' about it in here, students aren' s'pposed ter know. They'll think I've told yeh —'

'See you later, then,' said Harry.

Hagrid shuffled off.

'What was he hiding behind his back?' said Hermione thoughtfully.

'Do you think it had anything to do with the Stone?'

'I'm going to see what section he was in,' said Ron, who'd had enough of working. He came back a minute later with a pile of books in his arms and slammed them down on the table.

'*Dragons!*' he whispered. 'Hagrid was looking up stuff about dragons! Look at these: *Dragon Species of Great Britain and Ireland; From Egg to Inferno; A Dragon Keeper's Guide.*'

'Hagrid's always wanted a dragon, he told me so the first time I ever met him,' said Harry.

'But it's against our laws,' said Ron. 'Dragon-breeding was outlawed by the Warlocks' Convention of 1709, everyone knows that. It's hard to stop Muggles noticing us if we're keeping dragons in the back garden – anyway, you can't tame dragons, it's dangerous. You should see the burns Charlie's got off wild ones in Romania.'

'But there aren't wild dragons in *Britain*?' said Harry.

'Of course there are,' said Ron. 'Common Welsh Green and Hebridean Blacks. The Ministry of Magic has a job hushing them up, I can tell you. Our lot have to keep putting spells on Muggles who've spotted them, to make them forget.'

'So what on earth's Hagrid up to?' said Hermione.

*

When they knocked on the door of the game-keeper's hut an hour later, they were surprised to see that all the curtains were closed. Hagrid called, 'Who is it?' before he let them in and then shut the door quickly behind them.

It was stiflingly hot inside. Even though it was such a warm day, there was a blazing fire in the grate. Hagrid made them tea and offered them stoat sandwiches, which they refused.

'So – yeh wanted to ask me somethin'?'

'Yes,' said Harry. There was no point beating about the bush. 'We were wondering if you could tell us what's guarding the Philosopher's Stone apart from Fluffy.'

Hagrid frowned at him.

'O' course I can't,' he said. 'Number one, I don' know meself. Number two, yeh know too much already, so I wouldn' tell yeh if I could. That Stone's here fer a good reason. It was almost stolen outta Gringotts – I s'ppose yeh've worked that out an' all? Beats me how yeh even know abou' Fluffy.'

'Oh, come on, Hagrid, you might not want to tell us, but you *do* know, you know everything that goes round here,' said Hermione in a warm, flattering voice. Hagrid's beard twitched and they could tell he was smiling. 'We only wondered who had *done* the guarding, really,' Hermione went on. 'We wondered who Dumbledore had trusted enough to help him, apart from you.'

Hagrid's chest swelled at these last words. Harry and Ron beamed at Hermione.

'Well, I don' s'pose it could hurt ter tell yeh that ... let's see ... he borrowed Fluffy from me ... then some o' the teachers did enchantments ... Professor Sprout – Professor Flitwick – Professor McGonagall –' he ticked them off on his fingers, 'Professor Quirrell – an' Dumbledore himself did somethin', o' course. Hang on, I've forgotten someone. Oh yeah, Professor Snape.'

'Snape?'

'Yeah – yer not still on abou' that, are yeh? Look, Snape helped *protect* the Stone, he's not about ter steal it.'

Harry knew Ron and Hermione were thinking the same as he was. If Snape had been in on protecting the Stone, it must have been easy to find out how the other teachers had guarded it. He probably knew everything – except, it seemed, Quirrell's spell and how to get past Fluffy.

'You're the only one who knows how to get past Fluffy, aren't you, Hagrid?' said Harry anxiously.

'And you wouldn't tell anyone, would you? Not even one of the teachers?'

'Not a soul knows except me an' Dumbledore,' said Hagrid proudly.

'Well, that's something,' Harry muttered to the others. 'Hagrid, can we have a window open? I'm boiling.'

'Can't, Harry, sorry,' said Hagrid. Harry noticed him glance at the fire. Harry looked at it, too.

'Hagrid – what's *that*?'

But he already knew what it was. In the very heart of the fire, underneath the kettle, was a huge, black egg.

'Ah,' said Hagrid, fiddling nervously with his beard. 'That's – er ...'

'Where did you get it, Hagrid?' said Ron, crouching over the fire to get a closer look at the egg. 'It must've cost you a fortune.'

'Won it,' said Hagrid. 'Las' night. I was down in the village havin' a few drinks an' got into a game o' cards with a stranger. Think he was quite glad ter get rid of it, ter be honest.'

'But what are you going to do with it when it's hatched?' said Hermione.

'Well, I've bin doin' some readin',' said Hagrid, pulling a large book from under his pillow. 'Got this outta the library – *Dragon-Breeding for Pleasure and Profit* – it's a bit outta date, o' course, but it's all in here. Keep the egg in the fire, 'cause their mothers breathe on 'em, see, an' when it hatches, feed it on a bucket o' brandy mixed with chicken blood every half hour. An' see here – how ter recognise diff'rent eggs – what I got there's a Norwegian Ridgeback. They're rare, them.'

He looked very pleased with himself, but Hermione didn't.

'Hagrid, you live in a *wooden house*,' she said.

But Hagrid wasn't listening. He was humming merrily as he stoked the fire.

*

So now they had something else to worry about: what might happen to Hagrid if anyone found out he was hiding an illegal dragon in his hut.

'Wonder what it's like to have a peaceful life,' Ron sighed, as evening after evening they struggled through all the extra homework they were getting. Hermione had now started making revision time-tables for Harry and Ron, too. It was driving them mad.

Then, one breakfast time, Hedwig brought Harry another note from Hagrid. He had written only two words: *It's hatching.*

Ron wanted to skip Herbology and go straight down to the hut. Hermione wouldn't hear of it.

'Hermione, how many times in our lives are we going to see a dragon hatching?'

'We've got lessons, we'll get into trouble, and that's nothing to what Hagrid's going to be in when someone finds out what he's doing –'

'Shut up!' Harry whispered.

Malfoy was only a few feet away and he had stopped dead to listen. How much had he heard? Harry didn't like the look on Malfoy's face at all.

Ron and Hermione argued all the way to Herbology, and in the end, Hermione agreed to run down to Hagrid's with the other two during morning break. When the bell sounded from the castle at the end of their lesson, the three of them dropped their trowels at once and hurried through the grounds to the edge of the Forest. Hagrid greeted them looking flushed and excited.

'It's nearly out.' He ushered them inside.

The egg was lying on the table. There were deep cracks in it. Something was moving inside; a funny clicking noise was coming from it.

They all drew their chairs up to the table and watched with bated breath.

All at once there was a scraping noise and the egg split open. The baby dragon flopped on to the table. It wasn't exactly pretty; Harry thought it looked like a crumpled, black umbrella. Its spiny wings were huge compared to its skinny jet body and it had a long snout with wide nostrils, stubs of horns and bulging, orange eyes.

It sneezed. A couple of sparks flew out of its snout.

'Isn't he *beautiful*?' Hagrid murmured. He reached out a hand to stroke the dragon's head. It snapped at his fingers, showing pointed fangs.

'Bless him, look, he knows his mummy!' said Hagrid.

'Hagrid,' said Hermione, 'how fast do Norwegian Ridgebacks grow, exactly?'

Hagrid was about to answer when the colour suddenly drained from his face – he leapt to his feet and ran to the window.

'What's the matter?'

'Someone was lookin' through the gap in the curtains – it's a kid – he's runnin' back up ter the school.'

Harry bolted to the door and looked out. Even at a distance there was no mistaking him.

Malfoy had seen the dragon.

*

Something about the smile lurking on Malfoy's face during the next week made Harry, Ron and Hermione very nervous. They spent most of their free time in Hagrid's darkened hut, trying to reason with him.

'Just let him go,' Harry urged. 'Set him free.'

'I can't,' said Hagrid. 'He's too little. He'd die.'

They looked at the dragon. It had grown three times in length in just a week. Smoke kept furling out of its nostrils. Hagrid hadn't been doing his gamekeeping duties because the dragon was keeping him so busy. There were empty brandy bottles and chicken feathers all over the floor.

'I've decided to call him Norbert,' said Hagrid, looking at the dragon with misty eyes. 'He really knows me now, watch. Norbert! Norbert! Where's Mummy?'

'He's lost his marbles,' Ron muttered in Harry's ear.

'Hagrid,' said Harry loudly, 'give it a fortnight and Norbert's going to be as long as your house. Malfoy could go to Dumbledore at any moment.'

Hagrid bit his lip.

'I – I know I can't keep him for ever, but I can't jus' dump him, I can't.'

Harry suddenly turned to Ron.

'Charlie,' he said.

'You're losing it, too,' said Ron. 'I'm Ron, remember?'

'No – Charlie – your brother Charlie. In Romania. Studying dragons. We could send Norbert to him. Charlie can take care of him and then put him back in the wild!'

'Brilliant!' said Ron. 'How about it, Hagrid?'

And in the end, Hagrid agreed that they could send an owl to Charlie to ask him.

*

The following week dragged by. Wednesday night found Hermione and Harry sitting alone in the common room, long after everyone else had gone to bed. The clock on the wall had just chimed midnight when the portrait hole burst open. Ron appeared out of nowhere as he pulled off Harry's Invisibility Cloak. He had been down at Hagrid's hut, helping him feed Norbert, who was now eating dead rats by the crate.

'It bit me!' he said, showing them his hand, which was wrapped in a bloody handkerchief. 'I'm not going to be able to hold a quill for a week. I tell you, that dragon's the most horrible animal I've ever met, but the way Hagrid goes on about it, you'd think it was a fluffy little bunny rabbit. When it bit me he told me off for frightening it. And when I left, he was singing it a lullaby.'

There was a tap on the dark window.

'It's Hedwig!' said Harry, hurrying to let her in. 'She'll have Charlie's answer!'

The three of them put their heads together to read the note.

Dear Ron,
    How are you? Thanks for the letter – I'd be glad

*to take the Norwegian Ridgeback, but it won't be easy
getting him here. I think the best thing will be to send
him over with some friends of mine who are coming to
visit me next week. Trouble is, they mustn't be seen
carrying an illegal dragon.*

*Could you get the Ridgeback up the tallest tower at
midnight on Saturday? They can meet you there and
take him away while it's still dark.*

Send me an answer as soon as possible.

Love,

Charlie

They looked at each other.

'We've got the Invisibility Cloak,' said Harry. 'It
shouldn't be too difficult – I think the Cloak's big
enough to cover two of us and Norbert.'

It was a mark of how bad the last week had been
that the other two agreed with him. Anything to
get rid of Norbert – and Malfoy.

*

There was a hitch. By next morning, Ron's bitten
hand had swollen to twice its usual size. He didn't
know whether it was safe to go to Madam Pomfrey
– would she recognise a dragon bite? By the afternoon, though, he had no choice. The cut had
turned a nasty shade of green. It looked as if
Norbert's fangs were poisonous.

Harry and Hermione rushed up to the hospital
wing at the end of the day to find Ron in a terrible
state in bed.

'It's not just my hand,' he whispered, 'although
that feels like it's about to fall off. Malfoy told
Madam Pomfrey he wanted to borrow one of my

books so he could come and have a good laugh at me. He kept threatening to tell her what really bit me – I've told her it was a dog but I don't think she believes me – I shouldn't have hit him at the Quidditch match, that's why he's doing this.'

Harry and Hermione tried to calm Ron down.

'It'll all be over at midnight on Saturday,' said Hermione, but this didn't soothe Ron at all. On the contrary, he sat bolt upright and broke into a sweat.

'Midnight on Saturday!' he said in a hoarse voice. 'Oh no – oh no – I've just remembered – Charlie's letter was in that book Malfoy took, he's going to know we're getting rid of Norbert.'

Harry and Hermione didn't get a chance to answer. Madam Pomfrey came over at that moment and made them leave, saying Ron needed sleep.

*

'It's too late to change the plan now,' Harry told Hermione. 'We haven't got time to send Charlie another owl and this could be our only chance to get rid of Norbert. We'll have to risk it. And we *have* got the Invisibility Cloak, Malfoy doesn't know about that.'

They found Fang the boarhound sitting outside with a bandaged tail when they went to tell Hagrid, who opened a window to talk to them.

'I won't let you in,' he puffed. 'Norbert's at a tricky stage – nothin' I can't handle.'

When they told him about Charlie's letter, his eyes filled with tears, although that might have been because Norbert had just bitten him on the leg.

'Aargh! It's all right, he only got my boot – jus' playin' – he's only a baby, after all.'

The baby banged its tail on the wall, making the windows rattle. Harry and Hermione walked back to the castle, feeling Saturday couldn't come quickly enough.

*

They would have felt sorry for Hagrid when the time came for him to say goodbye to Norbert if they hadn't been so worried about what they had to do. It was a very dark, cloudy night and they were a bit late arriving at Hagrid's hut because they'd had to wait for Peeves to get out of their way in the Entrance Hall, where he'd been playing tennis against the wall.

Hagrid had Norbert packed and ready in a large crate.

'He's got lots o' rats an' some brandy fer the journey,' said Hagrid in a muffled voice. 'An' I've packed his teddy bear in case he gets lonely.'

From inside the crate came ripping noises that sounded to Harry as though teddy was having his head torn off.

'Bye-bye, Norbert!' Hagrid sobbed, as Harry and Hermione covered the crate with the Invisibility Cloak and stepped underneath it themselves. 'Mummy will never forget you!'

How they managed to get the crate back up to the castle, they never knew. Midnight ticked nearer as they heaved Norbert up the marble staircase in the Entrance Hall and along the dark corridors. Up another staircase, then another – even one of Harry's short cuts didn't make the work much easier.

'Nearly there!' Harry panted as they reached the corridor beneath the tallest tower.

Then a sudden movement ahead of them made them almost drop the crate. Forgetting that they were already invisible, they shrank into the shadows, staring at the dark outlines of two people grappling with each other ten feet away. A lamp flared.

Professor McGonagall, in a tartan dressing-gown and a hairnet, had Malfoy by the ear.

'Detention!' she shouted. 'And twenty points from Slytherin! Wandering around in the middle of the night, how *dare* you –'

'You don't understand, Professor, Harry Potter's coming – he's got a dragon!'

'What utter rubbish! How dare you tell such lies! Come on – I shall see Professor Snape about you, Malfoy!'

The steep spiral staircase up to the top of the tower seemed the easiest thing in the world after that. Not until they'd stepped out into the cold night air did they throw off the Cloak, glad to be able to breathe properly again. Hermione did a sort of jig.

'Malfoy's got detention! I could sing!'

'Don't,' Harry advised her.

Chuckling about Malfoy, they waited, Norbert thrashing about in his crate. About ten minutes later, four broomsticks came swooping down out of the darkness.

Charlie's friends were a cheery lot. They showed Harry and Hermione the harness they'd rigged up, so they could suspend Norbert between them.

They all helped buckle Norbert safely into it and then Harry and Hermione shook hands with the others and thanked them very much.

At last, Norbert was going ... going ... *gone*.

They slipped back down the spiral staircase, their hearts as light as their hands, now that Norbert was off them. No more dragon – Malfoy in detention – what could spoil their happiness?

The answer to that was waiting at the foot of the stairs. As they stepped into the corridor, Filch's face loomed suddenly out of the darkness.

'Well, well, well,' he whispered, 'we *are* in trouble.'

They'd left the Invisibility Cloak on top of the tower.

— CHAPTER FIFTEEN—

The Forbidden Forest

Things couldn't have been worse.

Filch took them down to Professor McGonagall's study on the first floor, where they sat and waited without saying a word to each other. Hermione was trembling. Excuses, alibis and wild cover-up stories chased each other around Harry's brain, each more feeble than the last. He couldn't see how they were going to get out of trouble this time. They were cornered. How could they have been so stupid as to forget the Cloak? There was no reason on earth that Professor McGonagall would accept for their being out of bed and creeping around the school in the dead of night, let alone being up the tallest astronomy tower, which was out-of-bounds except for classes. Add Norbert and the Invisibility Cloak and they might as well be packing their bags already.

Had Harry thought that things couldn't have been worse? He was wrong. When Professor McGonagall appeared, she was leading Neville.

'Harry!' Neville burst out, the moment he saw the other two. 'I was trying to find you to warn you, I heard Malfoy saying he was going to catch you, he said you had a drag–'

Harry shook his head violently to shut Neville up, but Professor McGonagall had seen. She looked more likely to breathe fire than Norbert as she towered over the three of them.

'I would never have believed it of any of you. Mr Filch says you were up the astronomy tower. It's one o'clock in the morning. *Explain yourselves.*'

It was the first time Hermione had ever failed to answer a teacher's question. She was staring at her slippers, as still as a statue.

'I think I've got a good idea of what's been going on,' said Professor McGonagall. 'It doesn't take a genius to work it out. You fed Draco Malfoy some cock-and-bull story about a dragon, trying to get him out of bed and into trouble. I've already caught him. I suppose you think it's funny that Longbottom here heard the story and believed it, too?'

Harry caught Neville's eye and tried to tell him without words that this wasn't true, because Neville was looking stunned and hurt. Poor, blundering Neville – Harry knew what it must have cost him to try and find them in the dark, to warn them.

'I'm disgusted,' said Professor McGonagall. 'Four students out of bed in one night! I've never heard of such a thing before! You, Miss Granger, I thought you had more sense. As for you, Mr Potter, I thought Gryffindor meant more to you than this. All three of you will receive detentions – yes, you too, Mr Longbottom, *nothing* gives you the right to walk around school at night, especially these days, it's very dangerous – and fifty points will be taken from Gryffindor.'

'*Fifty?*' Harry gasped – they would lose the lead, the lead he'd won in the last Quidditch match.

'Fifty points *each*,' said Professor McGonagall, breathing heavily through her long pointed nose.

'Professor – please –'

'You *can't* –'

'Don't tell me what I can and can't do, Potter. Now get back to bed, all of you. I've never been more ashamed of Gryffindor students.'

A hundred and fifty points lost. That put Gryffindor in last place. In one night, they'd ruined any chance Gryffindor had had for the House Cup. Harry felt as though the bottom had dropped out of his stomach. How could they ever make up for this?

Harry didn't sleep all night. He could hear Neville sobbing into his pillow for what seemed like hours. Harry couldn't think of anything to say to comfort him. He knew Neville, like himself, was dreading the dawn. What would happen when the rest of Gryffindor found out what they'd done?

At first, Gryffindors passing the giant hour-glasses that recorded the house points next day thought there'd been a mistake. How could they suddenly have a hundred and fifty points fewer than yesterday? And then the story started to spread: Harry Potter, the famous Harry Potter, their hero of two Quidditch matches, had lost them all those points, him and a couple of other stupid first-years.

From being one of the most popular and

admired people at the school, Harry was suddenly the most hated. Even Ravenclaws and Hufflepuffs turned on him, because everyone had been longing to see Slytherin lose the House Cup. Everywhere Harry went, people pointed and didn't trouble to lower their voices as they insulted him. Slytherins, on the other hand, clapped as he walked past them, whistling and cheering, 'Thanks Potter, we owe you one!'

Only Ron stood by him.

'They'll all forget this in a few weeks. Fred and George have lost loads of points in all the time they've been here, and people still like them.'

'They've never lost a hundred and fifty points in one go, though, have they?' said Harry miserably.

'Well – no,' Ron admitted.

It was a bit late to repair the damage, but Harry swore to himself not to meddle in things that weren't his business from now on. He'd had it with sneaking around and spying. He felt so ashamed of himself that he went to Wood and offered to resign from the Quidditch team.

'*Resign?*' Wood thundered. 'What good'll that do? How are we going to get any points back if we can't win at Quidditch?'

But even Quidditch had lost its fun. The rest of the team wouldn't speak to Harry during practice, and if they had to speak about him, they called him 'the Seeker'.

Hermione and Neville were suffering, too. They didn't have as bad a time as Harry, because they weren't as well known, but nobody would speak to them either. Hermione had stopped drawing attention to herself in class, keeping her head down and working in silence.

Harry was almost glad that the exams weren't far away. All the revision he had to do kept his mind off his misery. He, Ron and Hermione kept to themselves, working late into the night, trying to remember the ingredients in complicated potions, learn charms and spells off by heart, memorise the dates of magical discoveries and goblin rebellions ...

Then, about a week before the exams were due to start, Harry's new resolution not to interfere in anything that didn't concern him was put to an unexpected test. Walking back from the library on his own one afternoon, he heard somebody whimpering from a classroom up ahead. As he drew closer, he heard Quirrell's voice.

'No – no – not again, please –'

It sounded as though someone was threatening him. Harry moved closer.

'All right – all right –' he heard Quirrell sob.

Next second, Quirrell came hurrying out of the classroom, straightening his turban. He was pale and looked as though he was about to cry. He strode out of sight; Harry didn't think Quirrell had even noticed him. He waited until Quirrell's footsteps had disappeared, then peered into the classroom. It was empty, but a door stood ajar at the other end. Harry was halfway towards it before he remembered what he'd promised himself about not meddling.

All the same, he'd have gambled twelve Philosopher's Stones that Snape had just left the room, and from what Harry had just heard, Snape would be walking with a new spring in his step – Quirrell seemed to have given in at last.

Harry went back to the library, where Hermione was testing Ron on Astronomy. Harry told them what he'd heard.

'Snape's done it, then!' said Ron. 'If Quirrell's told him how to break his Anti-Dark Force spell –'

'There's still Fluffy, though,' said Hermione.

'Maybe Snape's found out how to get past him without asking Hagrid,' said Ron, looking up at the thousands of books surrounding them. 'I bet there's a book somewhere in here, telling you how to get past a giant three-headed dog. So what do we do, Harry?'

The light of adventure was kindling again in Ron's eyes, but Hermione answered before Harry could.

'Go to Dumbledore. That's what we should have done ages ago. If we try anything ourselves we'll be thrown out for sure.'

'But we've got no *proof*!' said Harry. 'Quirrell's too scared to back us up. Snape's only got to say he doesn't know how the troll got in at Hallowe'en and that he was nowhere near the third floor – who do you think they'll believe, him or us? It's not exactly a secret we hate him, Dumbledore'll think we made it up to get him sacked. Filch wouldn't help us if his life depended on it, he's too friendly with Snape, and the more students get thrown out, the better, he'll think. And don't forget, we're not sup-posed to know about the Stone or Fluffy. That'll take a lot of explaining.'

Hermione looked convinced, but Ron didn't.

'If we just do a bit of poking around –'

'No,' said Harry flatly, 'we've done enough poking around.'

He pulled a map of Jupiter towards him and started to learn the names of its moons.

*

The following morning, notes were delivered to Harry, Hermione and Neville at the breakfast table. They were all the same:

> *Your detention will take place at eleven o'clock tonight. Meet Mr Filch in the Entrance Hall.*
> *Prof. M. McGonagall*

Harry had forgotten they still had detentions to do in the furore over the points they'd lost. He half expected Hermione to complain that this was a whole night of revision lost, but she didn't say a word. Like Harry, she felt they deserved what they'd got.

At eleven o'clock that night they said goodbye to Ron in the common room and went down to the entrance hall with Neville. Filch was already there – and so was Malfoy. Harry had also forgotten that Malfoy had got a detention, too.

'Follow me,' said Filch, lighting a lamp and leading them outside. 'I bet you'll think twice about breaking a school rule again, won't you, eh?' he continued, leering at them. 'Oh yes ... hard work and pain are the best teachers if you ask me ... It's just a pity they let the old punishments die out ... hang you by your wrists from the ceiling for a few days, I've got the chains still in my office, keep 'em well oiled in case they're ever needed ... Right, off we go, and don't think of running off, now, it'll be worse for you if you do.'

They marched off across the dark grounds. Neville kept sniffing. Harry wondered what their punishment was going to be. It must be something really horrible, or Filch wouldn't be sounding so delighted.

The moon was bright, but clouds scudding across it kept throwing them into darkness. Ahead, Harry could see the lighted windows of Hagrid's hut. Then they heard a distant shout.

'Is that you, Filch? Hurry up, I want ter get started.'

Harry's heart rose; if they were going to be working with Hagrid it wouldn't be so bad. His relief must have showed in his face, because Filch said, 'I suppose you think you'll be enjoying yourself with that oaf? Well, think again, boy – it's into the Forest you're going and I'm much mistaken if you'll all come out in one piece.'

At this, Neville let out a little moan and Malfoy stopped dead in his tracks.

'The Forest?' he repeated, and he didn't sound quite as cool as usual. 'We can't go in there at night – there's all sorts of things in there – werewolves, I heard.'

Neville clutched the sleeve of Harry's robe and made a choking noise.

'That's your lookout, isn't it?' said Filch, his voice cracking with glee. 'Should've thought of them werewolves before you got in trouble, shouldn't you?'

Hagrid came striding towards them out of the dark, Fang at his heel. He was carrying his large crossbow, and a quiver of arrows hung over his shoulder.

'Abou' time,' he said. 'I bin waitin' fer half an hour already. All right, Harry, Hermione?'

'I shouldn't be too friendly to them, Hagrid,' said Filch coldly, 'they're here to be punished, after all.'

'That's why yer late, is it?' said Hagrid, frowning at Filch. 'Bin lecturin' them, eh? 'Snot your place ter do that. Yeh've done yer bit, I'll take over from here.'

'I'll be back at dawn,' said Filch, 'for what's left of them,' he added nastily, and he turned and started back towards the castle, his lamp bobbing away in the darkness.

Malfoy now turned to Hagrid.

'I'm not going in that Forest,' he said, and Harry was pleased to hear the note of panic in his voice.

'Yeh are if yeh want ter stay at Hogwarts,' said Hagrid fiercely. 'Yeh've done wrong an' now yeh've got ter pay fer it.'

'But this is servant stuff, it's not for students to do. I thought we'd be writing lines or something. If my father knew I was doing this, he'd –'

'– tell yer that's how it is at Hogwarts,' Hagrid growled. 'Writin' lines! What good's that ter anyone? Yeh'll do summat useful or yeh'll get out. If yeh think yer father'd rather you were expelled, then get back off ter the castle an' pack. Go on!'

Malfoy didn't move. He looked at Hagrid furiously but then dropped his gaze.

'Right then,' said Hagrid, 'now, listen carefully,

'cause it's dangerous what we're gonna do tonight an' I don' want no one takin' risks. Follow me over here a moment.'

He led them to the very edge of the Forest. Holding his lamp up high he pointed down a narrow, winding earth track that disappeared into the thick black trees. A light breeze lifted their hair as they looked into the Forest.

'Look there,' said Hagrid, 'see that stuff shinin' on the ground? Silvery stuff? That's unicorn blood. There's a unicorn in there bin hurt badly by summat. This is the second time in a week. I found one dead last Wednesday. We're gonna try an' find the poor thing. We might have ter put it out of its misery.'

'And what if whatever hurt the unicorn finds us first?' said Malfoy, unable to keep the fear out of his voice.

'There's nothin' that lives in the Forest that'll hurt yeh if yer with me or Fang,' said Hagrid. 'An' keep ter the path. Right, now, we're gonna split inter two parties an' follow the trail in diff'rent directions. There's blood all over the place, it must've bin staggerin' around since last night at least.'

'I want Fang,' said Malfoy quickly, looking at Fang's long teeth.

'All right, but I warn yeh, he's a coward,' said Hagrid. 'So me, Harry an' Hermione'll go one way an' Draco, Neville an' Fang'll go the other. Now, if any of us finds the unicorn, we'll send up green sparks, right? Get yer wands out an' practise now – that's it – an' if anyone gets in trouble, send up red sparks, an' we'll all come an' find yeh – so, be careful – let's go.'

The Forest was black and silent. A little way into it they reached a fork in the earth path and Harry, Hermione and Hagrid took the left path while Malfoy, Neville and Fang took the right.

They walked in silence, their eyes on the ground. Every now and then a ray of moonlight through the branches above lit a spot of silver blue blood on the fallen leaves.

Harry saw that Hagrid looked very worried.

'*Could* a werewolf be killing the unicorns?' Harry asked.

'Not fast enough,' said Hagrid. 'It's not easy ter catch a unicorn, they're powerful magic creatures. I never knew one ter be hurt before.'

They walked past a mossy tree-stump. Harry could hear running water; there must be a stream somewhere close by. There were still spots of unicorn blood here and there along the winding path.

'You all right, Hermione?' Hagrid whispered. 'Don' worry, it can't've gone far if it's this badly hurt an' then we'll be able ter – GET BEHIND THAT TREE!'

Hagrid seized Harry and Hermione and hoisted them off the path behind a towering oak. He pulled out an arrow and fitted it into his crossbow, raising it, ready to fire. The three of them listened. Something was slithering over dead leaves nearby: it sounded like a cloak trailing along the ground. Hagrid was squinting up the dark path, but after a few seconds, the sound faded away.

'I knew it,' he murmured. 'There's summat in here that shouldn' be.'

'A werewolf?' Harry suggested.

'That wasn' no werewolf an' it wasn' no unicorn, neither,' said Hagrid grimly. 'Right, follow me, but careful, now.'

They walked more slowly, ears straining for the faintest sound. Suddenly, in a clearing ahead, something definitely moved.

'Who's there?' Hagrid called. 'Show yerself – I'm armed!'

And into the clearing came – was it a man, or a horse? To the waist, a man, with red hair and beard, but below that was a horse's gleaming chestnut body with a long, reddish tail. Harry and Hermione's jaws dropped.

'Oh, it's you, Ronan,' said Hagrid in relief. 'How are yeh?'

He walked forward and shook the centaur's hand.

'Good evening to you, Hagrid,' said Ronan. He had a deep, sorrowful voice. 'Were you going to shoot me?'

'Can't be too careful, Ronan,' said Hagrid, patting his crossbow. 'There's summat bad loose in this Forest. This is Harry Potter an' Hermione Granger, by the way. Students up at the school. An' this is Ronan, you two. He's a centaur.'

'We'd noticed,' said Hermione faintly.

'Good evening,' said Ronan. 'Students, are you? And do you learn much, up at the school?'

'Erm –'

'A bit,' said Hermione timidly.

'A bit. Well, that's something.' Ronan sighed. He flung back his head and stared at the sky. 'Mars is bright tonight.'

'Yeah,' said Hagrid, glancing up too. 'Listen, I'm glad we've run inter yeh, Ronan, 'cause there's a unicorn bin hurt – you seen anythin'?'

Ronan didn't answer immediately. He stared unblinkingly upwards, then sighed again.

'Always the innocent are the first victims,' he said. 'So it has been for ages past, so it is now.'

'Yeah,' said Hagrid, 'but have yeh seen anythin', Ronan? Anythin' unusual?'

'Mars is bright tonight,' Ronan repeated while Hagrid watched him impatiently. 'Unusually bright.'

'Yeah, but I was meanin' anythin' unusual a bit nearer home,' said Hagrid. 'So yeh haven't noticed anythin' strange?'

Yet again, Ronan took a while to answer. At last, he said, 'The Forest hides many secrets.'

A movement in the trees behind Ronan made Hagrid raise his bow again, but it was only a second centaur, black-haired and -bodied and wilder-looking than Ronan.

'Hullo, Bane,' said Hagrid. 'All right?'

'Good evening, Hagrid, I hope you are well?'

'Well enough. Look, I've jus' bin askin' Ronan, you seen anythin' odd in here lately? Only there's a unicorn bin injured – would yeh know anythin' about it?'

Bane walked over to stand next to Ronan. He looked skywards.

'Mars is bright tonight,' he said simply.

'We've heard,' said Hagrid grumpily. 'Well, if either of you do see anythin', let me know, won't yeh? We'll be off, then.'

Harry and Hermione followed him out of the clearing, staring over their shoulders at Ronan and Bane until the trees blocked their view.

'Never,' said Hagrid irritably, 'try an' get a straight answer out of a centaur. Ruddy star-gazers. Not interested in anythin' closer'n the moon.'

'Are there many of *them* in here?' asked Hermione.

'Oh, a fair few ... Keep themselves to themselves mostly, but they're good enough about turnin' up if ever I want a word. They're deep, mind, centaurs ... they know things ... jus' don' let on much.'

'D'you think that was a centaur we heard earlier?' said Harry.

'Did that sound like hooves to you? Nah, if yeh ask me, that was what's bin killin' the unicorns – never heard anythin' like it before.'

They walked on through the dense, dark trees. Harry kept looking nervously over his shoulder. He had the nasty feeling they were being watched. He was very glad they had Hagrid and his crossbow with them. They had just passed a bend in the path when Hermione grabbed Hagrid's arm.

'Hagrid! Look! Red sparks, the others are in trouble!'

'You two wait here!' Hagrid shouted. 'Stay on the path, I'll come back for yeh!'

They heard him crashing away through the undergrowth and stood looking at each other, very scared, until they couldn't hear anything but the rustling of leaves around them.

'You don't think they've been hurt, do you?' whispered Hermione.

'I don't care if Malfoy has, but if something's got Neville ... It's our fault he's here in the first place.'

The minutes dragged by. Their ears seemed sharper than usual. Harry's seemed to be picking up every sigh of the wind, every cracking twig. What was going on? Where were the others?

At last, a great crunching noise announced Hagrid's return. Malfoy, Neville and Fang were with him. Hagrid was fuming. Malfoy, it seemed, had sneaked up behind Neville and grabbed him for a joke. Neville had panicked and sent up the sparks.

'We'll be lucky ter catch anythin' now, with the racket you two were makin'. Right, we're changin' groups – Neville, you stay with me an' Hermione, Harry, you go with Fang an' this idiot. I'm sorry,' Hagrid added in a whisper to Harry, 'but he'll have a harder time frightenin' you, an' we've gotta get this done.'

So Harry set off into the heart of the Forest with Malfoy and Fang. They walked for nearly half an hour, deeper and deeper into the Forest, until the path became almost impossible to follow because the trees were so thick. Harry thought the blood seemed to be getting thicker. There were splashes on the roots of a tree, as though the poor creature had been thrashing around in pain close by. Harry could see a clearing ahead, through the tangled branches of an ancient oak.

'Look –' he murmured, holding out his arm to stop Malfoy.

Something bright white was gleaming on the ground. They inched closer.

It was the unicorn all right, and it was dead. Harry had never seen anything so beautiful and sad. Its long slender legs were stuck out at odd angles where it had fallen and its mane was spread pearly white on the dark leaves.

Harry had taken one step towards it when a slithering sound made him freeze where he stood. A bush on the edge of the clearing quivered ... Then, out of the shadows, a hooded figure came crawling across the ground like some stalking beast. Harry, Malfoy and Fang stood transfixed. The cloaked figure reached the unicorn, it lowered its head over the wound in the animal's side, and began to drink its blood.

'AAAAAAAAAAARGH!'

Malfoy let out a terrible scream and bolted – so did Fang. The hooded figure raised its head and looked right at Harry – unicorn blood was dribbling down its front. It got to its feet and came swiftly towards him – he couldn't move for fear.

Then a pain pierced his head like he'd never felt before, it was as though his scar was on fire – half-blinded, he staggered backwards. He heard hooves behind him, galloping, and something jumped clean over him, charging at the figure.

The pain in Harry's head was so bad he fell to his knees. It took a minute or two to pass. When he looked up, the figure had gone. A centaur was standing over him, not Ronan or Bane; this one looked younger; he had white-blond hair and a palomino body.

'Are you all right?' said the centaur, pulling Harry to his feet.

'Yes – thank you – what *was* that?'

The centaur didn't answer. He had astonishingly blue eyes, like pale sapphires. He looked carefully at Harry, his eyes lingering on the scar which stood out, livid, on Harry's forehead.

'You are the Potter boy,' he said. 'You had better get back to Hagrid. The Forest is not safe at this time – especially for you. Can you ride? It will be quicker this way.

'My name is Firenze,' he added, as he lowered himself on to his front legs so that Harry could clamber on to his back.

There was suddenly a sound of more galloping from the other side of the clearing. Ronan and Bane came bursting through the trees, their flanks heaving and sweaty.

'Firenze!' Bane thundered. 'What are you doing? You have a human on your back! Have you no shame? Are you a common mule?'

'Do you realise who this is?' said Firenze. 'This is the Potter boy. The quicker he leaves this Forest, the better.'

'What have you been telling him?' growled Bane. 'Remember, Firenze, we are sworn not to set ourselves against the heavens. Have we not read what is to come in the movements of the planets?'

Ronan pawed the ground nervously.

'I'm sure Firenze thought he was acting for the best,' he said, in his gloomy voice.

Bane kicked his back legs in anger.

'For the best! What is that to do with us?

Centaurs are concerned with what has been fore-told! It is not our business to run around like donkeys after stray humans in our Forest!'

Firenze suddenly reared on to his hind legs in anger, so that Harry had to grab his shoulders to stay on.

'Do you not see that unicorn?' Firenze bellowed at Bane. 'Do you not understand why it was killed? Or have the planets not let you in on that secret? I set myself against what is lurking in this Forest, Bane, yes, with humans alongside me if I must.'

And Firenze whisked around; with Harry clutching on as best he could, they plunged off into the trees, leaving Ronan and Bane behind them.

Harry didn't have a clue what was going on.

'Why's Bane so angry?' he asked. 'What was that thing you saved me from, anyway?'

Firenze slowed to a walk, warned Harry to keep his head bowed in case of low-hanging branches but did not answer Harry's question. They made their way through the trees in silence for so long that Harry thought Firenze didn't want to talk to him any more. They were passing through a particularly dense patch of trees, however, when Firenze suddenly stopped.

'Harry Potter, do you know what unicorn blood is used for?'

'No,' said Harry, startled by the odd question. 'We've only used the horn and tail-hair in Potions.'

'That is because it is a monstrous thing, to slay a unicorn,' said Firenze. 'Only one who has nothing to lose, and everything to gain, would commit such a crime. The blood of a unicorn will keep you alive, even if you are an inch from death, but at a terrible price. You have slain something pure and defence-less to save yourself and you will have but a half life, a cursed life, from the moment the blood touches your lips.'

Harry stared at the back of Firenze's head, which was dappled silver in the moonlight.

'But who'd be that desperate?' he wondered aloud. 'If you're going to be cursed for ever, death's better, isn't it?'

'It is,' Firenze agreed, 'unless all you need is to stay alive long enough to drink something else – something that will bring you back to full strength and power – something that will mean you can never die. Mr Potter, do you know what is hidden in the school at this very moment?'

'The Philosopher's Stone! Of course – the Elixir of Life! But I don't understand who –'

'Can you think of nobody who has waited many years to return to power, who has clung to life, awaiting their chance?'

It was as though an iron fist had clenched sud-denly around Harry's heart. Over the rustling of the trees, he seemed to hear once more what Hagrid had told him on the night they had met: 'Some say he died. Codswallop, in my opinion. Dunno if he had enough human left in him to die.'

'Do you mean,' Harry croaked, 'that was *Vol–*'

'Harry! Harry, are you all right?'

Hermione was running towards them down the path, Hagrid puffing along behind her.

'I'm fine,' said Harry, hardly knowing what he was saying. 'The unicorn's dead, Hagrid, it's in that clearing back there.'

'This is where I leave you,' Firenze murmured as Hagrid hurried off to examine the unicorn. 'You are safe now.'

Harry slid off his back.

'Good luck, Harry Potter,' said Firenze. 'The planets have been read wrongly before now, even by centaurs. I hope this is one of those times.'

He turned and cantered back into the depths of the Forest, leaving Harry shivering behind him.

*

Ron had fallen asleep in the dark common room, waiting for them to return. He shouted something about Quidditch fouls when Harry roughly shook him awake. In a matter of seconds, though, he was wide-eyed as Harry began to tell him and Hermione what had happened in the Forest.

Harry couldn't sit down. He paced up and down in front of the fire. He was still shaking.

'Snape wants the stone for Voldemort ... and Voldemort's waiting in the Forest ... and all this time we thought Snape just wanted to get rich ...'

'Stop saying the name!' said Ron in a terrified whisper, as if he thought Voldemort could hear them.

Harry wasn't listening.

'Firenze saved me, but he shouldn't have done ... Bane was furious ... he was talking about interfering with what the planets say is going to happen ... They must show that Voldemort's coming back ... Bane thinks Firenze should have let Voldemort kill me ... I suppose that's written in the stars as well.'

'*Will you stop saying the name!*' Ron hissed.

'So all I've got to wait for now is Snape to steal

the Stone,' Harry went on feverishly, 'then Voldemort will be able to come and finish me off ... Well, I suppose Bane'll be happy.'

Hermione looked very frightened, but she had a word of comfort.

'Harry, everyone says Dumbledore's the only one You-Know-Who was ever afraid of. With Dumbledore around, You-Know-Who won't touch you. Anyway, who says the centaurs are right? It sounds like fortune-telling to me, and Professor McGonagall says that's a very imprecise branch of magic.'

The sky had turned light before they stopped talking. They went to bed exhausted, their throats sore. But the night's surprises weren't over.

When Harry pulled back his sheets, he found his Invisibility Cloak folded neatly underneath them. There was a note pinned to it:

Just in case.

— CHAPTER SIXTEEN —

Through the Trapdoor

In years to come, Harry would never quite remember how he had managed to get through his exams when he half expected Voldemort to come bursting through the door at any moment. Yet the days crept by and there could be no doubt that Fluffy was still alive and well behind the locked door.

It was swelteringly hot, especially in the large classroom where they did their written papers. They had been given special, new quills for the exams, which had been bewitched with an Anti-Cheating spell.

They had practical exams as well. Professor Flitwick called them one by one into his class to see if they could make a pineapple tap-dance across a desk. Professor McGonagall watched them turn a mouse into a snuff-box – points were given for how pretty the snuff-box was, but taken away if it had whiskers. Snape made them all nervous, breathing down their necks while they tried to remember how to make a Forgetfulness Potion.

Harry did the best he could, trying to ignore the stabbing pains in his forehead which had been bothering him ever since his trip into the Forest. Neville thought Harry had a bad case of exam nerves because Harry couldn't sleep, but the truth was that Harry kept being woken by his old nightmare, except that it was now worse than ever because there was a hooded figure dripping blood in it.

Maybe it was because they hadn't seen what Harry had seen in the Forest, or because they didn't have scars burning on their foreheads, but Ron and Hermione didn't seem as worried about the Stone as Harry. The idea of Voldemort certainly scared them, but he didn't keep visiting them in dreams, and they were so busy with their revision they didn't have much time to fret about what Snape or anyone else might be up to.

Their very last exam was History of Magic. One hour of answering questions about batty old wizards who'd invented self-stirring cauldrons and they'd be free, free for a whole wonderful week until their exam results came out. When the ghost of Professor Binns told them to put down their quills and roll up their parchment, Harry couldn't help cheering with the rest.

'That was far easier than I thought it would be,' said Hermione, as they joined the crowds flocking out into the sunny grounds. 'I needn't have learnt about the 1637 Werewolf Code of Conduct or the uprising of Elfric the Eager.'

Hermione always liked to go through their exam papers afterwards, but Ron said this made him feel ill, so they wandered down to the lake and flopped under a tree. The Weasley twins and Lee Jordan were tickling the tentacles of a giant squid, which was basking in the warm shallows.

'No more revision,' Ron sighed happily, stretching out on the grass. 'You could look more cheerful, Harry, we've got a week before we find out how badly we've done, there's no need to worry yet.'

Harry was rubbing his forehead.

'I wish I knew what this *means*!' he burst out angrily. 'My scar keeps hurting – it's happened before, but never as often as this.'

'Go to Madam Pomfrey,' Hermione suggested.

'I'm not ill,' said Harry. 'I think it's a warning ... it means danger's coming ...'

Ron couldn't get worked up, it was too hot.

'Harry, relax, Hermione's right, the Stone's safe as long as Dumbledore's around. Anyway, we've never had any proof Snape found out how to get past Fluffy. He nearly had his leg ripped off once, he's not going to try it again in a hurry. And Neville will play Quidditch for England before Hagrid lets Dumbledore down.'

Harry nodded, but he couldn't shake off a lurking feeling that there was something he'd forgotten to do, something important. When he tried to explain this, Hermione said, 'That's just the exams. I woke up last night and was halfway through my Transfiguration notes before I remembered we'd done that one.'

Harry was quite sure the unsettled feeling didn't have anything to do with work, though. He watched an owl flutter towards the school across the bright blue sky, a note clamped in its mouth. Hagrid was the only one who ever sent him letters. Hagrid would never betray Dumbledore. Hagrid would never tell anyone how to get past Fluffy ... never ... but –

Harry suddenly jumped to his feet.

'Where're you going?' said Ron sleepily.

'I've just thought of something,' said Harry. He had gone white. 'We've got to go and see Hagrid, now.'

'Why?' panted Hermione, hurrying to keep up.

'Don't you think it's a bit odd,' said Harry, scrambling up the grassy slope, 'that what Hagrid wants more than anything else is a dragon, and a stranger turns up who just happens to have an egg in his pocket? How many people wander around with dragon eggs if it's against wizard law? Lucky they found Hagrid, don't you think? Why didn't I see it before?'

'What are you on about?' said Ron, but Harry, sprinting across the grounds towards the Forest, didn't answer.

Hagrid was sitting in an armchair outside his house; his trousers and sleeves were rolled up and he was shelling peas into a large bowl.

'Hullo,' he said, smiling. 'Finished yer exams? Got time fer a drink?'

'Yes, please,' said Ron, but Harry cut across him.

'No, we're in a hurry. Hagrid, I've got to ask you something. You know that night you won Norbert? What did the stranger you were playing cards with look like?'

'Dunno,' said Hagrid casually, 'he wouldn' take his cloak off.'

He saw the three of them look stunned and raised his eyebrows.

'It's not that unusual, yeh get a lot o' funny folk in the Hog's Head – that's one of the pubs down in the village. Mighta bin a dragon dealer, mightn' he? I never saw his face, he kept his hood up.'

Harry sank down next to the bowl of peas.

'What did you talk to him about, Hagrid? Did you mention Hogwarts at all?'

'Mighta come up,' said Hagrid, frowning as he tried to remember. 'Yeah ... he asked what I did, an' I told him I was gamekeeper here ... He asked a bit about the sorta creatures I look after ... so I told him ... an' I said what I'd always really wanted was a dragon ... an' then ... I can' remember too well, 'cause he kept buyin' me drinks ... Let's see ... yeah, then he said he had the dragon egg an' we could play cards fer it if I wanted ... but he had ter be sure I could handle it, he didn' want it ter go ter any old home ... So I told him, after Fluffy, a dragon would be easy ...'

'And did he – did he seem interested in Fluffy?' Harry asked, trying to keep his voice calm.

'Well – yeah – how many three-headed dogs d'yeh meet, even around Hogwarts? So I told him, Fluffy's a piece o' cake if yeh know how to calm him down, jus' play him a bit o' music an' he'll go straight off ter sleep –'

Hagrid suddenly looked horrified.

'I shouldn'ta told yeh that!' he blurted out. 'Forget I said it! Hey – where're yeh goin'?'

Harry, Ron and Hermione didn't speak to each other at all until they came to a halt in the Entrance Hall, which seemed very cold and gloomy after the grounds.

'We've got to go to Dumbledore,' said Harry. 'Hagrid told that stranger how to get past Fluffy and it was either Snape or Voldemort under that cloak – it must've been easy, once he'd got Hagrid drunk. I just hope Dumbledore believes us. Firenze might back us up if Bane doesn't stop him. Where's Dumbledore's office?'

They looked around, as if hoping to see a sign pointing them in the right direction. They had never been told where Dumbledore lived, nor did they know anyone who had been sent to see him.

'We'll just have to –' Harry began, but a voice suddenly rang across the hall.

'What are you three doing inside?'

It was Professor McGonagall, carrying a large pile of books.

'We want to see Professor Dumbledore,' said Hermione, rather bravely, Harry and Ron thought.

'See Professor Dumbledore?' Professor McGonagall repeated, as though this was a very fishy thing to want to do. 'Why?'

Harry swallowed – now what?

'It's sort of secret,' he said, but he wished at once he hadn't, because Professor McGonagall's nostrils flared.

'Professor Dumbledore left ten minutes ago,' she said coldly. 'He received an urgent owl from the Ministry of Magic and flew off for London at once.'

'He's *gone*?' said Harry frantically. '*Now?*'

'Professor Dumbledore is a very great wizard, Potter, he has many demands on his time –'

'But this is important.'

'Something you have to say is more important than the Ministry of Magic, Potter?'

'Look,' said Harry, throwing caution to the winds,

'Professor – it's about the Philosopher's Stone –'

Whatever Professor McGonagall had expected, it wasn't that. The books she was carrying tumbled out of her arms but she didn't pick them up.

'How do you know –?' she spluttered.

'Professor, I think – I *know* – that Sn– that someone's going to try and steal the Stone. I've got to talk to Professor Dumbledore.'

She eyed him with a mixture of shock and suspicion.

'Professor Dumbledore will be back tomorrow,' she said finally. 'I don't know how you found out about the Stone, but rest assured, no one can possibly steal it, it's too well protected.'

'But Professor –'

'Potter, I know what I'm talking about,' she said shortly. She bent down and gathered up the fallen books. 'I suggest you all go back outside and enjoy the sunshine.'

But they didn't.

'It's tonight,' said Harry, once he was sure Professor McGonagall was out of earshot. 'Snape's going through the trapdoor tonight. He's found out everything he needs and now he's got Dumbledore out of the way. He sent that note, I bet the Ministry of Magic will get a real shock when Dumbledore turns up.'

'But what can we –'

Hermione gasped. Harry and Ron wheeled round. Snape was standing there.

'Good afternoon,' he said smoothly.

They stared at him.

'You shouldn't be inside on a day like this,' he

said, with an odd, twisted smile.

'We were —' Harry began, without any idea what he was going to say.

'You want to be more careful,' said Snape. 'Hanging around like this, people will think you're up to something. And Gryffindor really can't afford to lose any more points, can they?'

Harry flushed. They turned to go back outside, but Snape called them back.

'Be warned, Potter – any more night-time wanderings and I will personally make sure you are expelled. Good day to you.'

He strode off in the direction of the staff room.

Out on the stone steps, Harry turned to the others.

'Right, here's what we've got to do,' he whispered urgently. 'One of us has got to keep an eye on Snape – wait outside the staff room and follow him if he leaves it. Hermione, you'd better do that.'

'Why me?'

'It's obvious,' said Ron. 'You can pretend to be waiting for Professor Flitwick, you know.' He put on a high voice, 'Oh Professor Flitwick, I'm so worried, I think I got question fourteen·b wrong ...'

'Oh, shut up,' said Hermione, but she agreed to go and watch out for Snape.

'And we'd better stay outside the third-floor corridor,' Harry told Ron. 'Come on.'

But that part of the plan didn't work. No sooner had they reached the door separating Fluffy from the rest of the school than Professor McGonagall turned up again, and this time, she lost her temper.

'I suppose you think you're harder to get past

than a pack of enchantments!' she stormed. 'Enough of this nonsense! If I hear you've come anywhere near here again, I'll take another fifty points from Gryffindor! Yes, Weasley, from my own house!'

Harry and Ron went back to the common room. Harry had just said, 'At least Hermione's on Snape's tail,' when the portrait of the Fat Lady swung open and Hermione came in.

'I'm sorry, Harry!' she wailed. 'Snape came out and asked me what I was doing, so I said I was waiting for Flitwick, and Snape went to get him, and I've only just got away. I don't know where Snape went.'

'Well, that's it then, isn't it?' Harry said.

The other two stared at him. He was pale and his eyes were glittering.

'I'm going out of here tonight and I'm going to try and get to the Stone first.'

'You're mad!' said Ron.

'You can't!' said Hermione. 'After what McGonagall and Snape have said? You'll be expelled!'

'SO WHAT?' Harry shouted. 'Don't you understand? If Snape gets hold of the Stone, Voldemort's coming back! Haven't you heard what it was like when he was trying to take over? There won't be any Hogwarts to get expelled from! He'll flatten it, or turn it into a school for the Dark Arts! Losing points doesn't matter any more, can't you see? D'you think he'll leave you and your families alone if Gryffindor win the House Cup? If I get caught before I can get to the Stone, well, I'll have to go back to the Dursleys and wait for Voldemort to find me there. It's only dying a bit later than I would have done, because I'm never going over to the Dark Side! I'm going through that trapdoor tonight and nothing you two say is going to stop me! Voldemort killed my parents, remember?'

He glared at them.

'You're right, Harry,' said Hermione in a small voice.

'I'll use the Invisibility Cloak,' said Harry. 'It's just lucky I got it back.'

'But will it cover all three of us?' said Ron.

'All – all three of us?'

'Oh, come off it, you don't think we'd let you go alone?'

'Of course not,' said Hermione briskly. 'How do you think you'd get to the Stone without us? I'd better go and look through my books, there might be something useful ...'

'But if we get caught, you two will be expelled, too.'

'Not if I can help it,' said Hermione grimly. 'Flitwick told me in secret that I got a hundred and twelve per cent on his exam. They're not throwing me out after that.'

*

After dinner the three of them sat nervously apart in the common room. Nobody bothered them; none of the Gryffindors had anything to say to Harry any more, after all. This was the first night he hadn't been upset by it. Hermione was skimming through all her notes, hoping to come across one of the enchantments they were about to try and break. Harry and Ron didn't talk much. Both of them were thinking about what they were about to do.

Slowly, the room emptied as people drifted off to bed.

'Better get the Cloak,' Ron muttered, as Lee Jordan finally left, stretching and yawning. Harry ran upstairs to their dark dormitory. He pulled out the Cloak and then his eyes fell on the flute Hagrid had given him for Christmas. He pocketed it to use on Fluffy – he didn't feel much like singing.

He ran back down to the common room.

'We'd better put the Cloak on here, and make sure it covers all three of us – if Filch spots one of our feet wandering along on its own –'

'What are you doing?' said a voice from the corner of the room. Neville appeared from behind an armchair, clutching Trevor the toad, who looked as though he'd been making another bid for freedom.

'Nothing, Neville, nothing,' said Harry, hurriedly putting the Cloak behind his back.

Neville stared at their guilty faces.

'You're going out again,' he said.

'No, no, no,' said Hermione. 'No, we're not. Why don't you go to bed, Neville?'

Harry looked at the grandfather clock by the door. They couldn't afford to waste any more time, Snape might even now be playing Fluffy to sleep.

'You can't go out,' said Neville, 'you'll be caught again. Gryffindor will be in even more trouble.'

'You don't understand,' said Harry, 'this is important.'

But Neville was clearly steeling himself to do something desperate.

'I won't let you do it,' he said, hurrying to stand in front of the portrait hole. 'I'll – I'll fight you!'

'Neville,' Ron exploded, 'get away from that hole and don't be an idiot –'

'Don't you call me an idiot!' said Neville. 'I don't think you should be breaking any more rules! And you were the one who told me to stand up to people!'

'Yes, but not to *us*,' said Ron in exasperation. 'Neville, you don't know what you're doing.'

He took a step forward and Neville dropped Trevor the toad, who leapt out of sight.

'Go on then, try and hit me!' said Neville, raising his fists. 'I'm ready!'

Harry turned to Hermione.

'*Do something,*' he said desperately.

Hermione stepped forward.

'Neville,' she said, 'I'm really, really sorry about this.'

She raised her wand.

'*Petrificus Totalus!*' she cried, pointing it at Neville.

Neville's arms snapped to his sides. His legs sprang together. His whole body rigid, he swayed where he stood and then fell flat on his face, stiff as a board.

Hermione ran to turn him over. Neville's jaws were jammed together so he couldn't speak. Only his eyes were moving, looking at them in horror.

'What've you done to him?' Harry whispered.

'It's the full Body-Bind,' said Hermione miserably. 'Oh, Neville, I'm so sorry.'

'We had to, Neville, no time to explain,' said Harry.

'You'll understand later, Neville,' said Ron, as they

stepped over him and pulled on the Invisibility Cloak.

But leaving Neville lying motionless on the floor didn't feel like a very good omen. In their nervous state, every statue's shadow looked like Filch, every distant breath of wind sounded like Peeves swooping down on them.

At the foot of the first set of stairs, they spotted Mrs Norris skulking near the top.

'Oh, let's kick her, just this once,' Ron whispered in Harry's ear, but Harry shook his head. As they climbed carefully around her, Mrs Norris turned her lamp-like eyes on them, but didn't do anything.

They didn't meet anyone else until they reached the staircase up to the third floor. Peeves was bobbing halfway up, loosening the carpet so that people would trip.

'Who's there?' he said suddenly as they climbed towards him. He narrowed his wicked black eyes. 'Know you're there, even if I can't see you. Are you ghoulie or ghostie or wee student beastie?'

He rose up in the air and floated there, squinting at them.

'Should call Filch, I should, if something's a-creeping around unseen.'

Harry had a sudden idea.

'Peeves,' he said, in a hoarse whisper, 'the Bloody Baron has his own reasons for being invisible.'

Peeves almost fell out of the air in shock. He caught himself in time and hovered about a foot off the stairs.

'So sorry, your bloodiness, Mr Baron, sir,' he said greasily. 'My mistake, my mistake – I didn't see you

– of course I didn't, you're invisible – forgive old Peevsie his little joke, sir.'

'I have business here, Peeves,' croaked Harry. 'Stay away from this place tonight.'

'I will, sir, I most certainly will,' said Peeves, rising up in the air again. 'Hope your business goes well, Baron, I'll not bother you.'

And he scooted off.

'*Brilliant*, Harry!' whispered Ron.

A few seconds later, they were there, outside the third-floor corridor – and the door was already ajar.

'Well, there you are,' Harry said quietly. 'Snape's already got past Fluffy.'

Seeing the open door somehow seemed to impress upon all three of them what was facing them. Underneath the Cloak, Harry turned to the other two.

'If you want to go back, I won't blame you,' he said. 'You can take the Cloak, I won't need it now.'

'Don't be stupid,' said Ron.

'We're coming,' said Hermione.

Harry pushed the door open.

As the door creaked, low, rumbling growls met their ears. All three of the dog's noses sniffed madly in their direction, even though it couldn't see them.

'What's that at its feet?' Hermione whispered.

'Looks like a harp,' said Ron. 'Snape must have left it there.'

'It must wake up the moment you stop playing,' said Harry. 'Well, here goes ...'

He put Hagrid's flute to his lips and blew. It wasn't really a tune, but from the first note the beast's eyes began to droop. Harry hardly drew breath. Slowly, the dog's growls ceased – it tottered on its paws and fell to its knees, then it slumped to the ground, fast asleep.

'Keep playing,' Ron warned Harry as they slipped out of the Cloak and crept towards the trapdoor. They could feel the dog's hot, smelly breath as they approached the giant heads.

'I think we'll be able to pull the door open,' said Ron, peering over the dog's back. 'Want to go first, Hermione?'

'No, I don't!'

'All right.' Ron gritted his teeth and stepped carefully over the dog's legs. He bent and pulled the ring of the trapdoor, which swung up and open.

'What can you see?' Hermione said anxiously.

'Nothing – just black – there's no way of climbing down, we'll just have to drop.'

Harry, who was still playing the flute, waved at Ron to get his attention and pointed at himself.

'You want to go first? Are you sure?' said Ron. 'I don't know how deep this thing goes. Give the flute to Hermione so she can keep him asleep.'

Harry handed the flute over. In the few seconds' silence, the dog growled and twitched, but the moment Hermione began to play, it fell back into its deep sleep.

Harry climbed over it and looked down through the trapdoor. There was no sign of the bottom.

He lowered himself through the hole until he was hanging on by his fingertips. Then he looked up at Ron and said, 'If anything happens to me, don't follow. Go straight to the owlery and send Hedwig to Dumbledore, right?'

'Right,' said Ron.

'See you in a minute, I hope ...'

And Harry let go. Cold, damp air rushed past him as he fell down, down, down and –

FLUMP. With a funny, muffled sort of thump he landed on something soft. He sat up and felt around, his eyes not used to the gloom. It felt as though he was sitting on some sort of plant.

'It's OK!' he called up to the light the size of a postage stamp which was the open trapdoor. 'It's a soft landing, you can jump!'

Ron followed straight away. He landed sprawled next to Harry.

'What's this stuff?' were his first words.

'Dunno, sort of plant thing. I suppose it's here to break the fall. Come on, Hermione!'

The distant music stopped. There was a loud bark from the dog, but Hermione had already jumped. She landed on Harry's other side.

'We must be miles under the school,' she said.

'Lucky this plant thing's here, really,' said Ron.

'*Lucky!*' shrieked Hermione. 'Look at you both!'

She leapt up and struggled towards a damp wall. She had to struggle because the moment she had landed, the plant had started to twist snake-like tendrils around her ankles. As for Harry and Ron, their legs had already been bound tightly in long creepers without their noticing.

Hermione had managed to free herself before the plant got a firm grip on her. Now she watched in horror as the two boys fought to pull the plant off them, but the more they strained against it, the tighter and faster the plant wound around them.

'Stop moving!' Hermione ordered them. 'I know what this is – it's Devil's Snare!'

'Oh, I'm so glad we know what it's called, that's a great help,' snarled Ron, leaning back, trying to stop the plant curling around his neck.

'Shut up, I'm trying to remember how to kill it!' said Hermione.

'Well, hurry up, I can't breathe!' Harry gasped, wrestling with it as it curled around his chest.

'Devil's Snare, Devil's Snare ... What did Professor Sprout say? It likes the dark and the damp –'

'So light a fire!' Harry choked.

'Yes – of course – but there's no wood!' Hermione cried, wringing her hands.

'HAVE YOU GONE MAD?' Ron bellowed. 'ARE YOU A WITCH OR NOT?'

'Oh, right!' said Hermione, and she whipped out her wand, waved it, muttered something and sent a jet of the same bluebell flames she had used on Snape at the plant. In a matter of seconds, the two boys felt it loosening its grip as it cringed away from the light and warmth. Wriggling and flailing, it unravelled itself from their bodies and they were able to pull free.

'Lucky you pay attention in Herbology, Hermione,' said Harry as he joined her by the wall, wiping sweat off his face.

'Yeah,' said Ron, 'and lucky Harry doesn't lose his head in a crisis – "there's no wood", *honestly*.'

'This way,' said Harry, pointing down a stone passageway which was the only way on.

All they could hear apart from their footsteps was the gentle drip of water trickling down the walls.

The passageway sloped downwards and Harry was reminded of Gringotts. With an unpleasant jolt of the heart, he remembered the dragons said to be guarding vaults in the wizards' bank. If they met a dragon, a fully grown dragon – Norbert had been bad enough ...

'Can you hear something?' Ron whispered.

Harry listened. A soft rustling and clinking seemed to be coming from up ahead.

'Do you think it's a ghost?'

'I don't know ... sounds like wings to me.'

'There's light ahead – I can see something moving.'

They reached the end of the passageway and saw before them a brilliantly lit chamber, its ceiling arching high above them. It was full of small, jewel-bright birds, fluttering and tumbling all around the room. On the opposite side of the chamber was a heavy, wooden door.

'Do you think they'll attack us if we cross the room?' said Ron.

'Probably,' said Harry. 'They don't look very vicious, but I suppose if they all swooped down at once ... Well, there's nothing for it ... I'll run.'

He took a deep breath, covered his face with his arms and sprinted across the room. He expected to feel sharp beaks and claws tearing at him any second, but nothing happened. He reached the door untouched. He pulled the handle, but it was locked.

The other two followed him. They tugged and heaved at the door, but it wouldn't budge, not even when Hermione tried her Alohomora Charm.

'Now what?' said Ron.

'These birds ... they can't be here just for decoration,' said Hermione.

They watched the birds soaring overhead, glittering – *glittering*?

'They're not birds!' Harry said suddenly, 'they're *keys*! Winged keys – look carefully. So that must mean ...' he looked around the chamber while the other two squinted up at the flock of keys. '... Yes – look! Broomsticks! We've got to catch the key to the door!'

'But there are *hundreds* of them!'

Ron examined the lock on the door.

'We're looking for a big, old-fashioned one – probably silver, like the handle.'

They seized a broomstick each and kicked off into the air, soaring into the midst of the cloud of keys. They grabbed and snatched but the bewitched keys darted and dived so quickly it was almost impossible to catch one.

Not for nothing, though, was Harry the youngest Seeker in a century. He had a knack for spotting things other people didn't. After a minute's weaving about through the whirl of rainbow feathers, he noticed a large silver key that had a bent wing, as if it had already been caught and stuffed roughly into the keyhole.

'That one!' he called to the others. 'That big one – there – no, there – with bright blue wings – the feathers are all crumpled on one side.'

Ron went speeding in the direction that Harry was pointing, crashed into the ceiling and nearly fell off his broom.

'We've got to close in on it!' Harry called, not

taking his eyes off the key with the damaged wing. 'Ron, you come at it from above – Hermione, stay below and stop it going down – and I'll try and catch it. Right, NOW!'

Ron dived, Hermione rocketed upwards, the key dodged them both and Harry streaked after it; it sped towards the wall, Harry leant forward and with a nasty crunching noise, pinned it against the stone with one hand. Ron and Hermione's cheers echoed around the high chamber.

They landed quickly and Harry ran to the door, the key struggling in his hand. He rammed it into the lock and turned – it worked. The moment the lock had clicked open, the key took flight again, looking very battered now that it had been caught twice.

'Ready?' Harry asked the other two, his hand on the door handle. They nodded. He pulled the door open.

The next chamber was so dark they couldn't see anything at all. But as they stepped into it, light suddenly flooded the room to reveal an astonishing sight.

They were standing on the edge of a huge chessboard, behind the black chessmen, which were all taller than they were and carved from what looked like black stone. Facing them, way across the chamber, were the white pieces. Harry, Ron and Hermione shivered slightly – the towering white chessmen had no faces.

'Now what do we do?' Harry whispered.

'It's obvious, isn't it?' said Ron. 'We've got to play our way across the room.'

Behind the white pieces they could see another door.

'How?' said Hermione nervously.

'I think,' said Ron, 'we're going to have to be chessmen.'

He walked up to a black knight and put his hand out to touch the knight's horse. At once, the stone sprang to life. The horse pawed the ground and the knight turned his helmeted head to look down at Ron.

'Do we – er – have to join you to get across?'

The black knight nodded. Ron turned to the other two.

'This wants thinking about ...' he said. 'I suppose we've got to take the place of three of the black pieces ...'

Harry and Hermione stayed quiet, watching Ron think. Finally he said, 'Now, don't be offended or anything, but neither of you are that good at chess –'

'We're not offended,' said Harry quickly. 'Just tell us what to do.'

'Well, Harry, you take the place of that bishop, and Hermione, you go next to him instead of that castle.'

'What about you?'

'I'm going to be a knight,' said Ron.

The chessmen seemed to have been listening, because at these words a knight, a bishop and a castle turned their backs on the white pieces and walked off the board leaving three empty squares which Harry, Ron and Hermione took.

'White always plays first in chess,' said Ron, peering across the board. 'Yes ... look ...'

A white pawn had moved forward two squares.

Ron started to direct the black pieces. They moved silently wherever he sent them. Harry's knees were trembling. What if they lost?

'Harry – move diagonally four squares to the right.'

Their first real shock came when their other knight was taken. The white queen smashed him to the floor and dragged him off the board, where he lay quite still, face down.

'Had to let that happen,' said Ron, looking shaken. 'Leaves you free to take that bishop, Hermione, go on.'

Every time one of their men was lost, the white pieces showed no mercy. Soon there was a huddle of limp black players slumped along the wall. Twice, Ron only just noticed in time that Harry and Hermione were in danger. He himself darted around the board taking almost as many white pieces as they had lost black ones.

'We're nearly there,' he muttered suddenly. 'Let me think – let me think ...'

The white queen turned her blank face towards him.

'Yes ...' said Ron softly, 'it's the only way ... I've got to be taken.'

'NO!' Harry and Hermione shouted.

'That's chess!' snapped Ron. 'You've got to make some sacrifices! I take one step forward and she'll take me – that leaves you free to checkmate the king, Harry!'

'But –'

'Do you want to stop Snape or not?'

'Ron –'

'Look, if you don't hurry up, he'll already have the Stone!'

There was nothing else for it.

'Ready?' Ron called, his face pale but determined. 'Here I go – now, don't hang around once you've won.'

He stepped forward and the white queen pounced. She struck Ron hard around the head with her stone arm and he crashed to the floor – Hermione screamed but stayed on her square – the white queen dragged Ron to one side. He looked as if he'd been knocked out.

Shaking, Harry moved three spaces to the left.

The white king took off his crown and threw it at Harry's feet. They had won. The chessmen parted and bowed, leaving the door ahead clear. With one last desperate look back at Ron, Harry and Hermione charged through the door and up the next passageway.

'What if he's –?'

'He'll be all right,' said Harry, trying to convince himself. 'What do you reckon's next?'

'We've had Sprout's, that was the Devil's Snare – Flitwick must've put charms on the keys – McGonagall transfigured the chessmen to make them alive – that leaves Quirrell's spell, and Snape's ...'

They had reached another door.

'All right?' Harry whispered.

'Go on.'

Harry pushed it open.

A disgusting smell filled their nostrils, making both of them pull their robes up over their noses.

Eyes watering, they saw, flat on the floor in front of them, a troll even larger than the one they had tackled, out cold with a bloody lump on its head.

'I'm glad we didn't have to fight that one,' Harry whispered, as they stepped carefully over one of its massive legs. 'Come on, I can't breathe.'

He pulled open the next door, both of them hardly daring to look at what came next – but there was nothing very frightening in here, just a table with seven differently shaped bottles standing on it in a line.

'Snape's,' said Harry. 'What do we have to do?'

They stepped over the threshold and immediately a fire sprang up behind them in the doorway. It wasn't ordinary fire either; it was purple. At the same instant, black flames shot up in the doorway leading onwards. They were trapped.

'Look!' Hermione seized a roll of paper lying next to the bottles. Harry looked over her shoulder to read it:

Danger lies before you, while safety lies behind,
Two of us will help you, whichever you would find,
One among us seven will let you move ahead,
Another will transport the drinker back instead,
Two among our number hold only nettle wine,
Three of us are killers, waiting hidden in line.
Choose, unless you wish to stay here for evermore,
To help you in your choice, we give you these clues four:
First, however slyly the poison tries to hide
You will always find some on nettle wine's left side;
Second, different are those who stand at either end,

*But if you would move onwards, neither is your
friend;
Third, as you see clearly, all are different size,
Neither dwarf nor giant holds death in their insides;
Fourth, the second left and the second on the right
Are twins once you taste them, though different at
first sight.*

Hermione let out a great sigh and Harry, amazed,
saw that she was smiling, the very last thing he felt
like doing.

'*Brilliant,*' said Hermione. 'This isn't magic – it's
logic – a puzzle. A lot of the greatest wizards haven't
got an ounce of logic, they'd be stuck in here for
ever.'

'But so will we, won't we?'

'Of course not,' said Hermione. 'Everything we
need is here on this paper. Seven bottles: three are
poison; two are wine; one will get us safely through
the black fire and one will get us back through the
purple.'

'But how do we know which to drink?'

'Give me a minute.'

Hermione read the paper several times. Then she
walked up and down the line of bottles, muttering
to herself and pointing at them. At last, she clapped
her hands.

'Got it,' she said. 'The smallest bottle will get us
through the black fire – towards the Stone.'

Harry looked at the tiny bottle.

'There's only enough there for one of us,' he said.
'That's hardly one swallow.'

They looked at each other.

'Which one will get you back through the purple flames?'

Hermione pointed at a rounded bottle at the right end of the line.

'You drink that,' said Harry. 'No, listen – get back and get Ron – grab brooms from the flying-key room, they'll get you out of the trapdoor and past Fluffy – go straight to the owlery and send Hedwig to Dumbledore, we need him. I might be able to hold Snape off for a while, but I'm no match for him really.'

'But Harry – what if You-Know-Who's with him?'

'Well – I was lucky once, wasn't I?' said Harry, pointing at his scar. 'I might get lucky again.'

Hermione's lip trembled and she suddenly dashed at Harry and threw her arms around him.

'*Hermione!*'

'Harry – you're a great wizard, you know.'

'I'm not as good as you,' said Harry, very embarrassed, as she let go of him.

'Me!' said Hermione. 'Books! And cleverness! There are more important things – friendship and bravery and – oh Harry – be *careful*!'

'You drink first,' said Harry. 'You are sure which is which, aren't you?'

'Positive,' said Hermione. She took a long drink from the round bottle at the end and shuddered.

'It's not poison?' said Harry anxiously.

'No – but it's like ice.'

'Quick, go, before it wears off.'

'Good luck – take care –'

'GO!'

Hermione turned and walked straight through the

purple fire.

Harry took a deep breath and picked up the smallest bottle. He turned to face the black flames.

'Here I come,' he said and he drained the little bottle in one gulp.

It was indeed as though ice was flooding his body. He put the bottle down and walked forward; he braced himself, saw the black flames licking his body but couldn't feel them – for a moment he could see nothing but dark fire – then he was on the other side, in the last chamber.

There was already someone there – but it wasn't Snape. It wasn't even Voldemort.

CHAPTER SEVENTEEN

The Man with Two Faces

It was Quirrell.

'*You!*' gasped Harry.

Quirrell smiled. His face wasn't twitching at all.

'Me,' he said calmly. 'I wondered whether I'd be meeting you here, Potter.'

'But I thought – Snape –'

'Severus?' Quirrell laughed and it wasn't his usual quivering treble, either, but cold and sharp. 'Yes, Severus does seem the type, doesn't he? So useful to have him swooping around like an overgrown bat. Next to him, who would suspect p-p-poor st-stuttering P-Professor Quirrell?'

Harry couldn't take it in. This couldn't be true, it couldn't.

'But Snape tried to kill me!'

'No, no, no. *I* tried to kill you. Your friend Miss Granger accidentally knocked me over as she rushed to set fire to Snape at that Quidditch match. She broke my eye contact with you. Another few seconds and I'd have got you off that broom. I'd have managed it before then if Snape hadn't been muttering a counter-curse, trying to save you.'

'Snape was trying to *save* me?'

'Of course,' said Quirrell coolly. 'Why do you think he wanted to referee your next match? He was trying to make sure I didn't do it again. Funny, really ... he needn't have bothered. I couldn't do anything with Dumbledore watching. All the other teachers thought Snape was trying to stop Gryffindor winning, he *did* make himself unpopular ... and what a waste of time, when after all that, I'm going to kill you tonight.'

Quirrell snapped his fingers. Ropes sprang out of thin air and wrapped themselves tightly around Harry.

'You're too nosy to live, Potter. Scurrying around the school at Hallowe'en like that, for all I knew you'd seen me coming to look at what was guarding the Stone.'

'*You* let the troll in?'

'Certainly. I have a special gift with trolls – you must have seen what I did to the one in the chamber back there? Unfortunately, while everyone else was running around looking for it, Snape, who already suspected me, went straight to the third floor to head me off – and not only did my troll fail to beat you to death, that three-headed dog didn't even manage to bite Snape's leg off properly.

'Now, wait quietly, Potter. I need to examine this interesting mirror.'

It was only then that Harry realised what was standing behind Quirrell. It was the Mirror of Erised.

'This mirror is the key to finding the Stone,'

Quirrell murmured, tapping his way around the frame. 'Trust Dumbledore to come up with something like this ... but he's in London ... I'll be far away by the time he gets back ...'

All Harry could think of doing was to keep Quirrell talking and stop him concentrating on the Mirror.

'I saw you and Snape in the Forest –' he blurted out.

'Yes,' said Quirrell idly, walking around the Mirror to look at the back. 'He was on to me by that time, trying to find out how far I'd got. He suspected me all along. Tried to frighten me – as though he could, when I had Lord Voldemort on my side ...'

Quirrell came back out from behind the Mirror and stared hungrily into it.

'I see the Stone ... I'm presenting it to my master ... but where is it?'

Harry struggled against the ropes binding him, but they didn't give. He *had* to keep Quirrell from giving his whole attention to the Mirror.

'But Snape always seemed to hate me so much.'

'Oh, he does,' said Quirrell casually, 'heavens, yes. He was at Hogwarts with your father, didn't you know? They loathed each other. But he never wanted you *dead*.'

'But I heard you a few days ago, sobbing – I thought Snape was threatening you ...'

For the first time, a spasm of fear flitted across Quirrell's face.

'Sometimes,' he said, 'I find it hard to follow my master's instructions – he is a great wizard and I am weak –'

'You mean he was there in the classroom with you?' Harry gasped.

'He is with me wherever I go,' said Quirrell quietly. 'I met him when I travelled around the world. A foolish young man I was then, full of ridiculous ideas about good and evil. Lord Voldemort showed me how wrong I was. There is no good and evil, there is only power, and those too weak to seek it ... Since then, I have served him faithfully, although I have let him down many times. He has had to be very hard on me.' Quirrell shivered suddenly. 'He does not forgive mistakes easily. When I failed to steal the Stone from Gringotts, he was most displeased. He punished me ... decided he would have to keep a closer watch on me ...'

Quirrell's voice tailed away. Harry was remembering his trip to Diagon Alley – how could he have been so stupid? He'd *seen* Quirrell there that very day, shaken hands with him in the Leaky Cauldron.

Quirrell cursed under his breath.

'I don't understand ... is the Stone *inside* the Mirror? Should I break it?'

Harry's mind was racing.

What I want more than anything else in the world at the moment, he thought, is to find the Stone before Quirrell does. So if I look in the Mirror, I should see myself finding it – which means I'll see where it's hidden! But how can I look without Quirrell realising what I'm up to?

He tried to edge to the left, to get in front of the glass without Quirrell noticing, but the ropes around his ankles were too tight: he tripped and fell over. Quirrell ignored him. He was still talking to himself.

'What does this mirror do? How does it work? Help me, Master!'

And to Harry's horror, a voice answered, and the voice seemed to come from Quirrell himself.

'Use the boy ... Use the boy ...'

Quirrell rounded on Harry.

'Yes – Potter – come here.'

He clapped his hands once and the ropes binding Harry fell off. Harry got slowly to his feet.

'Come here,' Quirrell repeated. 'Look in the Mirror and tell me what you see.'

Harry walked towards him.

'I must lie,' he thought desperately. 'I must look and lie about what I see, that's all.'

Quirrell moved close behind him. Harry breathed in the funny smell that seemed to come from Quirrell's turban. He closed his eyes, stepped in front of the Mirror and opened them again.

He saw his reflection, pale and scared-looking at first. But a moment later, the reflection smiled at him. It put its hand into its pocket and pulled out a blood-red stone. It winked and put the Stone back in its pocket – and as it did so, Harry felt something heavy drop into his real pocket. Somehow – incredibly – *he'd got the Stone*.

'Well?' said Quirrell impatiently. 'What do you see?'

Harry screwed up his courage.

'I see myself shaking hands with Dumbledore,' he invented. 'I – I've won the House Cup for Gryffindor.'

Quirrell cursed again.

'Get out of the way,' he said. As Harry moved aside he felt the Philosopher's Stone against his leg. Dare he make a break for it?

But he hadn't walked five paces before a high voice spoke, though Quirrell wasn't moving his lips.

'He lies ... He lies ...'

'Potter, come back here!' Quirrell shouted. 'Tell me the truth! What did you just see?'

The high voice spoke again.

'Let me speak to him ... face to face ...'

'Master, you are not strong enough!'

'I have strength enough ... for this ...'

Harry felt as if Devil's Snare was rooting him to the spot. He couldn't move a muscle. Petrified, he watched as Quirrell reached up and began to unwrap his turban. What was going on? The turban fell away. Quirrell's head looked strangely small without it. Then he turned slowly on the spot.

Harry would have screamed, but he couldn't make a sound. Where there should have been a back to Quirrell's head, there was a face, the most terrible face Harry had ever seen. It was chalk white with glaring red eyes and slits for nostrils, like a snake.

'Harry Potter ...' it whispered.

Harry tried to take a step backwards but his legs wouldn't move.

'See what I have become?' the face said. 'Mere shadow and vapour ... I have form only when I can share another's body ... but there have always been those willing to let me into their hearts and minds

... Unicorn blood has strengthened me, these past weeks ... you saw faithful Quirrell drinking it for me in the Forest ... and once I have the Elixir of Life, I will be able to create a body of my own ... Now ... why don't you give me that Stone in your pocket?'

So he knew. The feeling suddenly surged back into Harry's legs. He stumbled backwards.

'Don't be a fool,' snarled the face. 'Better save your own life and join me ... or you'll meet the same end as your parents ... They died begging me for mercy ...'

'LIAR!' Harry shouted suddenly.

Quirrell was walking backwards at him, so that Voldemort could still see him. The evil face was now smiling.

'How touching ...' it hissed. 'I always value bravery ... Yes, boy, your parents were brave ... I killed your father first and he put up a courageous fight ... but your mother needn't have died ... she was trying to protect you ... Now give me the Stone, unless you want her to have died in vain.'

'NEVER!'

Harry sprang towards the flame door, but Voldemort screamed, 'SEIZE HIM!' and, next second, Harry felt Quirrell's hand close on his wrist. At once, a needle-sharp pain seared across Harry's scar; his head felt as though it was about to split in two; he yelled, struggling with all his might, and to his surprise, Quirrell let go of him. The pain in his head lessened – he looked around wildly to see where Quirrell had gone and saw him hunched in pain, looking at his fingers – they were blistering before his eyes.

'Seize him! SEIZE HIM!' shrieked Voldemort again and Quirrell lunged, knocking Harry clean off his feet, landing on top of him, both hands around Harry's neck – Harry's scar was almost blinding him with pain, yet he could see Quirrell howling in agony.

'Master, I cannot hold him – my hands – my hands!'

And Quirrell, though pinning Harry to the ground with his knees, let go of his neck and stared, bewildered, at his own palms – Harry could see they looked burnt, raw, red and shiny.

'Then kill him, fool, and be done!' screeched Voldemort.

Quirrell raised his hand to perform a deadly curse, but Harry, by instinct, reached up and grabbed Quirrell's face –

'AAAARGH!'

Quirrell rolled off him, his face blistering too, and then Harry knew: Quirrell couldn't touch his bare skin, not without suffering terrible pain – his only chance was to keep hold of Quirrell, keep him in enough pain to stop him doing a curse.

Harry jumped to his feet, caught Quirrell by the arm and hung on as tight as he could. Quirrell screamed and tried to throw Harry off – the pain in Harry's head was building – he couldn't see – he could only hear Quirrell's terrible shrieks and Voldemort's yells of 'KILL HIM! KILL HIM!' and other voices, maybe in Harry's own head, crying, 'Harry! Harry!'

He felt Quirrell's arm wrenched from his grasp, knew all was lost, and fell into blackness, down ... down ... down ...

*

Something gold was glinting just above him. The Snitch! He tried to catch it, but his arms were too heavy.

He blinked. It wasn't the Snitch at all. It was a pair of glasses. How strange.

He blinked again. The smiling face of Albus Dumbledore swam into view above him.

'Good afternoon, Harry,' said Dumbledore.

Harry stared at him. Then he remembered. 'Sir! The Stone! It was Quirrell! He's got the Stone! Sir, quick –'

'Calm yourself, dear boy, you are a little behind the times,' said Dumbledore. 'Quirrell does not have the Stone.'

'Then who does? Sir, I –'

'Harry, please relax, or Madam Pomfrey will have me thrown out.'

Harry swallowed and looked around him. He realised he must be in the hospital wing. He was lying in a bed with white linen sheets and next to him was a table piled high with what looked like half the sweet-shop.

'Tokens from your friends and admirers,' said Dumbledore, beaming. 'What happened down in the dungeons between you and Professor Quirrell is a complete secret, so, naturally, the whole school knows. I believe your friends Misters Fred and George Weasley were responsible for trying to send you a lavatory seat. No doubt they thought it would amuse you. Madam Pomfrey, however, felt it might not be very hygienic, and confiscated it.'

'How long have I been in here?'

'Three days. Mr Ronald Weasley and Miss Granger will be most relieved you have come round, they have been extremely worried.'

'But sir, the Stone –'

'I see you are not to be distracted. Very well, the Stone. Professor Quirrell did not manage to take it from you. I arrived in time to prevent that, although you were doing very well on your own, I must say.'

'You got there? You got Hermione's owl?'

'We must have crossed in mid-air. No sooner had I reached London than it became clear to me that the place I should be was the one I had just left. I arrived just in time to pull Quirrell off you –'

'It was *you*.'

'I feared I might be too late.'

'You nearly were, I couldn't have kept him off the Stone much longer –'

'Not the Stone, boy, you – the effort involved nearly killed you. For one terrible moment there, I was afraid it had. As for the Stone, it has been destroyed.'

'Destroyed?' said Harry blankly. 'But your friend – Nicolas Flamel –'

'Oh, you know about Nicolas?' said Dumbledore, sounding quite delighted. 'You *did* do the thing properly, didn't you? Well, Nicolas and I have had a little chat and agreed it's all for the best.'

'But that means he and his wife will die, won't they?'

'They have enough Elixir stored to set their affairs in order and then, yes, they will die.'

Dumbledore smiled at the look of amazement on Harry's face.

'To one as young as you, I'm sure it seems incredible, but to Nicolas and Perenelle, it really is like going to bed after a very, *very* long day. After all, to the well-organised mind, death is but the next great adventure. You know, the Stone was really not such a wonderful thing. As much money and life as you could want! The two things most human beings would choose above all – the trouble is, humans do have a knack of choosing precisely those things which are worst for them.'

Harry lay there, lost for words. Dumbledore hummed a little and smiled at the ceiling.

'Sir?' said Harry. 'I've been thinking ... Sir – even if the Stone's gone, Vol– ... I mean, You-Know-Who –'

'Call him Voldemort, Harry. Always use the proper name for things. Fear of a name increases fear of the thing itself.'

'Yes, sir. Well, Voldemort's going to try other ways of coming back, isn't he? I mean, he hasn't gone, has he?'

'No, Harry, he has not. He is still out there somewhere, perhaps looking for another body to share ... not being truly alive, he cannot be killed. He left Quirrell to die; he shows just as little mercy to his followers as his enemies. Nevertheless, Harry, while you may only have delayed his return to power, it will merely take someone else who is prepared to fight what seems a losing battle next time – and if he is delayed again, and again, why, he may never return to power.'

Harry nodded, but stopped quickly, because it made his head hurt. Then he said, 'Sir, there are some other things I'd like to know, if you can tell me ... things I want to know the truth about ...'

'The truth.' Dumbledore sighed. 'It is a beautiful and terrible thing, and should therefore be treated with great caution. However, I shall answer your questions unless I have a very good reason not to, in which case I beg you'll forgive me. I shall not, of course, lie.'

'Well ... Voldemort said that he only killed my mother because she tried to stop him killing me. But why would he want to kill me in the first place?'

Dumbledore sighed very deeply this time.

'Alas, the first thing you ask me, I cannot tell you. Not today. Not now. You will know, one day ... put it from your mind for now, Harry. When you are older ... I know you hate to hear this ... when you are ready, you will know.'

And Harry knew it would be no good to argue.

'But why couldn't Quirrell touch me?'

'Your mother died to save you. If there is one thing Voldemort cannot understand, it is love. He didn't realise that love as powerful as your mother's for you leaves its own mark. Not a scar, no visible sign ... to have been loved so deeply, even though the person who loved us is gone, will give us some protection for ever. It is in your very skin. Quirrell, full of hatred, greed and ambition, sharing his soul with Voldemort, could not touch you for this reason. It was agony to touch a person marked by something so good.'

Dumbledore now became very interested in a bird out on the window-sill, which gave Harry time to dry his eyes on the sheet. When he had found his voice again, Harry said, 'And the Invisibility Cloak – do you know who sent it to me?'

'Ah – your father happened to leave it in my possession and I thought you might like it.' Dumbledore's eyes twinkled. 'Useful things ... your father used it mainly for sneaking off to the kitchens to steal food when he was here.'

'And there's something else ...'

'Fire away.'

'Quirrell said Snape –'

'*Professor* Snape, Harry.'

'Yes, him – Quirrell said he hates me because he hated my father. Is that true?'

'Well, they did rather detest each other. Not unlike yourself and Mr Malfoy. And then, your father did something Snape could never forgive.'

'What?'

'He saved his life.'

'*What?*'

'Yes ...' said Dumbledore dreamily. 'Funny, the way people's minds work, isn't it? Professor Snape couldn't bear being in your father's debt ... I do believe he worked so hard to protect you this year because he felt that would make him and your father quits. Then he could go back to hating your father's memory in peace ...'

Harry tried to understand this but it made his head pound, so he stopped.

'And sir, there's one more thing ...'

'Just the one?'

'How did I get the Stone out of the Mirror?'

'Ah, now, I'm glad you asked me that. It was one of my more brilliant ideas, and between you and me, that's saying something. You see, only one who wanted to *find* the Stone – find it, but not use it – would be able to get it, otherwise they'd just see themselves making gold or drinking Elixir of Life. My brain surprises even me sometimes ... Now, enough questions. I suggest you make a start on these sweets. Ah! Bertie Bott's Every-Flavour Beans! I was unfortunate enough in my youth to come across a vomit-flavoured one, and since then I'm afraid I've rather lost my liking for them – but I think I'll be safe with a nice toffee, don't you?'

He smiled and popped the golden-brown bean into his mouth. Then he choked and said, 'Alas! Earwax!'

*

Madam Pomfrey, the matron, was a nice woman, but very strict.

'Just five minutes,' Harry pleaded.

'Absolutely not.'

'You let Professor Dumbledore in ...'

'Well, of course, that was the Headmaster, quite different. You need *rest*.'

'I am resting, look, lying down and everything. Oh, go on, Madam Pomfrey ...'

'Oh, very well,' she said. 'But five minutes *only*.'

And she let Ron and Hermione in.

'*Harry!*'

Hermione looked ready to fling her arms around him again, but Harry was glad she held herself in as his head was still very sore.

'Oh, Harry, we were sure you were going to – Dumbledore was so worried –'

'The whole school's talking about it,' said Ron. 'What *really* happened?'

It was one of those rare occasions when the true story is even more strange and exciting than the wild rumours. Harry told them everything: Quirrell; the Mirror; the Stone and Voldemort. Ron and Hermione were a very good audience; they gasped in all the right places and, when Harry told them what was under Quirrell's turban, Hermione screamed out loud.

'So the Stone's gone?' said Ron finally. 'Flamel's just going to *die*?'

'That's what I said, but Dumbledore thinks that – what was it? – "to the well-organised mind, death is but the next great adventure".'

'I always said he was off his rocker,' said Ron, looking quite impressed at how mad his hero was.

'So what happened to you two?' said Harry.

'Well, I got back all right,' said Hermione. 'I brought Ron round – that took a while – and we were dashing up to the owlery to contact Dumbledore when we met him in the Entrance Hall. He already knew – he just said, "Harry's gone after him, hasn't he?" and hurtled off to the third floor.'

'D'you think he meant you to do it?' said Ron. 'Sending you your father's Cloak and everything?'

'*Well*,' Hermione exploded, 'if he did – I mean to say – that's terrible – you could have been killed.'

'No, it isn't,' said Harry thoughtfully. 'He's a funny man, Dumbledore. I think he sort of wanted to give me a chance. I think he knows more or less everything that goes on here, you know. I reckon he had a pretty good idea we were going to try, and instead of stopping us, he just taught us enough to help. I don't think it was an accident he let me find out how the Mirror worked. It's almost like he thought I had the right to face Voldemort if I could ...'

'Yeah, Dumbledore's barking, all right,' said Ron proudly. 'Listen, you've got to be up for the end-of-year feast tomorrow. The points are all in and Slytherin won, of course – you missed the last Quidditch match, we were steamrollered by Ravenclaw without you – but the food'll be good.'

At that moment, Madam Pomfrey bustled over.

'You've had nearly fifteen minutes, now OUT,' she said firmly.

*

After a good night's sleep, Harry felt nearly back to normal.

'I want to go to the feast,' he told Madam Pomfrey as she straightened his many sweet-boxes. 'I can, can't I?'

'Professor Dumbledore says you are to be allowed to go,' she said sniffily, as though in her opinion Professor Dumbledore didn't realise how risky feasts could be. 'And you have another visitor.'

'Oh good,' said Harry. 'Who is it?'

Hagrid sidled through the door as he spoke. As usual when he was indoors, Hagrid looked too big to be allowed. He sat down next to Harry, took one look at him and burst into tears.

'It's – all – my – ruddy – fault!' he sobbed, his face in his hands. 'I told the evil git how ter get past

Fluffy! I told him! It was the only thing he didn't know an' I told him! Yeh could've died! All fer a dragon egg! I'll never drink again! I should be chucked out an' made ter live as a Muggle!'

'Hagrid!' said Harry, shocked to see Hagrid shaking with grief and remorse, great tears leaking down into his beard. 'Hagrid, he'd have found out somehow, this is Voldemort we're talking about, he'd have found out even if you hadn't told him.'

'Yeh could've died!' sobbed Hagrid. 'An' don' say the name!'

'VOLDEMORT!' Harry bellowed, and Hagrid was so shocked, he stopped crying. 'I've met him and I'm calling him by his name. Please cheer up, Hagrid, we saved the Stone, it's gone, he can't use it. Have a Chocolate Frog, I've got loads ...'

Hagrid wiped his nose on the back of his hand and said, 'That reminds me. I've got yeh a present.'

'It's not a stoat sandwich, is it?' said Harry anxiously and at last Hagrid gave a weak chuckle.

'Nah. Dumbledore gave me the day off yesterday ter fix it. 'Course, he shoulda sacked me instead – anyway, got yeh this ...'

It seemed to be a handsome, leather-covered book. Harry opened it curiously. It was full of wizard photographs. Smiling and waving at him from every page were his mother and father.

'Sent owls off ter all yer parents' old school friends, askin' fer photos ... Knew yeh didn' have any ... D'yeh like it?'

Harry couldn't speak, but Hagrid understood.

*

Harry made his way down to the end-of-year feast

alone that night. He had been held up by Madam Pomfrey's fussing-about, insisting on giving him one last check-up, so the Great Hall was already full. It was decked out in the Slytherin colours of green and silver to celebrate Slytherin's winning the House Cup for the seventh year in a row. A huge banner showing the Slytherin serpent covered the wall behind the High Table.

When Harry walked in there was a sudden hush and then everybody started talking loudly at once. He slipped into a seat between Ron and Hermione at the Gryffindor table and tried to ignore the fact that people were standing up to look at him.

Fortunately, Dumbledore arrived moments later. The babble died away.

'Another year gone!' Dumbledore said cheerfully. 'And I must trouble you with an old man's wheezing waffle before we sink our teeth into our delicious feast. What a year it has been! Hopefully your heads are all a little fuller than they were ... you have the whole summer ahead to get them nice and empty before next year starts ...

'Now, as I understand it, the House Cup here needs awarding and the points stand thus: in fourth place, Gryffindor, with three hundred and twelve points; in third, Hufflepuff, with three hundred and fifty-two; Ravenclaw have four hundred and twenty-six and Slytherin, four hundred and seventy-two.'

A storm of cheering and stamping broke out from the Slytherin table. Harry could see Draco Malfoy banging his goblet on the table. It was a sickening sight.

'Yes, yes, well done, Slytherin,' said Dumbledore. 'However, recent events must be taken into account.'

The room went very still. The Slytherins' smiles faded a little.

'Ahem,' said Dumbledore. 'I have a few last-minute points to dish out. Let me see. Yes ...

'First – to Mr Ronald Weasley ...'

Ron went purple in the face; he looked like a radish with bad sunburn.

'... for the best-played game of chess Hogwarts has seen in many years, I award Gryffindor house fifty points.'

Gryffindor cheers nearly raised the bewitched ceiling; the stars overhead seemed to quiver. Percy could be heard telling the other Prefects, 'My brother, you know! My youngest brother! Got past McGonagall's giant chess set!'

At last there was silence again.

'Second – to Miss Hermione Granger ... for the use of cool logic in the face of fire, I award Gryffindor house fifty points.'

Hermione buried her face in her arms; Harry strongly suspected she had burst into tears. Gryffindors up and down the table were beside themselves – they were a hundred points up.

'Third – to Mr Harry Potter ...' said Dumbledore. The room went deadly quiet. '... for pure nerve and outstanding courage, I award Gryffindor house sixty points.'

The din was deafening. Those who could add up while yelling themselves hoarse knew that Gryffindor now had four hundred and seventy-two points – exactly the same as Slytherin. They had drawn for the House Cup – if only Dumbledore had given Harry just one more point.

Dumbledore raised his hand. The room gradually fell silent.

'There are all kinds of courage,' said Dumbledore, smiling. 'It takes a great deal of bravery to stand up to our enemies, but just as much to stand up to our friends. I therefore award ten points to Mr Neville Longbottom.'

Someone standing outside the Great Hall might well have thought some sort of explosion had taken place, so loud was the noise that erupted from the Gryffindor table. Harry, Ron and Hermione stood up to yell and cheer as Neville, white with shock, disappeared under a pile of people hugging him. He had never won so much as a point for Gryffindor before. Harry, still cheering, nudged Ron in the ribs and pointed at Malfoy, who couldn't have looked more stunned and horrified if he'd just had the Body-Bind curse put on him.

'Which means,' Dumbledore called over the storm of applause, for even Ravenclaw and Hufflepuff were celebrating the downfall of Slytherin, 'we need a little change of decoration.'

He clapped his hands. In an instant, the green hangings became scarlet and the silver became gold; the huge Slytherin serpent vanished and a towering Gryffindor lion took its place. Snape was shaking Professor McGonagall's hand, with a horrible forced smile. He caught Harry's eye and Harry knew at once that Snape's feelings towards him hadn't changed one jot. This didn't worry Harry. It seemed as though life would be back to normal next year, or as normal as it ever was at Hogwarts.

It was the best evening of Harry's life, better than winning at Quidditch or Christmas or knocking out mountain trolls ... he would never, ever forget tonight.

*

Harry had almost forgotten that the exam results were still to come, but come they did. To their great surprise, both he and Ron passed with good marks; Hermione, of course, came top of the year. Even Neville scraped through, his good Herbology mark making up for his abysmal Potions one. They had hoped that Goyle, who was almost as stupid as he was mean, might be thrown out, but he had passed, too. It was a shame, but as Ron said, you couldn't have everything in life.

And suddenly, their wardrobes were empty, their trunks were packed, Neville's toad was found lurking in a corner of the toilets; notes were handed out to all students, warning them not to use magic over the holidays ('I always hope they'll forget to give us these,' said Fred Weasley sadly); Hagrid was there to take them down to the fleet of boats that sailed across the lake; they were boarding the Hogwarts Express; talking and laughing as the country-side became greener and tidier; eating Bertie Bott's Every-Flavour Beans as they sped past Muggle towns; pulling off their wizard robes and putting on jackets and coats; pulling into platform nine and three-quarters at King's Cross Station.

It took quite a while for them all to get off the platform. A wizened old guard was up by the ticket barrier, letting them go through the gate in twos and threes so they didn't attract attention by all bursting out of a solid wall at once and alarming the Muggles.

'You must come and stay this summer,' said Ron, 'both of you – I'll send you an owl.'

'Thanks,' said Harry. 'I'll need something to look forward to.'

People jostled them as they moved forwards towards the gateway back to the Muggle world. Some of them called:

'Bye, Harry!'

'See you, Potter!'

'Still famous,' said Ron, grinning at him.

'Not where I'm going, I promise you,' said Harry.

He, Ron and Hermione passed through the gateway together.

'There he is, Mum, there he is, look!'

It was Ginny Weasley, Ron's younger sister, but she wasn't pointing at Ron.

'Harry Potter!' she squealed. 'Look, Mum! I can see –'

'Be quiet, Ginny, and it's rude to point.'

Mrs Weasley smiled down at them.

'Busy year?' she said.

'Very,' said Harry. 'Thanks for the fudge and the jumper, Mrs Weasley.'

'Oh, it was nothing, dear.'

'Ready, are you?'

It was Uncle Vernon, still purple-faced, still moustached, still looking furious at the nerve of Harry, carrying an owl in a cage in a station full of ordinary people. Behind him stood Aunt Petunia and Dudley, looking terrified at the very sight of Harry.

'You must be Harry's family!' said Mrs Weasley.

'In a manner of speaking,' said Uncle Vernon. 'Hurry up, boy, we haven't got all day.' He walked away.

Harry hung back for a last word with Ron and Hermione.

'See you over the summer, then.'

'Hope you have – er – a good holiday,' said Hermione, looking uncertainly after Uncle Vernon, shocked that anyone could be so unpleasant.

'Oh, I will,' said Harry, and they were surprised at the grin that was spreading over his face. '*They don't know we're not allowed to use magic at home. I'm going to have a lot of fun with Dudley this summer ...*'